By

BERT ENTWISTLE

RHYOLITE PRESS, LLC

This is a work of fiction. All the names, places and events are fictional and are products of the author's imagination or are used fictitiously. Any similarity to an actual person, whether living or dead, is coincidence and entirely unintentional.

Copyright © Bert Entwistle, 2012

All Rights Reserved. No portion of this book may be reproduced in any form or by any electronic or mechanical means, including information storage and retrieval systems, without permission from the publisher, except by a reviewer who may quote brief passages in a review.

Published in the United States of America by Rhyolite Press, LLC
P.O. Box 2406
Colorado Springs, Colorado 80901
www.rhyolitepress.com

The Drift / Bert Entwistle
Revised Edition
November 2012

Library of Congress Control Number: 2012948346

ISBN 978-0-9839952-2-7

PRINTED IN THE UNITED STATES OF AMERICA

Cover design and book design/layout by Donald R. Kallaus

Author photo, © Donald R. Kallaus, 2012

To Nancy

*My beautiful bride of forty-three years.
You have endured my often erratic
and generally eccentric lifestyle all these years.
I couldn't do it without you.*

Author's Note

This novel is a work of fiction, created from something that has been lurking around in the darkest recesses of my now-ancient brain for years. It has tried to escape before, but never made it past my bullheaded efforts to keep it at bay. Finally, I gave in to its constant nagging and let it spill out onto my keyboard and into a book.

I got the idea around the mid-eighties, after a trip down a Cripple Creek gold mine. After writing a few chapters, I filed it away, only to revive it long enough to add a few more words every two or three years. By the time gambling came to Colorado in 1991, I had to revise it from a sleepy little tourist town to a gambling town, so it's been a pretty long trip for me.

I am basically a journalistic-style writer, never having to contend with much more than a few thousand words at time. The thing about journalism work is that the people printing the articles tend to frown on writers making things up just for the fun of it. Since I've always wondered if making things up just for the fun of it was cool (it seems to be), I thought I'd give it a try.

Although this is a work of fiction, I have tried to blend it in with historical fact, to try to anchor the time and place. Cripple Creek is obviously a real place, as are other places mentioned, like Ellis Island and Colorado City. But the basic story is just a creation that lived inside my mind all these years.

There are a few real historical characters used in the book that were part of Cripple Creek's colorful history. Most of the places Vitor visited on his trip, as well as the ship he sailed on, are all real. All of the contemporary characters except for one, are just people I made up. The one exception is the character of R.D. Turner. With the permission of his family, in real life, he was pretty much as I wrote him.

    Bert Entwistle
    Colorado Springs, Colorado 2012

drift (drift)–noun

A) Horizontal or nearly horizontal passageway in a mine running through or parallel to a vein.

B) A secondary mine passageway between two main shafts or tunnels.

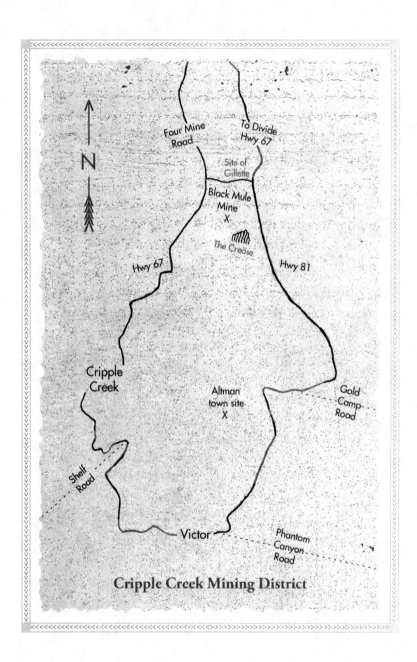

Chapter 1

It was a plain-looking rental truck, the type someone might use to move their possessions on any given weekend. An unusually cold fall day in Colorado, the intermittent rain and snow had left it caked with mud, the wipers doing little good against the freezing temperatures. More than three days of driving, mostly at night, along rough back roads, had left the driver mentally and physically exhausted. Rounding a tight bend on the narrow canyon road, he felt the rear end come loose on the wet surface and cramped the wheel hard to compensate.

Sliding over the edge sideways, the dual tires sprayed gravel helplessly as the truck rolled three times down the steep embankment. The driver died instantly after the second rollover, pinned inside the crushed cab. Several large pines stopped the truck's momentum, leaving it sitting upright. In the back, three of the fifty-gallon drums split open and drained into the dirt.

When the truck failed to show up at the scheduled time, the four rough-looking men left the mine to search for it. Within an hour, they found the wreck over the side of Phantom Canyon Road, near an abandoned railroad work site. Moving quickly, they transferred the remaining sealed drums from the rental to their own trucks. Before leaving, the heavyset man searched through the cab and removed the driver's wallet, watch, and cell phone. Using his knife, he pried open the glove box and grabbed a .380 automatic pistol, two spare clips, and an envelope, stuffing all of it into his coat pockets. With the job complete, he climbed back in his Jeep and followed the freshly loaded trucks through the trees and onto the road. The last thing the men needed was to meet up with the cops, or some nosy locals.

Chapter 2

At exactly the wrong moment the football-sized piece of rock under his boot went south.

So did Jack Bannister.

As he hit the ledge flat on his belly, the breath exploded from his mouth. Choking violently, he slipped backward over the edge. Rolling and bouncing in a wild rush down the steep incline, he came to a stop at the base of the cliff. Rocks and dirt showered down around his head. When he pulled his left hand out from under him and attempted to sit up, a large piece of granite landed square on the end of his little finger. Blood squirted out where the nail used to be, and pain streaked up his arm like a rifle shot.

Sitting up and seeing the blood running down his hand, he jammed his finger against his shirt and screamed, "Jesus Christ almighty, what the hell else could go wrong today?"

Crawling off the loose rock, he stood up on shaky legs, blood leaking from a dozen assorted wounds. However painful it might be, the thought of his lightning ride down the steep hillside forced him to smile. Like the pilots always say, *any landing you can walk away from is a good one. All things considered,* he thought, *this was a pretty good landing.* Wrapping his bandanna around his throbbing little finger, he started the climb back to the truck.

When he got home he would tell Jessie to forget the damn treasure hunt. Years of chasing this legend and they had nothing to show for it but sore feet and empty gas tanks.

And one busted finger.

The way he saw it, the so-called treasure of the golden armor was nothing but a dusty old legend, and they were just wasting their time.

When his pickup finally came into view, he saw three men standing alongside it. The biggest one had a handgun strapped to his side and a radio in his hand. If this is the sheriff, he might have a first-aid kit and some aspirin, reasoned Jack.

Spotting him walking toward the truck, the owner of the radio spoke first. "Is this your truck?"

"Yeah, it sure is. I'm really glad to see you guys; I could use a little help," he said, holding up his bloody hand. "Had a little hiking accident."

The stranger stepped close to Jack's face and stared at him. "You're on private ground. Now get in your truck and get the hell out of here."

"Mister, this is public land and I can come and go as I please . . ."

The punch landed squarely in Bannister's aching belly before he could finish the sentence. For the second time today he was gasping for breath. The two smaller men stuffed him in his pickup and waited while he fumbled for the keys. When they backed away from the cab, he spotted the MAC-10 under the coat of the nearest man.

Must be more than just a couple of good old boys out on a joy ride, thought Bannister, it had been a long time since he'd seen this much firepower. Turning his battered old pickup onto the gravel road, he noticed a black

Jeep parked in the trees. A silver sign on the door read PMV, Inc.

* * *

Struggling to get his boots off took the last of his strength and he slid into the huge claw-foot bathtub, Levi's and all. Steaming hot water surrounded him, and for a moment he thought maybe it was all a bad dream. Remembering his finger covered with the filthy red bandanna, he twisted the makeshift bandage a little tighter, deciding it was something that could wait a while longer. For now, he would soak his poor, pitiful body and wait for Jessie to get home.

He didn't hear the car drive up or the kitchen door close. When the bathroom door banged open, he jerked his head above the rim in time to see his bird dog bounding for the tub. "No Maggie, get out!" It was too late. The dog was head and shoulders over the tub, licking and barking, obviously thrilled to see him.

"What's going on, Bannister, you trying to shrink-fit those Levi's or what?" said a feminine voice from the doorway.

"Is that all the thanks I get for trying to find your family fortune?" he replied . . . with what little smile he could muster.

Jessie Lopez leaned over the tub and noticed the water swirling red around his hand.

"Jesus, Jack, let me see that hand." She gently unwrapped the bandanna and the blood flowed faster. "Come on, get up," she ordered. "We're going to the clinic and get this sewed up."

"Is that all you live for, to order me around?"

"Shut up, old man, and do as I say, or I throw Maggie the rest of the way in the tub." As she helped him out of his wet clothes her curiosity got the best of her. "Jack, were you really looking for the treasure or did you just get your butt thrown from a horse?"

"It's a long story, Jess; I'll fill you in on the way to the doc-in-the-box."

His description of the small clinic with one bed and one doctor was comical, if not accurate. Living so far from a large city, they were lucky to have even one doctor as close as Cripple Creek. At least they wouldn't have to drive all the way to Colorado Springs.

* * *

"Mister Bannister, I'm afraid the first joint of that little finger is history," the doctor said flatly. "We can sew it up just fine, but you need a blast of antibiotics to fight off infection. Drop your pants and roll over, please."

"Right, why not? What's a little more pain to a tough guy like me?" As the doctor filled the syringe, Bannister fell back on the table, out cold.

After twenty minutes, Jessie shook his shoulder gently. "Wake up tough guy; the doctor needs the table."

Bannister looked around the room for a moment, waiting for his head to clear. "What the hell did you do to me, doc?"

"Just a little thread and a couple quarts of penicillin, nothing serious. Now get your prescription filled and let this nice lady take you home. See to it he gets plenty of rest. If he has any problems give me a call."

"Thanks, Doctor," said Jessie, "we appreciate your help."

Standing up to leave, he realized his hand was wrapped up nearly the size of a softball. "Tell me, doc, how long have you lived here?"

"About a year—why do you ask?"

"Have you ever heard of a company called PMV, Inc.?"

"Sure, they own a mining operation up on the mountain. I take care of their medical claims. The letters stand for 'Precious Metal Ventures.'"

Bannister was out the door heading for his truck before Jessie realized he was gone. When she got to the pickup, he was sitting behind the wheel. "Keys," he said quietly.

"Jack, you can't drive in this condition, now move over."

"Keys," he repeated, his voice hardening.

She knew it was no use. When he was in this mood it was better to let him work it out. They rode quietly for twenty minutes, the chill night air blowing through the truck.

"It doesn't add up, Jess. Three guys with automatic weapons, supposedly guarding some kind of mining operation? There hasn't been a worthwhile claim over on that side of the mountain in years."

"Sure," said, Jessie, nodding in agreement. "Those guys just thought they were showing off for a tourist; forget them and let's get home. I'm hungry."

"I suppose so; there can't be much up there worth guarding anyway."

After a long night's sleep, Bannister woke up feeling like lukewarm death. If there was a spot without a bump, bruise, or cut, he couldn't find it. After a handful of aspirin and a couple of Alka-Seltzers, he hobbled over to the fireplace, only to find there was no fresh wood anywhere. As he saw it, he could go out in the cold for more wood, or he could stand here and watch Jessie get dressed. No contest.

"Bannister, I feel like the centerfold in a girly magazine. If you don't have anything else to do, go get some wood, but quit staring at me."

"Staring at you is one of my favorite pastimes; besides, it keeps me out of the bars and home on those cold Colorado nights." He grinned as she pulled a thick wool sweater over her head. "Do you need any help? I'm great with buttons, snaps, and zippers."

"Thanks, but I can manage nicely without you. Now go get the wood. And don't mess around with the axe; you wouldn't want to lose any more little pink parts."

Jack laughed out loud at her reference to his recent ordeal. "Thanks for your concern about my fingers, I'll try and be careful."

Opening the kitchen door was a signal to Maggie; it was time to be fed. She shot by him on a dead run and headed for the closet where the food was kept. "Okay Maggie, okay, we all have our priorities—food before firewood." He bent down and rubbed the old dog's head.

With this chore done, he went for the wood. Stepping back inside the cabin, he found Jessie already engrossed in a pile of paperwork and old maps. "The search for the golden armor goes on, I see."

"One of us has to keep the faith," she said, without looking up.

Dropping the last pieces of piñon in the fireplace, he sat down beside her. "Last night, I decided to come home and tell you the legend was bull and we should give it up."

She turned away from the table and looked at him. "Do you really believe that?"

Buttoning up his wool shirt, he stretched out his arm and studied his new bandage. "Well—I guess there must be a few places we haven't checked."

"God, Jack, for a minute I thought you really might be getting old. I never heard you give up on anything before."

"Must have been the sore finger talking. If that golden armor is there, you, me, and Maggie will find it." Changing the subject quickly he asked, "What's the plan for today, are we really going down to the big city? How about we stay here and see if we can come up with some creative ways to keep warm."

She shook her head as she poured fresh coffee in his mug. "This is the only warm thing you get this morning, and hurry it up if you plan on riding to town with me."

"In case you didn't notice, Miss Lopez, it's Sunday. We really don't have to go anywhere."

He sounded like one of her old bosses when he used "Miss Lopez" so formally, like it was a sin to be single. "Well, Mister Bannister, if you want to leave your butt parked in that chair all day, go right ahead. I, however, am going out for breakfast and I'll even buy."

Pulling on a well-worn pair of cowboy boots, he grabbed his keys and headed for the door. "For a free meal I'll even drive." The truck coughed slowly to life. While he waited for it to warm up, he rearranged the junk in the seat to make room for a passenger.

Jessie surveyed the mess, "You sure there's room for me?"

"Room for you, me, and Willie Nelson," he said, plugging in the tape.

After a short ride through the trees, they pulled onto the blacktop and headed for the city. The ride would take less than an hour.

As they slowed for the first curve, a black Jeep covered with mud came headlong down the canyon with its wheels centered on the double yellow, aimed straight at the pickup.

Bannister jerked the wheel hard to the right and plunged into the bar ditch. Crashing and swaying, he took out a dozen fence posts and a hundred feet of wire. Jessie laid over in the seat as the truck went through the aspens, blindly plowing down small trees and brush.

When he sensed the truck was beginning to lose momentum, he pointed it back to the ditch and jammed both feet on the brake pedal. The truck dug into the soft ground and lurched to a stop. "Did you see the sign on that bastard's door?"

Jessie responded in a shaky voice, "I couldn't see anything but a blur."

"God, I'm sorry, Jess, you okay?"

"I'm fine, just a couple of minor bumps. What did you say about a sign?"

"PMV, Inc., the same as I saw up on the bench road. Maybe even the same jerks I met yesterday," said Bannister, with an icy tone in his voice.

"Well," she said with a sense of relief, "they're gone now. I doubt if you'll ever hear from them again."

"That's twice, it won't happen a third time."

She knew better than to ask what he was planning. It was sure to be something she didn't want to hear about.

Chapter 3

The small oak sign on the door read:

Jackson H. Bannister
United States
Environmental Research Agency

The three rooms overflowed with ten years of assorted records and junk of all kinds. With the high ceiling, dark paneling, and old-fashioned stone fireplace, the office looked like it had fallen out of a Sherlock Holmes story.

Bannister brushed past one of the more recent piles and dropped into an ancient leather chair. A computer, printer, and an answering machine were the room's only concessions to the modern world. Pushing the play button on the answering machine, he leaned back in the chair and waited for the day's news.

"Jack, I got your message and should have something today on the headwaters cleanup problem." The voice paused for several seconds. "We can take a ride up there next week if you want, but it might require taking the fishing gear with us."

He made a short note on his calendar as the machine continued. "If we keep the pressure on, I think they will come around without any legal action. Let me know when you're ready to go." The message was good news. With this business out of the way, his investigator, Rocky Batton, could be used on another, more pressing problem—like PMV, Inc.

As the machine finished its morning's business, Bannister started in on his. It was easy to remember why he preferred fieldwork to a desk job. The director had called it a promotion, but Jack knew chasing environmental bad guys from a desk wasn't near as much fun as it was in the field. With the paperwork out of the way, he called Jessie to cancel his lunch date and left a message for Rocky to call him at home.

Walking to the door, he looked at the piles of papers, files, and strange objects collected from all over the West. *Next week,* he thought, he'd sort through this stuff—*next week for sure.* He laughed out loud as he closed the door on the clutter. *Next week for sure.*

* * *

"Come on in, I've got elk steaks in the skillet and biscuits in the oven."

"Thanks," said Bannister taking in the smells of the kitchen. "I could stand a little something to eat."

Bright gray eyes peered out from under a red welder's cap and a full gray beard. R. D. Turner was a longtime friend and fishing buddy of Jack's. "What brings you all the way out here, besides elk steaks?"

"Elk steaks, a warm fire, and a little conversation would do fine," he said, pulling up a chair.

"Well, start in on these backstraps and let's hear about that big Band-aid on your paw," said the old man. Although his name was R. D. Turner, everyone always called him Turner, or sometimes, just to tease him, Old Timer or Old Man, although he never gave his age to anyone—just one of a few mysteries surrounding him and his past.

"A little treasure-hunting adventure, nothing serious."

"Is that what this is about? The golden armor?" There was nothing he liked better than to give him a hard time about the treasure.

"No, not exactly."

"Well, let's hear it then."

"You remember the last time we were up on the bench road?" said Bannister, pouring them both a cup of the strong black coffee the old man liked so well.

"Sure," said Turner, "we walked into Little Slide Lake. If I remember correctly I caught most of the fish that day."

"I see your memory is working as good as ever," said Bannister. "Have you been up there in the last year or two?"

Turner nodded his head as he turned off the stove. "I was up there about two months back. Those sorry-ass developers have fenced off the trailhead and cut off access to half the country we used to hunt and fish in." Dropping the sizzling steaks on Bannister's plate, Turner continued. "They cut in a new road and there's a lot of heavy truck traffic on it. It leads through a new fence and into a shiny new shaft house at that old Black Mule mine. Shit, that part of the mountain was worked out sixty years ago; I can't believe there's anything left up there worth all that trouble."

"What do you say we take Rattler for a little ride? After we eat our elk steaks and biscuits of course," said Bannister cutting up his steak.

A smile spread across Turner's face; he was always up for an adventure. "You finish up here and I'll make sure the Jeep is ready to go."

As the green, vintage Willys Jeep that he called Rattler backed out of the garage, Bannister grabbed a couple of fishing rods and a tackle box.

"Are you wanting to try Little Slide again, Jack?"

"They're just a little eyewash, in case someone wonders why we're up there."

As they turned onto the gravel, Bannister opened his small backpack and pulled out a pair of field glasses and a 9mm Browning Hi-Power pistol.

"Can I take it that you ain't bringing that along to ventilate tin cans?"

Bannister slid the clip into the gun. When he heard the metallic click, he looked at his old friend. "Just in case they don't buy the fishing story. Call it Plan B."

* * *

Bannister and Turner concealed themselves in the rocks until well after dark, and watched the truck leave the building and head down the canyon. "That's two trucks in the last hour. What do you figure they're hauling out of there?" asked Turner.

"My guess is they aren't hauling anything out."

"You mean them sons o' bitches are hiding something inside that old mine?"

Before Bannister could answer, the door opened again and four men left the building. A dirty black Jeep followed the two pickup trucks through the fence, stopping just long enough to lock the gate. Bannister stared hard through the field glasses.

"Someone you know, Jack?"

Bannister shook his head. "More like someone I'm about to know. Turner, you think you can get Rattler up that fire scar on the backside and over to the main gravel road?"

"Wouldn't be the first time," said Turner, "but where you gonna be?"

"I'll meet you where the creek crosses the gravel in an hour or so."

"Okay Jack, but take your Browning; you never know when you'll have to go to Plan B."

Bannister concealed himself in the rocks for a few more minutes to look the place over. From the outside, it didn't look any different from a hundred other mining operations he'd seen before. It was a typical tin building with a few old tires and a pile of steel cables lying along one side. It had been built completely around the shaft with the headframe sticking through the roof. A concrete powder magazine was set back in the trees a hundred yards from the entrance, and a smaller attached building contained the air compressors and controls for the electrical and ventilation systems.

The site had a new electric service and was completely surrounded with an eight-foot chain-link fence and a good gate with a metal sign attached to it. In large block letters it said: PMV, Inc. PRIVATE PROPERTY NO TRESPASSING.

When Bannister decided no one was about to return, he stood up and stretched his legs. Pushing the Browning down in his waistband and grabbing a small flashlight, he cleared the fence easily and began to pick his way down the ridge. Stopping at the last of the trees, he watched for any signs of life. The building looked quiet except for a thin sliver of light coming from a side door.

Through the small opening in the window, he could see a single light fixture hanging from the ceiling. He popped the small window open with his pocketknife, reached inside for the lock, and was inside in an instant. Walking to the back of the room, he squatted down and took in everything. Except for the electric forklift, a battery charger, and a few odds and ends, the room was almost empty. Bannister was almost disappointed; he wasn't sure what he expected to find, but this clean, almost sterile-looking operation didn't set right.

At the back of the building, he came to the shaft with a miner's cage big enough for half a dozen men. Disappearing down the shaft next to the cage were the usual power and air lines. The headframe and all the supports were new, as were the cables and lighting. It was a big investment for a supposedly worked-out claim. The new cage was unusual in this district; it operated electrically, able to run on regular power or emergency generator power.

He stepped in the cage and pushed the door closed. God, how he hated these kind of places. *If man were meant to be in these holes he would have been made to hang from the ceiling,* thought Bannister. Gritting his teeth, he pushed the power switch to the "on" position and pulled the lever down. The winch started its slow descent, and Bannister watched as each level rolled by. Spotting some equipment, he stopped at the level marked "800."

Sitting outside of the cage was an air-operated rock drill and a low, flat cart on rubber tires. He knew this was worse than any needle-in-the-haystack hunt. This operation had dozens of miles of tunnels, and whatever might be hidden down here could take weeks or even months to find.

The new lights and timbers had ended at the entrance to the cage, and this was what he expected to see. A few small lights hung by the wires, and the pipes, and ductwork disappeared into the darkness of the tunnel. He dug out his flashlight and flicked it on.

This was the only level that showed any sign of recent work. He would take a quick look around and then get out. While he walked behind his small light beam, the tunnel ended with a right-hand turn into another slightly smaller one. He stared into the blackness wanting a better reason to go in deeper.

The deafening blast cut his thoughts short. The tunnel seemed to come alive with vibrations and falling debris. Pipes and wires snapped back and forth like they had a life of their own, and air rushed out like a monstrous propeller wash.

Bannister bolted from the opening. A violent, choking cloud of dust filled the tunnel and raced for the entrance, overtaking him in an instant. The shock wave blew by and ran for another fifty yards before it died, knocking him flat against the ground.

If there was a hint of light anywhere, it was impossible to find it. Fine dust and rocky debris covered him completely and his head pounded uncontrollably. Taking small breaths through his bandanna, he tried to filter out some of the dust. Blackness like he'd never experienced engulfed his senses, and the urge to panic could barely be contained. He moved slowly on his hands and knees, using his left hand to feel the edge of the tunnel as he went. Resting against the wall, he wondered if this was even the right direction.

Jesus Christ, this is like something Poe would write about, thought Bannister. As the dust began to settle, he thought he could see a slight speck of light. Crawling closer, he realized it was coming from the bulb at the cage. *This is my last time in one of these holes*, he decided. *Definitely my last time.*

* * *

The green Willys Jeep sat across the creek with its back to the trees. Its driver was slumped down in the seat with his hat pulled over his eyes. After a quick rinse in the icy water, Bannister pulled the passenger door open and collapsed in the seat. Without looking up, Turner reached for the key and started the engine. Gunning it twice, he rolled through the bar ditch and onto the road.

"So, Jack, tell me—how was your evening?"

"Just another day in the life of Action Jack Bannister, Environmental Detective," he said, as he watched the fine dark grit blow off his jacket and swirl lazily out the wing window.

Turner broke into a wide grin and pressed down harder on the gas pedal. As the Jeep slid through the corners of the gravel road, Bannister laid out the details of his evening's adventure in the mine shaft.

"So what are you gonna do now?"

"Find some aspirin."

"Sounds like a nitro headache to me, Jack."

Bannister looked puzzled. "What's a nitro headache?"

"The nitro in dynamite gives the miners a major headache. In the old days, they all carried a pocket full of aspirin with them when they were blasting."

"What do you mean the old days?"

"Whoever packed those holes is an old-time powderman. They all use ammonium nitrate charges now, have for twenty years. It don't give headaches."

"Well, I don't plan on being around during any more blasting, but I do intend on finding out all there is to know about PMV, Inc."

"Why not just go in there with guns and dogs and a bunch of big mean cops?"

"The lawyers would have a field day with that. Truth is, I didn't see a single thing that looked illegal."

"What about the blast?" asked Turner.

Bannister shrugged his shoulders. "It's their mine, and they can blast it all they want." Before he could continue, the Jeep lurched into the next corner with all four tires sliding sideways. "Turner, you in a big hurry or what?"

Without taking his eyes off of the road, Turner downshifted once and shot through the curve. "Got me a fresh 350 V8 put under the hood last week. Runs pretty good, don't you think?"

Tightening his grip on the shoulder harness, Bannister managed to squeak out a weak, "Yeah, real good," before the next curve.

* * *

Rocky Batton, Bannister's field investigator and long time friend, stood in the doorway of the office, all six feet six and 280 pounds of him.

Fifty pounds heavier than when Bannister met him in Army Basic Training, he was, to say the least, imposing looking. Thick black hair just starting to turn gray, a crooked nose, and enormous hands the size of hams gave him the look of a barroom brawler, which was just one of his many talents.

When they stood in line next to each other that first day of Basic Training at Fort Campbell, it was almost comical. Bannister, at six feet and one-hundred-sixty pounds, looked like the original 90-pound weakling in all the body-builder ads.

"Bannister—you hiding in this shitpile somewhere?"

"Yeah, I'm back here, and who or what are you calling a shitpile?"

"This place you call an office, that's what."

"Well, if you worried less about my office and more about catching bad guys, the whole country might be the better for it," said Bannister.

"Nice repair job on that finger; you been treasure hunting again?"

Bannister forced back a grin. "Jessie couldn't wait to give you the good news I see."

"No, I had biscuits and gravy at the diner this morning, and I ran into Turner."

Picking up a stack of file folders from the only extra chair, and depositing them on Jack's desk, Rocky sat down. "I heard you had a little adventure last night."

"To answer your first question first, yes, I was doing a little treasure hunting, and my finger will be just fine, thank you; a bit shorter maybe, but just fine. As for your second question, it was an interesting evening, but not much of an adventure for a daring guy like me."

"So, did you find anything worth going down there for?" asked

Rocky, shifting to business.

"Nothing obvious, but my gut tells me something is rotten. I want you to find out who owns PMV, Inc."

"I already know who owns it," said Rocky, pressing back against the chair.

"Please feel free to enlighten me."

"Jamison Carhartt the third, patriarch of the well-to-do Colorado Springs mining family."

Jack wrote the name on his pad. "What else do you know about this bird?"

"Well, not all that much, really. He's something of a benefactor to the Pioneers Museum and some local charities. His name is in the paper every now and then, typical-old-money rich guy, I guess."

"By the end of the week I want to know everything there is to know about Mr. Carhartt, his family, and his business dealings," said Bannister.

"One more thing Rock . . ."

He knew from the tone that his boss was getting serious. "What is it Jack?"

"These guys carry automatic weapons."

"I got the picture—I'll pay close attention." He'd known Jack too long to doubt his gut feelings; their butts had been saved more than once by listening to his little voice.

"Well, hit the road, I ain't paying you all that money to park it in my chair."

"I'm going, I'm going. And Jack—you better forget that golden armor before you run out of fingers."

Bannister cracked a small smile, plugged in a Garth Brooks tape, and buried himself in the day's paperwork.

Chapter 4

It would be a long night; there were thirteen drums left to take down and only two drums could fit on the lift at one time. Stripping off their coats and heavy shirts, the four men threw them in a pile, laid their guns on top, and grabbed a couple bottles of water. Working steadily, it took several hours to move all of the drums down the shaft and into position.

The heavyset man, clearly the leader, moved with the confidence of an experienced powderman. He had already cut a small slit in the end of each stick of dynamite to be used for the primers. Ten shots on each rib and sixteen in the back would be enough for the job. The holes had already been drilled out to ten feet deep, and several were left empty in the rear of the blast area to give the charges a space to explode against.

After the last drum was in place, dynamite would make them disappear forever. No more than a day's worth of trash collection, as the guys called it, could be left exposed at a time. Each site was prepared in advance for closure well before the trash was brought down.

After pressing the electric time-delay cap into the slit of one stick to form a primer, he put three more sticks in each hole. Using a long wooden pole, he shoved the charges to the end, leaving a coil of colored wire hanging from the rock. The rest of the holes were packed with more explosives. Four cases, nearly 200 pounds, would do the job if his calculations were correct. Working quickly now, he tied the wires together and connected them to the timer. The charges would explode sequentially from the back to the front. He set the time on the way out of the building. In forty-five minutes the trash would be gone forever. In forty-five minutes they would be in Frankie's, sipping cold ones.

* * *

The familiar click of pool balls and incessant drone of the slot machines punctuated the men's conversation. With a fresh draft in front of him, the heavyset man at the bar reached into an envelope and removed nine 100-dollar bills. He raised his glass in a mock toast, "Here's to a good night's work." Handing three bills to each of his crew, he called the waitress to the table and ordered another round.

In the back of the bar, near the jukebox, a large man with an unruly shock of black hair sat nursing a beer. Rocky Batton made a few scratches in his notebook and sipped at his beer. After an hour, there wasn't much to note except for a couple of miners spending a little money on a Saturday night.

It was time to call it an evening; maybe tomorrow he could turn up something in town. The locals in these places usually have a good sense of anything strange going on. Parked alongside his four-wheel drive at the rear of the parking lot was a black Jeep with a silver sign on the door: PMV, Inc. Recording the tag number and a short description of the four miners in his book, he squeezed into his Blazer and headed for home.

* * *

Jessie Lopez sat at her desk in the tiny room once used as a judge's chambers. The nineteenth-century Colorado Springs courthouse had been saved from demolition in the 70s, and the Pioneers Museum moved in shortly after. As curator, she was responsible for day-to-day operations, as well as bringing in new exhibits.

"Where do you want this stuff, lady?" The man said, as he shifted his two-wheel dolly to an upright position and waited for an answer. The oversized black steamer trunk and a small wooden chest had been donated by a family in New York. Their great uncle left Russia for the Cripple Creek goldfields more than a hundred years ago and never returned home.

Inside the boxes were more than four years of the glory days of the mining district history in the form of letters, news clippings, and other material of the period. Directing the mover to put them in the office, she opened the small chest first. The letters, wrapped in old newspaper from New York City, were dated from 1892 to 1896. On the top of the chest, written in a very old hand, was a faded name: V. Serinov.

She was startled by the creak of the heavy oak door swinging open.

"What's the chance of you buying a poor hungry guy some breakfast?" said Bannister while he held the door open, allowing the morning light to fill the room.

"Bannister, your timing is perfect. What do you make of the language in this letter?"

Holding the letter to the light, he studied it for a moment. "No doubt, it's Russian, pretty old style, but definitely Russian."

"That's what I thought too."

"What, may I ask, does all this have to do with the price of breakfast?"

"I sometimes think your head is one big bowl of biscuits and gravy. Is food all you think about?"

"Well, every now and then, I think about warm fires and flannel sheets, if you know what I mean," said Bannister with a grin like the Cheshire cat.

She looked at him with just a trace of a smile. "I stand corrected. The price of breakfast will be the translation of these letters."

Bannister zipped up his jacket and held the door wide open. "If we hurry, we can catch Rocky before he eats Darla out of house and home."

* * *

Rocky sat at the tiny corner table with his notebook open. Steam from his coffee cup clouded the window next to him as he read through the entries. Jessie slid in next to Rocky and gave him a hug.

He put his long arm around her. "Hi, doll, who's this guy following you?"

"Well he's hardly big enough for my bodyguard, so I guess he's my chauffeur."

"And, Russian translator," added Bannister.

Dropping the menus on the table, Darla reached across to fill the cups. "What's that on your hand, Jack? You been treasure hunting again?"

Rocky grinned at the exchange. "Shit, Bannister, you're getting to be downright famous."

"Yeah, with you as my press agent. So what have you got on PMV, Inc.?"

"So far, about ten pages in my book, but nothing all that bad. From the outside looking in, it appears to be a pretty straightforward mining venture."

Bannister sat with his hands cupping the hot mug. "What about our man, what's his name . . . Carhartt?"

"Jamison Carhartt the third. Son of Carhartt the second. Made his money in mining, and branched out into real estate and aviation."

"Is Carhartt the second still around?"

"Died about four years ago; seems to be very well respected around here."

Jessie looked up from the letters. "If you're talking about the Carhartt family, of Carhartt Aviation, I can tell you they have been very good to the museum."

Bannister looked surprised at this information. "Jess, do you know this guy personally?"

"Sure, he attends most of the museum events and has been more than generous with funds for new exhibits. In fact, he helped arrange for the donation of the letters you're about to translate."

"Jack, you still think he's a bad guy?" asked Rocky, taking his first sip of coffee.

"If he turns out to be clean, I'll give you my season passes to the Bronco games. You got anything else?"

"I'm gonna hold you to that, Bannister. I spent a little time in the Cripple Creek bars and talked to the locals. As bad as the economy is right now, they're happy to get any kind of work."

Jack sensed there was more. "What do you think, Rocky?"

"I get a feeling that all is not well with PMV, Inc., but no one is talking. However, they must pay well. I saw three of their employees at the local bar with handful's of cash and a shiny new Jeep."

Bannister felt the hair bristle up on the back of his neck. "Was it black, with a silver PMV, Inc. sign?"

"That's the one. I've got the tag number and the descriptions."

"By God, Rock, you're Okay. Bring the information by the office and we'll find out who these guys are. Jess, can you arrange an introduction to Mr. Carhartt the third?"

"No problem. I'll just tell him you're the person that offered to translate the letters, but just ask him about flying—he'll talk all day."

"Jess, I haven't done any serious work in Russian for almost thirty years."

She patted him on the hand, smiling broadly. "The museum can't afford anyone else, and so, rusty or not, you get the job."

Even after ten years, saying no to her was almost impossible. Bannister knew when he was beaten.

The humor of the scene didn't escape Rocky. "Jack Bannister, ex-Green Beret, mountain climber, bull rider, scuba diver, and environmental expert, beaten into submission by a hundred-and-ten-pound museum curator!"

Bannister looked pained. "Well, at least she has to pay for breakfast."

"Sorry, Jack. Gotta go. Be a doll and take care of this please." Jessie Lopez dropped her bill in his lap and was out the door before he could say anything.

"I handled that well, don't you think?"

"Yeah, Jack, a lot better than usual."

Chapter 5

Jamison Carhartt III stood on the pavement next to the helicopter. "Mr. Bannister, glad you could fly with me today."

"Just call me Jack, please. I appreciate the offer; I hope Jessie's request isn't inconvenient."

"No, not at all. Jessie tells me you're translating the letters for the museum. Where did you learn your Russian?"

"It was just one of those things the army thought I should know back in the days of the Cold War."

Climbing into the chopper, Carhartt buckled in and began checking off the controls. "I hear you and Jessie are treasure hunters; any luck so far?"

"Only bad luck, if that counts."

The rotors started to spin as the pilot spoke to the tower: "NB-three-seven-three-seven-Charles, requesting clearance for takeoff." After the tower gave its okay, Carhartt continued. "The Sebring II is the latest addition to our fleet; it has a four-hundred-and-fifty-mile range and can do over three hundred miles per hour. Do you like flying, Jack?"

"I flew a little in Vietnam, but nothing as fancy as this. The Hueys were the hot ride at the time."

"Did you fly gunships?"

"Mostly dust-off duty—I don't think they would have trusted me with a machine gun back then," said Bannister, settling into the seat.

"That was scary work, did you get hurt?"

"Well, I only lost one of Uncle Sam's machines the whole time I was flying, but all I got out of it was a few stitches and bruises." Changing the subject, Bannister asked Carhartt about his years of flying.

"Copters have come a long way since then. The company has had several over the years but nothing like this one—this is really an amazing machine. I look for any excuse I can to go up; it's really my first love. Would you like a ride over Cripple Creek?"

"Sure," said Bannister, watching the ground rapidly fall away. "Our treasure hunting is in the area of Bull Hill, along the northeast side. Maybe I can pick up some clues from the bird's-eye view."

They followed the path of Gold Camp Road as it wound around the south side of Pikes Peak toward what was billed at the turn of the century as the World's Greatest Gold Camp. The mountain between the towns of Victor and Cripple Creek was covered with hundreds of scars and old structures. It was a testament to what men can do when they set their mind to it, and what they can do if gold is involved.

"Do you still do much mining Mr. Carhartt?"

"Not too much anymore. We have a couple of claims, but outside of a few small deposits, they're pretty well played out." The chopper followed the road with Pikes Peak rising over 14,000 feet on the right and miles of foothills and canyons on the left. "There's still gold here, but right now we haven't found enough to make it worthwhile to work seriously."

It was obvious to Bannister that Carhartt loved to fly, and that this was an incredible machine. It was smooth and quiet, complete with the world's most sophisticated electronics and every bell and whistle ever made. It was, at the least, thought Bannister, a very expensive toy—the type of thing only the most prosperous businesses could afford. As they moved above the peaks and valleys around Battle Mountain, the chopper banked left and right, showing off what the machine was capable of.

"Let me show you how smooth it is when we hover." Maneuvering the helicopter above a series of rough vertical granite outcrops, he held it as still and quiet as anything Bannister had ever seen.

"Somehow," said Bannister, "it's like we're not really in a chopper. If I can't hear the thump of the rotors and don't have to yell over the noise, it's not the same."

Carhartt noticed him staring intently at the rock formations below. "Impressive country don't you think? The rocks are Pikes Peak granite. This group is unusual in that it is almost perfectly vertical and laced through with veins and pockets of quartz—mostly smoky quartz as well as some amazonite and turquoise. Some beautiful specimens have come from around here."

Bannister nodded his head, taking it all in. "They are impressive from up here. I see them in a whole new light."

Maintaining the helicopter in the same spot gave Bannister a good view of the rocky peaks below. "The tallest point is called the Crease," said Carhartt. "The early miners named it that. I guess they thought it looked like a fold or crease in the vertical layers of rock; the dark rock on one side contrasts with the lighter granite on the other side." They hovered for a few more minutes and Bannister took it all in. "Seen enough, Jack? I need to get back to the office and back to the paperwork."

"Actually, I could spend all day up here, but I guess I can't find that golden armor from a helicopter."

Carhartt pulled up and banked right, pointing the Sebring back toward Colorado Springs. "Tell me about the treasure, Jack—do you think it's the real deal? Or is it just a dusty old legend?"

Bannister smiled broadly at the question. "I guess that depends if you want my answer or listen to Jessie explain it. Her family has been telling and retelling a story for generations that has her descendent, a mysterious Mexican ancestor, traveling with an early Spanish expedition that came through here. The story has it that they either buried or somehow lost a large quantity of gold and a custom-made piece of Spanish armor crafted from local gold and turquoise."

"If they buried it for security purposes, wouldn't they have been planning to come back and get it?"

Jack nodded his head. "That's been my opinion all along. I figure if there was a treasure, they came back and got it, end of story. However it's become a passion for Jess and if it makes her happy . . ."

"I understand how that goes, Jack, believe me, I understand."

Chapter 6

Jessie Lopez was sitting on the couch reading a book with Maggie curled up beside her when Bannister finally got home. The fire was already lit and the kitchen smelled like roasted chile peppers, a prime ingredient in most of her cooking.

Bannister plopped down on the couch and pulled off his boots, reaching over and rubbing the bird dog's belly. "Hi girls, what's for supper?"

Looking over her reading glasses at him, Jessie gave her standard answer to his question. "Food—If you don't like it, Maggie will eat it for you."

After a dinner of homemade tamales and green chile, Bannister threw a few sticks of wood in the fireplace and made himself comfortable next to Jessie and Maggie. "I see things are normal around here." Pulling the dog toward him and onto his lap he began to rub her ears. When he raised his arm, she crawled away, laying her head in her Jessie's lap.

"Et tu, Maggie? A guy doesn't have a chance around here. Oh, well, I guess I don't blame you for your choice."

"Well," asked Jessie, "how was your ride with Jamie? Did you learn anything?"

"Jamie? You call him Jamie?"

"Of course; we're old friends. He's done a lot for the museum, I told you that."

"For your information, your pal Jamie and I had a nice ride over the district today," said Bannister teasingly. "I really don't know if I learned much; we just had a friendly conversation about helicopters and treasure hunting. I think he was just checking me out—he might have heard about my run-in with his guys. It's hard to say.

"So then you have a little time to start on the letters, right?"

"The letters?"

"The Russian letters? Did you forget already?"

"Oh, yeah," said Bannister. "The Russian letters."

The stack of letters sat on the table with a faded piece of ribbon around them. As he unwrapped the binding he noticed the date on the first letter he picked up: April 12, 1892, posted in New Jersey.

"They're in chronological order," said Jessie. "The Russian miner's great-grandnephew put the packets together a year at a time. He could read the dates on the postmarks, but he can't read Russian."

"He may not be the only one who can't read it," said Bannister. "This is a difficult language at best. With a hundred-year-old dialect, poor handwriting, and faded paper, it's going to be a challenge. It could take years to do all of them."

"Well, I guess you better get started if you're going to finish before you retire."

Maggie looked up at Bannister, as though to confirm what Jessie just said. "Okay, girls, I got the picture."

* * *

After two hours of skimming through the earliest of the letters, Bannister became engrossed in this long-dead immigrant's story of his flight from Russia and trip to Colorado. He could make out about half of the words and wrote them down in English on a yellow legal pad, leaving plenty of space to fill in the missing pieces later, when he'd dig out his Russian books.

The phone jolted Bannister back to the present; the caller ID told him it was Rocky. "Hey, Rock, what's going on?"

"I'm at an accident site with the Teller County sheriff. It looks like a rental truck crashed on a curve. The driver was killed."

"You think there's some connection to our guy?"

"I got nothing solid yet, just a feeling. It looks like the truck was carrying a bunch of fifty-gallon drums. A couple split open and spilled out; the HazMat guys think it might be trichloroethylene. Judging from the scene, someone else was here and removed the rest of the drums."

Bannister made a few notes as he listened. "Okay, Rocky, I'll see you in my office in the morning. Bring me a copy of the police report and whatever you can find out about this guy and his truck."

"I'll be there."

Chapter 7

Rocky was waiting for Jack when he got to the door of his office. "What took you so long? I've been here for half an hour; you're never late."

"A very old Russian miner kept me up past my bedtime," said Bannister. Rocky looked puzzled. "I'll fill you in later; it doesn't have anything to do with our case. What have you got on the truck wreck? Did it turn out to be a trichloroethylene spill? Anything on the driver yet?"

Rocky shook his head. "Hell no, it was the middle of the night, Bannister—what did you expect?"

"Well make it your first priority for today. Did you find anything new about Carhartt the third?"

"Just bits and pieces. The most interesting piece so far is the fact that Carhartt Aviation hasn't turned a profit on their mining division, PMV, Inc., in years. The flying business is barely in the black and the real estate group is all but dead." Rocky pointed to the figures from the file he handed his boss. "It looks like he may have subsidized the company with some fresh cash recently. No idea where it came from yet."

Bannister sat down and studied the file for a moment, reading Rocky's notes carefully. "I don't see anything here on the guy in the black Jeep. Make that your first priority for today."

"You just told me to make the driver and the truck my first priority."

"So now you've got two first priorities for today. You got a problem with that?"

"No problem, boss. I know it must be tough to do your job with a missing pinkie finger, I'll carry the load for you." Batton grinned from ear to ear as he backed his way out the door. "So what does the boss have planned for today, if I might ask?"

Bannister stood up and picked up his keys and a notepad off his desk. "I have a date with a miner."

"A miner? The Russian miner?"

"No, a Cripple Creek miner. I think he's from Kentucky. He's going to teach me something about the district gold mines."

* * *

Bannister bounced along the gravel road, his pickup leaving a long, swirling tail of gravel dust behind him. In the distance, he could see the area where he and Jessie had spent so many weekends searching for the golden armor. As he drove in and out of the trees and across the flanks of Battle Mountain, he tried to visualize the district as it might have been in 1894, much as it might have been when Vitor Serinov described it in his letters home.

Bannister drove through a gate marked Golden Peak Exploration. The road wound through a small valley and ended at a pair of trailers parked on either side of a tall, skinny building containing the headframe and miner's cage. Odds and ends of mining equipment of various ages and conditions were scattered around the property, mixed in with tons and tons of broken rock.

A thin, middle-aged man, about five foot seven, with a gray-streaked beard and sunglasses, came out of the trailer and greeted Bannister at the door. "You must be Jack. I'm Allan Rogers. My friends call me A.J., and sometimes they call me a few other names too."

"A.J., good to meet you. I'm Jack Bannister. I appreciate your finding time to visit with me."

The two men walked inside the office trailer and sat down on folding chairs at the rear of the office. "So, what can I help you with, Jack? You said you wanted to pick my brain about the mines in the district."

"Yes, I'm the Rocky Mountain field director for the U.S. Environmental Research Agency. You probably know we've been involved in mapping these old mines for years. When we run out of money we stop for a while. When the politicians give us a little more, we start up again."

"How does that affect me? Do you need the engineering reports and maps of our operation?"

"I'll be straight with you," said Bannister. "Those are some of the things I need, but mostly I want to talk a little about the mountain itself. I heard you're the resident historian on this area?"

A.J. Rogers was a legend in the business, running hard rock operations all over the West. "I have a geology degree from Colorado State, but my real love is history. I particularly like the era of exploration of the West, and the mountain men and Indians of the period."

Bannister took a liking to the miner right away—something about his straightforward manner and love of the West. "So how did you end up making a career of gold mining?"

"Well, I started over on the old Gold Coin mine on the other side of Battle Mountain when I got out of high school. I was a miner's helper for one summer. Basically I helped out mucking on a small exploration drift. We didn't find much gold, but I was hooked on looking for it." Removing his sunglasses, he rubbed his eyes and put his feet up on another chair. "I've worked silver and gold mines all over the West for the last thirty years. Except for a vacation in Southeast Asia, courtesy of the government, and college, it's all I've ever done."

Bannister immediately understood Roger's comment about his vacation. He was a Vietnam vet, and it was another reason to like him. "I think we had the same travel agency, A.J."

Rogers ran his fingers through his matted hair, permanently distressed by a lifetime of wearing a hard hat. "I always thought this district looks kind of like it's been hit by a bunch of B-52s."

"I never thought of it that way before, but you're right, it does look bombed out, but at least no one is trying to kill you," said Bannister.

"Just the rock Jack, just the rock."

"A.J., I'm looking into possible contamination of the drainage downstream from the Cripple Creek District, possibly from something inside these old mines."

"What makes you think it's from the mines? It may be from a problem with the leach piles. They use cyanide to separate the gold from the rock. The big open-pit operation run by Phoenix Drilling is the only outfit making any money around here; they could be leaking something into the drainage."

"Our engineers have been doing a lot of testing, and it looks like it's coming from the drainage tunnel—I think they call it the Carlton Tunnel. Are you familiar with it?"

"You bet. The drainage tunnels are the reason so many people made so much money from this place. The Roosevelt was built in 1907, and the Carlton was built in 1941 and is more than six miles long. It's at seven-thousand feet and below most of the mines. It takes away all the water problems the miners suffered from in the early days."

"If I understand this right, something coming out of it could be from any mine in the district?"

A.J. smiled at Bannister's apparent lack of knowledge on the district. "Jack, you need a trip underground, let's talk as we go down." Throwing him a stained, yellow hard hat, he got up from the chair and headed out the door.

Bannister cringed at the thought of another trip into the darkness of a gold mine; the last time was more excitement than he really needed. Walking toward the mine entrance, he adjusted the hard hat the best he could and pushed it down on his head.

This mine was the site of the original Gold Ingot claim from the 1890s, now one of several leased by Golden Peak Exploration. A.J. made trips to each of their district claims about twice a week, moving his three small crews from claim to claim as needed. When they would find a vein that looked promising, they worked it for a while.

Bannister stepped into the cage and A.J. pulled the door closed with a dull clang. Reaching through a hole in the cage he pulled a rope, ringing a series of bells telling the winch operator where to stop him. This was the old way of signaling, but it was still used by a lot of the older operations around the district.

Bannister didn't talk all the way down the shaft. The small steel cage rattled and shook and the lights of each stop blurred by as they dropped. The ride to the 1,100-foot level tightened his belly and had him holding his breath all the way down. When A.J. opened the cage, he stepped out and put his hand on the nearest piece of rock to steady himself.

"You alright, Jack?" asked A.J. as he closed up the cage and rang the bell again. "It's not your first time in a hard rock mine, is it?"

"No, I've been in them before but I don't like it all that much. I think I'm a little claustrophobic. Our agency works on these kinds of problems all the time; I just never seem to get used to it."

The Drift

Rogers clipped his light onto his hard hat and handed another one to Bannister. "To answer your last question, yes, the Carlton and Roosevelt Tunnels drain the whole of the Cripple Creek Mining District. The bulk of the valuable claims were on Globe Hill, Gold Hill, Raven Hill, Bull Hill, and of course, Battle Mountain."

"The district must be one hell of a maze underground. How many different mines and miles of tunnels are we talking about here, A.J.?"

"Not tunnels, drifts. We call them drifts. The sides are called ribs and the top is called the back. The end of the drift where they're drilling is called the face. Your question is a good one—the last time I heard there were about four-hundred individual shafts, some of them over three-thousand feet deep and maybe twenty-five hundred miles of drifts. As far as a maze, you're right. Believe it or not, most of them are interconnected, that's why there's such a fresh air flow down here today," continued A.J. "Although that's not the case every single day. Depending on the weather and a few other factors, the air can be bad too; we monitor it around the clock. Also, that's how the high graders worked in the old days. They used to travel around from mine to mine looking to pocket some rich ore."

When they got to the end of the first drift they turned right, following the narrow rails to another intersection. They turned right again and Bannister could hear the unmistakable sound of an air drill working on rock. As they got closer, he saw the two small specks of light bouncing along the rock walls in concert with the jarring motion of the drill.

When they got close enough, the two miners shut down the air to the drill and the drift got deathly quiet.

Walking up to the grease and dust-covered men standing in the end of the drift, A.J. asked them how they were coming along. The youngest-looking face peered out from under the light on his hard hat, his long ponytail trailing down behind him. "Right on time, boss, we just finished the drilling. We should be ready to shoot it in about an hour."

Both men were barely in their thirties—much younger than Bannister thought they would be. All his past experiences seemed to be with grizzled-looking older guys, men that looked like they had spent an entire lifetime in the darkest reaches of a hard rock mine.

"Good enough," said A.J., "be safe. I'll have a helper get the muck cart ready. Let him know if you need something."

Bannister was surprised that two such young men did everything from the drilling to the blasting, pretty much unsupervised. "These guys put the dynamite in the holes and detonate it and everything?"

"Jack, we haven't used dynamite in this industry since the eighties-too unstable, and the guys hated it. We use ammonium nitrate now days. It's much more stable and easy to use."

"Ammonium nitrate? Isn't that the bomb material you hear about on the news, the stuff the terrorists use?"

"The very same. People using explosives for legitimate work have used it for years, but the publicity from the bombing in Oklahoma City put it in everyone's mind. Now the new rules make it harder to get. They document everything now; you're in the system if you buy it."

Bannister followed A.J. down the drift and back toward the junction, digesting this fresh information. "Is dynamite still available to the public?"

"Should be easier to get than ammonium, plus there's plenty of it around if you need it."

"A.J., do you know what a nitro headache is?"

Laughing out loud at the thought of dynamite-induced headaches, he nodded his head yes. It was something he knew all too well. "The nitro in dynamite can give you a whopper of a headache, that's one of the reasons the miners love ammonium nitrate so much—no headaches. How do you know about nitro headaches, Jack?"

"Just something an old miner told me about once; I'd hate to have one myself."

"If someone is still using dynamite, it must be because they're trying to use up an old stockpile, otherwise there would be no reason to use it."

Bannister looked at A.J. as they stepped in the cage. "You wouldn't think so would you?"

Chapter 8

Rocky Batton drained the last of the coffee from his mug as he sifted through his notes.

"What do we have on the accident so far?" said Bannister sitting down on the stool across from Rocky.

"Good morning to you too, Jack—had your coffee yet?" said Batton, with a bit of early morning sarcasm.

"Anything on the driver yet?" asked Bannister, ignoring the coffee comment.

"No, but the El Paso County Sheriff's office will call as soon as they get something. Detective Hammond is working on it as we speak."

"Good, now we can finish our coffee and take a little ride."

* * *

Standing on the highest point of Bull Hill, near the site of Altman, the two men took in their surroundings: it was a beautiful view, one that Bannister always loved. You could see all the way to the Arkansas River Valley and the Sangre De Cristo Mountains to the south and the Continental Divide at the Collegiate Range to the west. The summit of

Pikes Peak watched over them from behind.

The area was as rich with extraordinary history and scenery as it was with its gold. From the earliest Native Americans and Spanish explorers to Zebulon Pike and the mountain men, this was a place that drew many people to it all throughout history, for many different reasons.

As they stared at the scenery, the two were jarred back to reality by a loud thump and a tall swirling cloud of dust in the distance. One of the newest mining ventures was an open pit operation on Battle Mountain. For more than a hundred years, it had all been confined to miles and miles of shafts and drifts wandering throughout the district—now the landscape was changing fast.

Cripple Creek was now known for gambling, and Battle Mountain—sometimes referred to as the richest mountain in the West—stood between Cripple Creek and Victor, the town on the opposite side of the mountain. The famous mountain was slowly being eaten away from the top down, the open-pit mining operation gradually chewing its way through more than a century of old claims.

"Rocky, what do you know about the Carlton Tunnel?" asked Bannister.

"Well, not all that much. I heard it was built to take away the water problem in the mines. I think it ends up in the Arkansas River."

"That's it exactly," said Bannister pointing down the canyon. "We've been finding traces of heavy metals and stuff like trichloroethylene where it drains into the river,.."

"We found trych at the accident site the other day, but that shouldn't figure in this deal, Jack."

"Not the barrels that were broken, Rocky, but what if there were others that went somewhere else? Maybe those made their way into the mines somehow?"

"So you think that the bad guys hid them in the mines? Like you said, there are hundreds of miles of tunnels in there. It would be worse than finding a needle in a haystack."

"Drifts, Rocky, they're called drifts, and there are more than twenty-five-hundred miles of them and over four-hundred shafts, some of them three-thousand feet deep."

"You think those pricks are hiding this poison in the mine? Well, where do we start?"

"I think at the Cripple Creek District Museum. They have a lot of maps and models of the mountain and how they all tie together."

* * *

Cripple Creek, Colorado, is a small town sitting on a high plateau alongside of Battle Mountain. Gold was discovered in 1890 by an itinerant cowboy named Bob Womack, in a valley called Poverty Gulch. Within months after the strike, the rush was on and it soon became known as The World's Greatest Gold Camp.

As the mines played out and gold prices fell, the town assumed a new role as a sleepy tourist town. The town stands at nearly 9,500 feet above sea level, and in the center of spectacular scenery. Cripple Creek became someplace for locals to take their friends and family when they came on vacation. In 1991, when the state approved casino gambling, Cripple Creek entered its newest incarnation as a gambling hot spot. Bannister never thought much of the gambling industry but he appeared to be in the minority; there were always plenty of people to fill the casinos.

* * *

Rocky looked something like a bear as he bent over the model of the district mines. The museum in Cripple Creek maintained the glass model of the district as it was in the boom times of the late nineties. His fingers followed the lines of one operation into another, and then another and another.

"What are you thinking?" asked Bannister, as he watched him concentrating on the maze of lines going every direction.

"Couple of things, boss. How to get into the mine's for one, how to explore them, and how to know exactly what we're looking for," he said, without looking up. "Like I said, we have our work cut out for us."

"I have a call in to a new friend, a mine expert. He can help us get in and teach us how to get around. I'm still not sure exactly what we're looking for, but I have a couple of thoughts to keep me busy this weekend," said Bannister. "That, the golden armor, and Jessie's Russian project will take up most of the weekend I'm sure." He added. "By the way, I still haven't heard anything on the truck driver. You will have all that for me on Monday—Right?"

Rocky dutifully nodded his head. "Yes, boss, I'll call the detective this afternoon. Where are you going from here?"

"Back to the doc-in-a-box to have my stitches taken out, then back to the ranch for a little R and R—if that's okay with you . . ?"

"Sure, boss, fine with me, I know you gotta take care of what fingers you got left . . ."

Chapter 9

Hoping to numb the throbbing in his hand, Bannister threw down a couple of aspirin, followed by a few swallows of beer, and laid his head back on the couch. That's where Jessie found him when she got home. She glanced down at him as she walked into the kitchen, followed closely by Maggie, the dog's nose going a hundred miles an hour looking for a treat.

After setting out two plates and preparing supper, Jessie walked over to Bannister and shook him gently. "Come on, cowboy, let's get something to eat—you need your strength. There's a lot of work to do tonight." Maggie followed her back to the kitchen like a shadow, claws clicking along the hardwood floor, still waiting for her treat.

"What do you mean a lot of work to do?" asked Bannister between yawns. "I've been working all day; I need a break."

"You have a lot to catch up on—have you forgotten the Russian miner that went missing?" she said, setting a steaming hot dish in front of him.

"That old Russian isn't going anywhere. If no one has found him in the last hundred years, I don't think I'll find him tonight."

"But you will start looking—won't you . . ?"

"Yes," said Bannister, settling into the kitchen chair. "I guess I will. Pass the tortillas please."

* * *

Bannister finished up, walked into the living room, and sank down into the couch opposite the fireplace. Jessie came in and curled up on the other end with a book, and Maggie jumped up and plopped down next to her. As the warmth from the wood fire began to fill the cabin, he opened the small chest and started to sort out the contents. The packets of letters were waiting for him, neatly organized by Jessie.

The oldest packet contained five letters; the earliest was dated April 12, 1892, and postmarked in New Jersey. Bannister could tell it was nineteenth century Russian cursive, written by a strong hand. Russian school kids learned to write at a young age and the cursive of the time was full of tall uppercase letters done with a flourish. The lowercase letters were much smaller and plainer.

The letter was addressed to Kapeka Serinov, in a village called Miass in southern Russia. Thumbing through his vintage world atlas, he found it just above the border of Kazakhstan in the Ilmen Mountains.

Bannister took a fresh pad of paper and began to copy the letter in Russian, leaving plenty of space to write in the English translation. It was slow, tedious work, but he realized he could still understand many of the words from his days as a translator. After he finished copying the letter, he opened his Russian/English dictionary and began to piece together each sentence in English.

By the time he ran out of firewood, Jessie and Maggie were already in bed and he knew he was hooked on this amazing story of a Russian migrant on a journey to the United States and the hope of a better life. A classic story of immigration began to emerge from the pages of the letters, and by the time he finished the first one, he had followed the young miner, Vitor Serinov, from southern Russia to a seaport in Germany.

From what he could tell from the written words and reading between the lines, it looked like Serinov left his home in Miass around the end of December in 1891. Although traveling across Russia and Poland in the dead of winter would be an ordeal even today, the writer never showed any sign of pain or suffering, talking only in excited and positive terms. He recorded how he arrived in Stetten, Germany, on January 27, 1982, and bought passage on the *SS Polaria* to America.

After some research, he found that the town named Stetten in 1892 was now called Sczcecin and located in Poland. It was a port city on the Baltic Sea and a hub of transportation for the area.

As Bannister looked up each word and began to fill in the story, it was obvious that this was a tough, driven young man who was on a mission that eventually took him to the goldfields of Cripple Creek, Colorado, and into a mystery that had been ongoing for more than a hundred years.

* * *

Bannister woke up to the hot comfort of a blazing fire and the smell of coffee. He'd spent the night on the couch dreaming about the miner and his adventure. "So Bannister," said Jessie from the kitchen, "did you find the missing miner?"

"Not yet, but I still have a pile of letters to read; we'll find him eventually, I'm sure of that." Jack Bannister was fifty-nine years old and looked ten years younger. With his thick hair now gray, and a faded scar along the left side of his chin from his time in Vietnam, he was still lean and in good shape. Although lately his knees had begun to bother him when he got up in the morning, and his hearing was not what it once was, he still felt pretty good.

Jessie Lopez was fourteen years his junior and looked even younger.

The Drift

She was a classic Mexican beauty. At five foot eight, she was a little taller than most of her family, with thick black hair falling nearly to her waist, and just starting to show a few flecks of gray. At 110 pounds, her figure was exactly the same as it was when they had met ten years ago. Her large, riveting black eyes are what caught his attention the first time they met, and still drew him to her today.

Her family had immigrated to the United States from central Mexico around 1900 and landed in the San Luis Valley of south-central Colorado. They owned several farms around the valley and a small grocery business in nearby Manassas. After graduating from the University of Colorado, she went on to get her masters in American history. When a job as curator of the Pikes Peak Pioneers Museum opened up about ten years ago, she took it, and turned it from a nice local attraction into a world-class museum of western history.

That's when she met Jack Bannister. Through his family connections, he helped arrange the transfer of an important gift from a prominent local ranching family to the museum, and he never gave her a minute's rest until she agreed to go out with him. She moved into his cabin near Cripple Creek three months later.

* * *

The weekend went by quickly and they stayed in the cabin the whole time. Bannister worked on the first packet of letters and Jessie alternated between museum work and working on her files of the golden armor, the family treasure legend.

Her intense commitment to the treasure story was typical of everything she did in her life. Her relentless drive and pursuit of her goals weren't going to be derailed, and all who knew her understood that well. But she had a very special, personal connection with everyone she met, and could charm anyone from the deliveryman to the richest businessmen in the state. "She could charm the skin off a snake without getting bit if it meant a donation for the museum," cracked Rocky one day after watching her work.

Bannister was just as intense in his work, but did lack a bit in the charm department—at least according to Rocky and Jessie. Much more pragmatic and straightforward, he had a tendency to drive straight ahead nonstop when a little diplomacy might help. He also had a reputation for instantly understanding the situation at hand and cutting out all the distractions to get quickly to the root of the problem and find a solution. That's why the director wanted him to run things in Colorado and was now pressing him to take over the whole western states region.

For now, he had a good woman, a good job, and a good dog. That was more than enough for him, though he was beginning to wonder about the dog.

While flipping through the pages of his dictionary, the phone jarred him out of nineteenth-century Russia and back into the present. "Okay, I got it, I'll see you back in the office at 8:00 A.M.," said Bannister.

"Was that Rocky?" asked Jessie without looking up.

"Yeah, he has a little more information on the crash and on the mining operation. Let's plan on coffee at the diner about seven."

"Sure Jack, that sounds good. But you're buying, you know that, right?"

Chapter 10

The building on the southwest corner of Pikes Peak and Tejon was the original Colorado National Bank building built in 1909, and it was often called Colorado Springs' first high-rise. At seven stories, it was the highest at that time, and the first steel-frame building in the county. Bannister's corner office was on the sixth floor. It also had a great view of Pikes Peak-in some ways it all matched Bannister's personality perfectly.

Rocky sat down across from the desk and opened his notebook. "I found out that the driver killed in the crash, a guy named Harley Craig Pattison, age forty-two, had been arrested and convicted several times on theft, fraud, and armed robbery—just another dirtbag."

Bannister sipped his coffee while looking over his notes. "Did you find out where he was from?"

"It looks like he was originally from New Jersey."

"So we have a missing load of trichloroethylene and who knows what else. We have traces of it at the outlet of the Carlton drainage tunnel as well as a mix of other things I can't even pronounce. We know that it's coming from somewhere inside of the twenty-four hundred miles of drifts connecting hundreds of these old claims," said Bannister, looking at his map of the district. "We also know that with the recent increase in the price of gold, there's been a lot more digging and blasting going on lately."

"Maybe the new mining has damaged an old stash of chemicals stored inside a mine somewhere?"

"Or—maybe, Rocky, someone has been hiding this poison in a mine somewhere and it's just now starting to show up. And just maybe that someone is PMV, Inc."

"Jack, that's a bit of a stretch, don't you think? I know how you feel about them, but we haven't found anything bad about those guys yet. In fact, so far, I can't find anyone with much to say about them at all."

"It may be nothing, but my gut feeling says there's a connection here. Let's take a ride up to the district and look over the operations that are working now. I can introduce you to my new friend; he's an old-time hard rock miner, and he may have a few answers for us."

"You got it, boss, your truck or mine?"

"You drive, my hand hurts—maybe I can get a little nap on the way."

"You want to do a little treasure hunting while we're up there, boss?" said Rocky, trying to force back a grin.

"Just stop talking and drive. If I ever need your help treasure hunting, I'll ask for it!"

* * *

Leaving the main highway at the remains of the ghost town of Gillette, they rode through a beautiful valley dotted with scattered ruins and mine sites. The road wound its way around the hills past a few more ghost towns like Goldfield, to Victor, which was nearly a ghost town at one time, but was now partially revived by the current gold boom. A few resident citizens were now mixed in with the new working miners, and a few more were hoping to find work. The Phoenix Drilling Co. open-pit project had several hundred people on the payroll at any given time.

As Rocky turned onto a freshly graded gravel road, Bannister couldn't help but notice just how wide and smooth it was. *This is the best I ever saw this road, somebody must be making a little money around here*, thought Bannister. The road twisted through the remains of dozens of abandoned claims, climbing up and through acre after acre of tailings, punctuated by the remains of steel headframes and rotting timbers guarding the ancient shafts. It was a photographer's paradise, but mostly unusable for anything else.

Piles of rusty brown tailings and waste rock were piled in every available spot, evidence of more than a century of labor by thousands of men who came for gold. Most ended up working for wages and disappearing into the footnotes of history—just like Jessie's missing Russian miner.

Following Bannister's directions, Rocky turned down a smaller graded road, through the Golden Peak Exploration gate, and pulled up next to the largest trailer. They found A.J. Rogers at his desk, buried behind a pile of paperwork, with the phone up to his ear. He motioned for them to have a seat and finished up his conversation.

"Hi Jack, good to see you again—more questions on the mining business?"

"A few," said Bannister. "A.J., this is my investigator, Rocky Batton. He chases down all the bad guys for me."

"Good to meet you, Rocky," said A.J., extending a hand. "Jack told me that he thinks there may be something fishy going on at one of these claims. You're welcome to look anywhere you want on Golden Peak property; so far I haven't seen much in the way of bad guys—or much in the way of gold for that matter."

Like Bannister, Rocky liked A.J. immediately. He knew they were about the same age and had all served about the same time. To Rocky he just felt like a straight shooter.

"A.J., I was wondering if you use trichloroethylene in your business?" asked Bannister.

"That's some kind of cleaning solvent, isn't it?"

"Among other things, but you don't use it in your business do you?"

"Not that I know of, Jack. But you might check with open-pit guys. I'm not up on all the stuff they use over there. If something has escaped their operation, it would end up in the same watershed."

"Do you think there's any way to test the water above the open-pit operation? That would narrow down our search area a lot."

"Come with me—I'll take you and Rocky to the overlook so you can get a feel for what the open pit looks like. Maybe that'll give you a little better idea what you're dealing with."

After a short trip up the mountain, they turned into a small graveled parking lot at an abandoned headframe. The local historical society set up an informational display and an overlook point directly above the Phoenix Drilling operation on Battle Mountain.

They stepped up to the fence and looked down into an enormous crater where the top of Battle Mountain used to be. Giant trucks were hauling load after load of rock out of the pit and down to the crusher plant on the south side of the mountain. Wide flat areas the size of football fields were being drilled and loaded with explosives in preparation for the next blast.

After spending a few minutes taking it all in, Bannister shook his head in amazement. "At this rate, in a few years you'll be able to see Cripple Creek from Victor. There won't be any mountain left. This is hard for someone who loves living in this beautiful state."

"Even as a lifelong gold miner, I tend to agree with you, Jack. This is pretty ugly, but the plans are to restore the mountain when they're done. I know the coal companies can do it, so I imagine it can be done here as well. There are those who called the old mine scars a blight too, so I guess it's all in the eye of the beholder. The rumor is they're making more than a million dollars a day, so as long as the gold market is good, this monster will just keep getting bigger."

Bannister stared at the pit for a moment longer before he finally spoke. "A.J., is the drainage tunnel below this deal?"

"Way below. This might be a thousand feet deep. The Carlton Tunnel is several thousand feet below this. It really doesn't connect directly to any mine in particular; it just collects the drainage from the whole district."

"Another thing," continued A.J. "If you look closely at the sides, you can see where the pit mine has exposed many of the old drifts. In fact, they're always in danger of exposing something every time they start to remove another layer of rock. I think they use ground-penetrating radar to try and find the hidden drifts and stopes, so they won't have any equipment fall through."

"What's a stope?" asked Bannister. "Another mining term?"

"Yep, a stope is a branch off of a drift. When we find a vein we follow it. It could go up or down or at any possible angle. We try and get below the vein so we can get gravity on our side. It might be just big enough for one man to work or might be as large as your truck, depending if it's good ore or not."

Rocky shook his head and said what everyone else was thinking. "The chances of finding the source of the contaminant just went from a needle in a haystack to a needle in a whole field of haystacks."

Bannister seemed lost in thought when A.J. nudged him. "Anthing else I can do for you, Jack?"

"Probably, but that's about it for today I think, unless you have any ideas about where to go from here—any thoughts on that?"

"Only one, Jack, and I doubt if you would like it. That's for you to go down and start exploring for yourself."

"You're right about that, I don't like it."

Chapter 11

The overhead door on the tin building slammed shut with a thud. The rental truck was backed into the building next to the black Jeep. Inside the truck was the usual collection of fifty-gallon drums, cleaned of any identifying marks and sealed with proper lids and locking rings. Each drum was secured with a new padlock.

The biggest man was the resident explosives expert, directing the placing of the charges. However, they had done this many times, and needed little instruction. The new electric lift could take down two drums and two men in one trip. The lift allowed them to operate the controls themselves and stop at whatever level they were currently working. After they brought the load down, they wheeled the drums to the end of the drift that was already prepared. The process was repeated over and over all night until the drift was full and ready to shoot.

As the last barrel was removed from the truck, the leader noticed that it didn't have a padlock on it. He put his hand up in front of the driver's face. "Put it back on, right now—you know the rules."

The driver tried to argue but was cut off in mid-sentence. "Nothing goes down there that isn't sealed and locked. Now get out of here and don't come back if you can't get it right."

This trash collection business had been working successfully for almost five years and had made them all a lot of money. But the boss's rules were strict; the only thing that goes into this mine comes in sealed barrels. That way nobody knows what is being disposed of and nobody can be made to talk about the contents.

Although the drums all looked the same from the outside, it was anybody's guess what might be inside of them. Some weighed nearly 400 pounds and were obviously liquid, and some were anywhere from a few pounds and up. The running joke was that Jimmy Hoffa lived in one drift and Amelia Earhart in another—anything was possible if you had a good imagination. The fact that nobody knew what was in them was the perfect part of the operation. Judging from the license plates on the delivery trucks, the drums came from all over the country.

The second rule was that nothing can be put into the mine until the explosives were in place, and each load had to be sealed the same day. The third rule was that all the trucks had to be plain rental units from agencies used only once by the customer. All barrels must be sealed and cleaned off before they could even go into the truck. If there was a problem with the chain of operation, it could be easily severed and there was no path to the big boss. These rules had kept things running smoothly and mostly unnoticed by the locals. The boss charged so much per load to make them disappear forever and had more business than it was possible to handle.

The Black Mule mine was 1,800 feet deep with about 14 miles of drifts and stopes, and there was no end to what they could hide down there. If they played their cards right, they would be rich in another year or two and nobody would be the wiser.

With the timer set, all four men walked out of the portal and toward the Jeep. It had been a long night moving all the drums to the right spot and they were exhausted. As they locked the gate and started their drive to Cripple Creek, they failed to notice a short old man, with a full gray beard and a dirty red welder's hat, tucked back in the trees watching intently.

After they were out of sight, Turner picked his way back through the rocks and trees, climbed into Rattler, and fired it up. In twenty minutes, he was at Bannister's cabin.

* * *

"They're for sure putting something down that old mine," said Turner, as he headed for the couch. "There were two trucks tonight, one right after another."

"Did you get any license plate numbers?"

"Why hell, yes, I got the numbers! What do you think I was doing out there all night—howling at the moon?"

Jessie had been working on paperwork when she heard the exchange and burst out laughing. "You tell him, Turner—and tell him if he doesn't start paying you pretty soon, you'll be looking for another job!"

Bannister ignored the humor at his expense and took the numbers. "If they're like the truck that crashed last week, then they're rentals. I suspect they're just another dead end, but I'll have Rocky run them tomorrow. You'd just as well stay here tonight; the couch is plenty soft and there's a big breakfast in it for you if you want."

"That okay with you, Jess?" asked Turner. "I don't want to bother you none, I know you got one big pain in the butt to take care of already."

"For you, I would even make blueberry pancakes, and—biscuits and gravy."

"You talked me into it, and while I'm here, I'll throw on a little more

The Drift

wood and we can talk about what's going on up on the mountain."

The three of them sat down on the long, overstuffed couch in front of the roaring fire, Jessie with a hot cup of tea, and Bannister and Turner sipping on a cold beer. Maggie claimed her usual place on Jessie's lap. The conversation eventually got around to Cripple Creek, as it often did when they were together, and the history of the mining district. Even now, the Cripple Creek District ranked as the fifth greatest American gold producer of all times.

Jessie Lopez was born and raised on a farm in the San Luis Valley in southern Colorado. Jack was born in Illinois and moved here in the seventies right after the army, and Turner, although often as mysterious about his history as he was his age, came from Iowa as a kid. They all had two important things in common: they loved history, and they loved the West.

Bannister and Turner had no real family left where they came from and saw no good reason to return. Jessie was just the opposite. The San Luis Valley was overflowing with family, and they were a close-knit bunch. Although she had never had kids, she herself was the sixth of seven and always said she had more than enough siblings, nieces, and nephews in her life to make up for no kids of her own.

Bannister had learned to love the Hispanic influence in his life and looked forward to their trips south. Her family was a like a nonstop, three-ring circus with people coming and going at all hours, showing off the newest family, members, and insisting they come to their house for supper. The different siblings were all farmers and ranchers; two of them raised ranch horses and still did things the traditional way, working their cattle from horseback. Jack was always made to feel like part of the family and he treasured the relationship.

* * *

As the fire died down, so did the conversation. Jessie finished her last cup of tea and stood up. "It's time for bed, boys; I've got work to do in the morning. If I don't get a little sleep there won't be any blueberry pancakes for breakfast."

As she headed for the bedroom, Bannister pulled the still-sleeping bird dog over to him and started to rub her ears. Finally waking up to the situation, Maggie wiggled out of his grasp, jumped off the couch, and followed Jessie into the bedroom.

Turner got a huge smile from this. "Does that dog even like you, Jack?"

"She has to like me, she's my dog!"

"Well, she may have been your dog once . . ." said Turner, choking back a laugh.

"She's still my dog. She's just having a little trouble remembering exactly who's the boss around here." At that, Bannister got up and followed Jessie and Maggie into the bedroom.

Turner watched both of them following Jessie and could hold it back no longer; he broke into a loud, cackling laugh. "Looks to me like you both know who the boss really is, Jack—and it sure ain't you!" With that, he pulled his hat down over his eyes and fell instantly asleep.

Chapter 12

Bannister met Rocky at Darla's early the next morning. After draining one pot of coffee, they were well into another one when they finished their breakfast. For an hour they discussed what was going on at the Black Mule mine—or at least what they thought was going on.

What they knew for sure was that it was operated by PMV, Inc., which was owned by Carhartt Aviation. After a thorough check through all the old mining records, as well as the county and state records and permits, everything was current and straightforward. The bills were all paid and the company kept a low profile around the district.

Darla Rios, the owner of the diner, was a tiny, slim, forty-five year old Hispanic woman, originally from New Mexico. After years of working at a local electronics firm, the company went out of business and left her without a job, a common thing for Colorado Springs in the eighties and nineties.

With her severance pay in hand, she went looking for a new career. She found a 1950s style diner for sale in the heart of downtown

Colorado Springs. She bought it immediately, and set up a breakfast and lunch business five days a week. She ran it alone, cooking and waiting on customers at the same time. With nothing but word of mouth for advertising, her business took off on the power of her red chile, great burgers, and outgoing personality. With only twelve seats, the diner was always full.

As the breakfast crowd began to thin, she couldn't resist poking a little fun at her two friends huddled together so seriously. "You guys staying for lunch too?" she teased.

"It's about the only way to beat the three-piece suits that plug up the place in the afternoon," said Bannister without looking up. "We get a lot of work done here, Darla."

"Well, maybe it wouldn't do you two any harm to clean up a little, maybe wear a suit now and then," she said, trying her best to get a rise out of them. "You could use the guys from the lunch crowd as your models."

Rocky laughed at the thought of wearing a three-piece suit to work. "Shoot Dar, Bannister don't even own a tie and I outgrew my last suit in high school."

"Just a testimonial to your eating here for so many years," said Rios. "You're a model of what good cooking can do for a man. Now if you would just marry me, I'd have you out of those outdated clothes in no time..."

The two had been flirting like this for years, and Bannister was beginning to wonder if there wasn't a little more to their relationship than he knew about. If so, it would be a good match he thought. Rocky was the only person he ever heard address her as Dar; there could be something there. Tiny little Darla and Rocky the giant—it was something to smile about.

* * *

Sitting in Bannister's office, the two continued their conversation on the Cripple Creek problem. "Rock, I think the only way to get to Carhartt Aviation is through the guys that drive around in the Jeep. I think these PMV guys are the weak spot in the armor; a little pressure on the ones that look to be the followers of the team might be the answer. How about watching them for a few days and see which one looks like the weakest of the group? After awhile, let him see you until he gets a little nervous and watch what develops."

"I can handle that, boss," said Rocky. "It'll be fun to screw with these guys a little."

Bannister knew this was right up Rocky's alley; he loved this detective stuff and was totally at home hunting down criminals.

As Rocky headed out, Bannister stopped him at the door. "Rock, you might as well crash at the cabin while you're working on this. I'll call Jessie and tell her that you're coming, and she needs more food." As he started to leave, Bannister had one more thing to add. "Rocky, I know I said this before, but be careful with these guys, be sure you have your gun and badge."

"I got it, boss, anything else—or can I go now?"

"I'll see you at the cabin tonight—now get the hell out of here, I got somewhere I gotta be."

Chapter 13

It was Friday night and Bannister had already been working on the Russian letters for over an hour, while Jessie and Maggie were worked on their own project—the never-ending search for the golden armor. The first letter covered the time Vitor Serinov left Miass, to shortly after he docked in New Jersey, at Ellis Island. Serinov was among the first immigrants to come through its portals. In April 1892, Ellis Island had been built by the federal government as the new center for all immigration. Previous to 1892 individual states had managed their immigration issues themselves.

The first entry on the ship talked about its size. "I today found passage to America. The *SS Polaria* is very large, and will hold many more people than our small town. Made of iron, with two tall masts front and rear and an enormous smokestack in the center, it looks like it could sail anywhere on earth where there is water—it looks very safe."

More than a thousand people were booked on the *SS Polaria* for the trip to America. They were mostly Poles and Germans with a lesser mix of Russians and others. Many Russian Jews were leaving their homes ahead of the terror called Alexander the Third. The czar was a tyrant and anti-Semite who restricted every move of the Jewish population and repealed all the more liberal policies of his father.

Serinov gave his information to the clerk, and he entered it into the logbook of the ship. "Today I became an official passenger. I paid them six English pounds passage, and they asked to know where I was going, and I said Colorado, USA. They wanted to know my profession and I told them miner, and they even wanted to know how much money I had. I had traded my Russian money for English money, as I was told it would be easier to use for passage. I told them two pounds but I didn't tell them of the other two I had sewn into my coat. They said they wanted all immigrants to have a certain amount before they can go. I thought this strange but I told them."

The boat was beginning to swell with immigrants; the Russian Jews stood out as the poorest of the lot, a testament of their harsh life in Russia. Many of these had their fares paid for by various relief organizations. The Germans looked to be the fittest and more prosperous of the passengers; though, as the writer noted in his letter, "All are notably of a working-class variety." The rest, including Serinov, fell somewhere in between in appearance and prosperity. The space below the decks was cramped with other single men, but no one complained—they were going to America.

Serinov noted the date as January 29, 1892. "As we began to leave port, I was much surprised to see many hundreds of people gathered to watch us depart. Two stowaways were caught and returned to shore on the tugboat that was towing us."

On the third day, the *SS Polaria* put to in the harbor at Swansea, Wales, to take on a full load of coal and tinplate destined for America. "We made quick time of disembarking, all of us wanting the feel of solid ground under our feet. We all needed, if for only a few hours, to get away from the seasickness and the closeness of our fellow passengers."

The passengers wandered the streets of Swansea, only to draw the curiosity and comments of the locals, who rarely saw such an odd collection of foreigners. When it was time to board, the passengers had experienced all they wanted of Swansea and its residents, and no doubt the residents had their curiosity of the foreigners quenched too. As they marched back to their respective berths, they didn't even care to watch the ship head out into the open ocean.

Single men slept, played local games, wrote letters, and filled their journals. Families kept busy with games and studies for the children. It would be more than two weeks before they would see the shores of America. Serinov's journal-like letters were mixed in with his personal thoughts. They would suddenly appear as though he just couldn't hold them back any longer—his wife was always close by in his mind. "My beautiful wife Kapeka, it is cold and lonely and damp in this iron ship. I so wish you were with me on this journey. I promise I will find our new home and send for you soon. I love you very much."

He had always loved her name—it meant "Little Stork"—and he envisioned an equally beautiful daughter with the same name. "I will name our successful mine The Little Stork, in honor of my girls," he wrote. Though not mentioned specifically in the letter, it appeared that his wife was expecting and Serinov was hoping for a girl. "It will become a famous place, and we will build our home on a hill above it for all to see, and we will have many friends to entertain and to share our happiness with."

After the first few days at sea, the mood of the travelers became much quieter, with many unable to get up and around due to seasickness. Even the children grew quieter, seldom leaving their parents side. The incessant rocking of the ship, and dull, vibrating drone of the engines were, at times, almost too much for many to tolerate.

"After our sixth day out from Swansea, the excitement had worn off of the faces of most of my fellow passengers. Their look was more that of quiet resolution, just wanting to get this trip over and set foot in America," wrote Serinov.

He noted that the conditions were not truly bad; it was just that most had never left their homeland before, let alone spent any time on a ship in the middle of the Atlantic Ocean with a thousand strangers. He also wrote that "the ship had plenty of fresh water and perhaps strangely enough, more soap than he had seen anywhere. It appears the captain wants a clean bunch of passengers."

He continued the entry of the day. "The food is passable and filling, but rather bland. Not like you and I have become used to. Most take their meals with them back to their berth. This is a problem for some, for if they fail to keep their area clean, they invite the smallest stowaways in." He was referring to the never-ending supply of rats that inhabited every ship of the day.

"At night, you can sometimes feel them burrowing through your blanket looking for bits of food or a place to nest. The thought of sharing my nights with live rats is very uncomfortable to me, but most of us are more or less used to it by now. We heard that one of the German children had her ear badly chewed by one, so we pull a sock down over our head and ears when we sleep."

With the New World always in his mind, he was able to keep his focus and shut out the day-to-day boredom that came with long sea voyages. When he was not writing, he was visiting with other passengers. Despite the many different languages, they were able to communicate with a few basic words and gestures. In the family area, he witnessed his first live birth. "A young German family by the name of Bauer gave birth to a little girl they called Elica. It was the talk of the ship. They said it meant "noble" in the German language."

"Many passengers and several midwives were there to help with the birth, and many more came by to give their congratulations and offer a few small gifts," wrote Serinov. "I had nothing to offer but my support if they needed it, but it was truly some kind of shipboard miracle, this I know for sure."

After about twelve days out from Swansea, the ocean got rough, and a brutally cold wind filled with razor-sharp ice and snow raked the ship for two straight days. "Those that weren't sick at the start of the voyage were now laid low. The heaving of the bow and the crashing back into the water bruised and battered most of the travelers. We all bundled in everything we had, and held tight on to our pallets."

Serinov began to show signs of acute seasickness for the first time in the voyage. "I am now myself sick and feel nearly unable to get up and walk about. This giant ship is tossed about like a feather in a gale, and leans perilously from side to side as the swells hit it. I can only hope and pray we get there soon."

The passengers were buzzing about spotting several ships and their first look at land in weeks. "The word today is that we will be in America soon. At last, solid ground beneath my feet. As we crowded the rails of the ship and the land grew closer, I spotted the Bauer family with baby Elica—what a wonderful start for a beautiful baby girl. Soon, my love, it will be you, and I, and our baby girl together in Colorado, I promise, I love you."

As the great iron ship slowed and began to enter the harbor, two tugboats came to meet them and deliver a pilot for the last part of the trip. The ship slowed even more and headed toward the Ellis Island Immigration Center.

"Suddenly, the passengers began to get quiet, reflecting perhaps on what was about to happen next in their journey for a new life. After a few minutes, a deafening roar from the crowd drowned out any thoughts I may have had at that moment, and I rushed to the front of the ship to see what was the cause of the sudden excitement," wrote Serinov.

"There, before me, was the great American lady, holding her blazing golden torch high in welcome. For that moment, I could hear nothing but my own heart beating wildly, all else was lost in a moment of emotion like nothing I have ever experienced before. She was so magnificent, so beyond anything I am able to put into words at this moment." As the ship slid past the statue, Serinov suddenly realized that he was not the only one crying. "A great many of the passengers were also overcome with the moment. Kapeka, soon you will experience it too, very soon. I love you."

As the tugs maneuvered the ship into the dock, the passengers pressed toward the exit with baggage and children tightly in hand. "We were made to wait until the gangway was in place and they were ready for the lot of us," noted Serinov. "The building was a new and beautiful structure built of wood, very large, with tall towers on the four corners and was alive with activity of all sorts."

As the passengers slowly disembarked, they entered the first of many doors and stops required to complete their passage. The medical stop was the most intimidating; many of the passengers had never seen a real doctor before. "I felt like a cow being examined before slaughter. They poked things into my eyes and ears and mouth very quickly before they let me go on. Some passengers received large letters chalked onto their coats, I am not sure of the significance of that, but they were led into a different area."

"We waited in the lines while they checked to see if I was healthy, to see if I was legal, and to see if I had any money—they are very concerned that we are all poor and have nowhere to go." Serinov moved through the mass of immigrants, waiting as patiently as possible for his turn. "The noise of thousands of people all talking at once, in more languages than I ever heard, nearly overwhelmed me. People translating were trying to talk louder and those calling out names even louder—it both scared me a little and excited me at the same time."

The next stop was the money exchange station where he traded his English money for American money. "This felt very good to me, like I now belonged," noted Serinov. From here he went to the train station, where he could buy a ticket to many different places, depending if he had family somewhere or what kind of work he was looking for. After asking if there was a ticket to Colorado, he was disappointed to find Pennsylvania was far as the train could go. "The agent told me that there was coal mine work there, so I bought a ticket, and plan to keep on to Colorado from there."

Most of the day was required to process the passengers from the *SS Polaria*, and after the new immigrants were released, a smaller ferry boat took them to the mainland and the train stations. The ferries docked right at the train terminal and the new Americans, as Serinov chose to call them, were directed to the proper platform. "More trains, people, and buildings than you or I could ever imagine, line the banks of the harbor. But it is not Colorado and I am moving on. We shall be together soon Kapeka. I love you, Vitor."

Somewhere near the train terminal, Vitor was able to send his letter on its way to his wife, Kapeka, in the village of Miass, Russia. The postmark said April 12, 1892, Jersey City, New Jersey, USA.

Chapter 14

The sawed-off baseball bat came down hard on the side of Rocky Batton's head, tearing at his ear and filling it with blood. The next blow was stopped in mid-swing by his giant hand. Jerking the bat away from the drunken miner, he broke it in half and threw the pieces across the floor. Grabbing the man by the belt and the collar, he slammed him headfirst into the wall where he dropped to the floor in a pile of legs and arms. The night bartender and another customer grabbed the man's cuffs and dragged him out the back door to let him sleep it off in the cold night air.

The waitress brought Rocky a damp towel and pressed it against the side of his head. "You took quite a shot there, mister, you gonna be okay?"

Rocky looked up at the face of a pleasant, middle-aged woman with dyed black hair and a bit too much makeup. "Yes, ma'am, I think so. Thank you." He walked to the restroom and cleaned up as much as possible. After a little inspection, he could see that he might need a few stitches, but decided it could wait awhile.

When he returned to his booth, it had been cleaned up and a fresh glass of beer was waiting for him. "Anything else I can get for you, honey?" asked the waitress.

"Any chance you might have a Band-aid so I can slow the bleeding down a little?"

"Sure, give me just a minute."

When she left, the bartender and another miner walked over and sat down across from him. The bartender stuck out his hand to Rocky and introduced himself. "I'm Buck Tyler; I just want to thank you for the help on that deal. That guy's usually a pain in the ass after a few drinks, but after tonight I think he may just mellow out a bit."

The other man offered his hand and introduced himself only as Dave. "Thanks man, I thought he was about to deliver the coup de grace on my head when you stepped in. What made you do it?"

"It looked to me like he was about to hurt you bad, and you didn't have a bat of your own—so, I guess I just hate an unfair fight. I'm Rocky, good to meet you."

The waitress returned with tape and gauze and proceeded to patch up the torn ear and temporarily stop the blood flow. "Thank you, ma'am, I really appreciate it. I'm Rocky."

"No, Rocky, thank you. "It's about time that someone took out the trash around here," she said, shooting the bartender a hard sideways look. "I'm Sharon, I'll get you another beer; you want something to eat to go along with it?"

"No thanks, just a beer would be fine."

Rocky and his new pal, Dave, spent the next hour talking sports and women and eventually gold mining. Rocky judged him to be about forty years old. He was medium height and stocky with thinning brown hair and a small gold earring in his left ear. His right leg bounced nervously up and down, almost uncontrollably while sitting in the booth, and he was a serious chain-smoker. "You work in the gold mines, Dave? It always seemed a little claustrophobic down there to me."

"Yeah, it pays decent, but it's not all that scary. Where I work is just mostly a small prospect operation; we just have a few guys and we search for new veins in old works. We drill for a couple of days, then shoot it and search for good ore—pretty straightforward stuff."

"Any big finds yet?" asked Rocky.

"Not nearly enough to get rich on, but there's always a chance, I guess."

Rocky continued the covert interrogation of his new friend. "Do you handle the dynamite and set it off?"

"No, I'm just a driller and mucker. Someone tells us where to drill, how many holes, and how deep; they put in the charges and wire them up. Then they tell us where they want the next one and we do it all over again."

"Sounds like hard work to me, but we all gotta do what we gotta do to make a buck nowadays," said Rocky, draining the last of his beer.

"What do you do to make a buck, Rocky?"

"Well, I'm mostly an office pinkie these days. I work for a branch of the federal government that monitors water quality for rivers in the West. Right now I'm checking the tributaries to the Arkansas River and the river itself; we don't want any minnows gettin' sick you know." Rocky kept his story close to reality so it would be easier to keep it straight. "I'll be around for a few more weeks until I gather up all the numbers and turn them in to Washington, and then I'll move upstream to do the same in the Leadville area. It only takes a few minutes to get a sample, but there are a couple of hours of paperwork for each one."

"That don't sound like all that bad of a deal to me, Rocky. At least you're not coming home with crashing headaches after working down there—and, at least you get to breathe fresh air and see a little sunshine on your shift."

"You're right about that, and when I get the samples for the day, I can come here and have a beer and a sandwich while I enter everything into my computer. Not a bad deal for a broken-down old guy like me," he said with a chuckle.

"Hell, Rocky, I don't know old you are, but I sure didn't see any sign of a broken-down old guy when you tuned up that drunk—I can only imagine what you must have been like when you were a young guy."

Rocky looked at him with a slight grin on his face. "Yeah, back in the old days I did a bit of fighting, it was almost mandatory growing up in my part of New Jersey. If they ever saw you as scared they would make your life a living hell. Everybody there was a scrapper; some of the smallest guys were the most fearless ones on the street. What happened here tonight was just instinct, I guess, but I don't like to see anyone sucker punched—it just ain't right."

"Well, I got to thank you again; you really saved my butt tonight."

"No problem," said Rocky. "I've been kind of using this spot as a home base. Some of the booths have a place to plug in my computer; that way I can relax, have supper, and get my paperwork entered before I head back to the big city."

"I've seen you around a couple of times before. I wondered what kind of interesting stuff you were doing on the laptop," said Dave. "I thought maybe you were looking at pretty girls or something."

"No pretty girls on this computer, the government would have my balls if they caught me doing that. I'd hate to lose this gig; I'm too old to start looking for another one. Well, I have to head down the mountain. Maybe I'll see you here again, Dave," said Rocky, extending his hand one more time before making his exit.

"I'm usually here when I'm not down in the hole or in bed, so I'm sure we'll see each other again."

With that, Rocky stepped out into the cool night air, noticing that the drunk was already gone. As he climbed into his Blazer, he decided it had been a pretty good start to this part of his investigation. Actually, it was kind of fun in a strange sort of way.

* * *

Turning off the pavement and onto the gravel, Rocky could see the Milky Way brilliantly lit in the night sky. It was always great to get away from the city and up to Jack's place. Like all big cities, the lights of Colorado Springs washed out most of the stars, but up here, the sky looked just as Mother Nature had intended. Rocky leaned against his truck for a few more minutes taking it all in, and was rewarded with several shooting stars for his trouble. "That has to be a good sign," he said out loud to no one in particular. He walked to the front door of the cabin, pounded twice, and stepped inside.

Jessie was nowhere in sight, but Jack sat on the couch surrounded by letters, papers, and books. Without looking up, he told Rocky to grab what he wanted from the kitchen and get comfortable. "Rock, tell me you have some good news about the PMV miners," said Bannister, finally looking up and noticing the bandage on his ear. "What the hell did you do, try and arrest all of them at once?"

"No, I stopped for a beer at Driller's Casino, and came up with a real creative way to get close to one of our boys—it involved a Louisville Slugger and a drunk," said Rocky, unconsciously touching the bandage on his left ear. "Your pal at the doc-in-the-box put a little thread in it for me; it'll be fine."

"So did you get anything useful from him after the baseball bat deal, or was he the one swinging it?"

"No, he was the intended victim. I was able to step in and save him from a nasty beating, and this was just a little collateral damage. But, Dave is my very good buddy now, and I believe he will work nicely as a PMV source."

"You're sure he's one of the guys in the old Black Mule operation?"

"Hell yes, I'm sure," said Rocky. "He was telling me how much he hated the headaches from the blasting, so they must be using dynamite. Didn't you say something about headaches from dynamite, and everyone else uses something else?"

"No doubt the guys in the Black Mule operation are using dynamite instead of the new stuff. Most likely they're using up old stock, I don't imagine they want to call any extra attention to themselves buying something they can get by without," said Bannister, putting down his paperwork and motioning for Rocky to sit down.

"I traced the black Jeep with the silver PMV, Inc. sign yesterday," said Rocky, getting comfortable. "It belongs to the Carhartt Aviation outfit. It's all legal, no problem there."

"What about the rental truck and the dead guy?" asked Bannister.

"Another dead end, just an average rental. The driver had a few rubs with the law, but no connection to any of our guys that I can find."

"So what was your new friend, Dave, like?"

"I think he's the lowest rung on the ladder, just an average guy that needed a job. My guess is he's doing most of the grunt work. He says they're only prospecting old claims, and he just drills and cleans up. Someone else sets the charges. But there's no doubt he has to know what's going on down there; it's a small space and there're only a couple of guys doing all the work."

The two men spent another half hour talking about Batton's day before the conversation turned to other things. "So where's Jessie tonight, still at the museum?"

Bannister nodded his head. "She's setting up a new display on the mining history of the district and a related display on the homes in Colorado Springs that were built by the wealthy mine owners. Also," continued Bannister, "she has managed to get Jamison Carhartt the third involved, so I'll be spending some quality time with him—I think I feel a new friendship coming on. Jessie also wants some new photographs from above, and he'll take me up to get them."

"Are you a museum director now?"

"Just a very interested volunteer, Rock. It can't hurt to get to know him a little better. Besides, that's about the only time I get to see Jess anymore."

"So what's Turner up to? He still working for you?"

"Yeah, he likes all that lurking around in the hills watching the operation for me. He's come up with tag numbers and lots of info; he thinks he's a short, bearded James Bond," said Bannister, grinning at the picture he just created.

"He's a lot like a bulldog when you put him on something, that's for sure. Speaking of dogs, where's Maggie tonight? With Jessie?"

"No, she's in the bedroom, probably sleeping on Jessie's pillow." Bannister whistled and called for her and she came bounding into the living room, jumped up on the couch, and curled up next to Rocky.

Rocky let out a loud booming laugh as she pulled herself higher up onto his lap. "Looks to me like you're now number three on Maggie's list, and falling fast, Jack."

Bannister looked at the dog and stood up shaking his head. "On that note, goodnight, I'm going to bed."

Chapter 15

Bannister opened up the next letter in the packet, and started the laborious procedure of translation all over again. It was posted in the Pennsylvania town of Enslava, in the late summer of 1892. It started with a train ride from New Jersey to the coal mining district, generally referred to as "coal patches," in Clearfield County, Pennsylvania.

After noting with some sadness that he missed Kapeka, Serinov started to talk about the area and finding work in the local mines. "The country in Pennsylvania is beautiful, with many mountains and full of many kinds of trees, except for near the towns, where the hills are nearly barren. I found work in the first mine I went to; they mine soft coal. They have many employees, and are much larger than I have seen before. I have been assigned a job at the newest level, and we are just starting to work on a new vein."

Enslava was a small, relatively new mining town that often turned into thick, sticky black muck after a hard rain. Coal dust coated everything within a mile and keeping clean was nearly impossible for everyone. Serinov was not experienced in coal mines, but he was used to the hard work and difficult conditions inside other types of mines, and took it in stride. As long as it was a paying job, and would help him get to Colorado, was all he cared about. "My wife Kapeka and my beautiful daughter, I am making some money, nearly enough to start sending you some each month. And, I will soon have enough saved to start for Colorado."

After sleeping in an empty railroad car for the first week, Serinov finally got a space in the company housing. "It is very crowded," he wrote. "But, it is dry and has fresh water showers. I spent a few cents for a bar of American soap. It is said to be special soap to get off the coal dust, and it appears to help a little."

After a few weeks, Vitor fell into a routine—ten hours in the mine, six days a week. He quickly discovered what was meant by company town. The site of Enslava was very isolated, and the mine owners built the town for their workers. Like all company towns, they also built and owned everything—from the family houses and the barracks for single men, to the sawmill and railhead that carried the coal to the market. They paid in cash and everything the workers bought for the month was marked on their pay envelope. The rent, groceries, clothes, and any supplies were taken from the pay before the workers got anything. Serinov wrote to his wife that even though his English was getting better, he still didn't understand the pay system that well. "It appears that I sometimes pay for items that are unneeded or unwanted. As well as rent and supplies, I must pay twenty-five cents every month for Catholic priest services. I have not yet seen a priest and would not need him if I had," complained Serinov. "The nights are getting cool and we all put our extra pennies together and buy coal from the company for our stove. My wage of one dollar and fifty-four cents per day does not really go as far as I would like."

The town, like many in these coal patches, was built in a narrow valley with one rough road in, and a railroad spur next to it for shipping the coal. It was crude and barren and lacked anything of color to show even a touch of humanity. It was just the clapboard buildings the company had built, and depending on the weather, life-choking dust or ankle-deep black mud. There was no paint on the outside of any building and the inside was little better. A single stove heated most buildings and the same coal that paid their wages fueled them—if they could afford it.

Although Serinov was an hourly employee, there were those that worked on contract, meaning they were paid by the ton. This was not uncommon, and the rate of pay was better, but the miners had to buy all their own supplies, including the explosives used in the mine. But, he was not offered this work, and really knew very little about blasting. He told Kapeka about this and how many other things he had to pay for. "We must even pay for such things as oil and cotton for our lamps. There is nothing that I can purchase that can stop my head from hurting while working in the mine. If there was, I would buy all I could."

Saving money proved to be extremely difficult, as the monthly expenses sometimes exceeded their earnings. "One of the men on my shift today said that he got the snake on his pay envelope, meaning he had spent more than he had earned that month," wrote Serinov. The snake was a curved line drawn across the envelope when it didn't contain any money. Sometimes the debt from one month had to be carried over to the next. "I am working hard to not get bit by the snake; so far I have succeeded."

Although life was difficult in the Enslava mines, it really wasn't much different from his life in Russia. When the winter set in, he noted it was "easier than the winter in Russia, and not as much snow." He saved what he could from his meager wages, and for lack of a better place to put it, he made a small pouch with a string and carried it around his neck under his shirt. He soon realized that most of the other workers also had a similar method of safekeeping theirs.

By the time spring began to show itself, he had endured months of the damp, dark confines of the coal mine, lit only by the lantern on his head. He wrote to his wife of his readiness to move from Enslava in April of 1893. "I am very tired of this ugly town with the ugly name. It is dirty and dangerous, and I have seen the 'Black Maria' rolling through town with the bodies of my fellow workers three times already; that is enough for me."

The Black Maria was a freight wagon, with the back covered with a roof and pulled by a team of two enormous black draft horses. It was all black, including the tack, except for a window on either side, and was used as an ambulance, or a hearse, as the situation dictated. The company used it to carry injured or dead workers from the mine to the small hospital, although Serinov had seen only the bodies of the dead miners killed through its windows. People moved away, or turned their heads when they saw it coming, they understood that someone was taking their last ride, and they hoped it wasn't someone they knew.

By May of 1893, Serinov was ready to move on. This place had done little more than keep him alive through the winter—it was time to push on to Colorado. He wrote his next letter to his wife and "beautiful baby girl" telling them that he needed "to see the sun and the prairies and would be heading to Colorado soon." He caught a ride on a coal car out of the mountains and started to walk west. After catching an occasional ride on a wagon and working short jobs in eastern Ohio and central Indiana, he landed back in the coal business in southern Illinois. The job was short lived, as he remembered why he had developed a hate for coal—and seeing the Black Maria his first day on the new job.

After a month in the mine, Serinov and another miner took a trip to Cairo, Illinois. Cairo sat at the confluence of the Ohio and the Mississippi Rivers and was surrounded by tall walls and large berms of earth to keep back the water during the spring floods. Both men found work on the railroads and decided to try this new life for a while.

Cairo was as exciting as any place Serinov had ever been. The railroad had several lines going to places with all kinds of exciting names. Steamboats were lined up as far as he could see, and people everywhere were on the move. Teamsters loaded and unloaded every kind of merchandise: from coal and lumber to new furniture, as well as barrels and crates full of food and hardware.

Cairo proved to be a such a draw to the coal miners that they settled into a comfortable routine for nearly a year, working on the rails by day and spending their nights in the city, eating most of their evening meals at the local beer halls. The owners put out a table full of food and they could help themselves for the cost of a five-cent beer.

Serinov's letters home began to slow, from every month or so, to about every two or three months, but he always started them with, "To my wife Kapeka and my beautiful baby girl." He always finished with a reference to his Colorado dream. "I am finally able to save some money to make the trip to Colorado," he said in his last letter mailed from Cairo.

Chapter 16

Turner stared intently from his spot above the road, peering out between the granite boulders and the pines on the hillside. He had a comfortable, well-concealed spot and had been documenting the trucks coming into the Black Mule shaft house. Two hundred yards back into the trees, he had a small, well-camouflaged tent and a few supplies. Some nights he would spend at Bannister's cabin and some in the tent, depending on his mood at the time. He really was a throwback to the mountain man era, a time he secretly wished he could have lived in.

A retired plumber and pipefitter, he had traveled around the country working on big construction projects, including the Alaska oil pipeline. After retirement, he was always looking for something to do in the mountains of Colorado. Bannister liked him from the first time they met while fishing on a remote high lake, and he loved that he was a walking encyclopedia of everything Colorado.

Turner had kept meticulous notes on the trucks, the licenses, and descriptions of any of the people associated with them. Most came after dark, stayed an hour or less, and often left with a truck that rode noticeably higher. A black Jeep and two older pickups were always parked back near the powder storage bunker. Usually, only one rental truck came every two or three days, but now and then two might come at the same time. When the driver left, a worker closed the overhead door, locked the gate behind the truck, and disappeared back inside.

The workers spent three or four hours in the mine before they finished for the night. When they left, the last man out was always the big guy in the Jeep; he snapped the lock shut, took one last look around, and headed off into the night. That night Turner walked back to his tent and crawled inside, filing all his notes and observations for the night. He stared up at the stars for a minute and then pulled his sleeping gear out of the tent, and threw it out on the ground. *No reason to miss this star show*, he thought. After a few minutes of watching the stars, he pulled down his cap and was fast asleep.

* * *

Jessie had her crew setting up displays in preparation for the new mining exhibit. The main floor of the old courthouse had been turned into a walking tour of the Cripple Creek District starting with the Native Americans, and traveling through the discovery of gold by Bob Womack in Poverty Gulch in 1890. The second floor of the exhibit took the visitor from the boom days of the district to the present, including the current open-pit operation on Battle Mountain. For those interested, there was also a walking tour available of the early homes built by the successful miners.

The grand opening of the new display was a smashing success, with all of the city dignitaries and the who's who of the Colorado Springs business world in attendance. Jessie had become something of a local celebrity herself, and she played her part perfectly. While everyone there seemed to be working an angle on someone, Jessie worked her magic on them. Smiling, shaking hands, and touching people on their arms while posing for pictures was part of her charm, and it always worked well for her, raising nearly half a million dollars for the museum since she took over.

As Jack watched her, he spied Jamison Carhartt walking his way, with a drink in one hand and a slim, fragile looking blonde in the other. "Hello, Jack, this is my wife, Clarice."

After the introductions, Clarice went off to visit with some of the other women, and Carhartt pointed at a couple of empty chairs. "Let's grab a chair, Jack; we need to visit a bit. Jessie is quite the master manipulator when it comes to getting what she wants, isn't she?"

"Tell me about it," chuckled Bannister. "I put up with it every day and I can never say no to her. She's all brains and drive wrapped up in a real pretty package."

"Well, she's got me scheduled for another chopper trip over the district to get more pictures from above. She says you're the photographer?"

"Really? Then I guess I am. As you can see, it won't do any good to try and get out of it. Just tell me when you are available and I'll try to make it."

"I'll give you a call next week and see what I can work out. How's the treasure hunting working out, are you having any better luck?" he said, draining the last of his wine.

"No, it's been on hold with all this new museum stuff going on, but after Jess gets back to normal, we will be chasing the legend of the golden armor harder than ever, you can be sure of that."

"Can you tell me a little more about the legend?"

"Well," said Bannister, taking a swallow of his beer, "the story that has been passed down from generation to generation is about a mysterious ancestor named Juan Soto, who was part of an early Spanish expedition.

After months of marching, and a lot of hardship, they had found nothing of real value. Somewhere along the line, they came to camp around the west side of what is now Pikes Peak. The family history says that they either found gold and turquoise or traded the local Indians for it. One of the members of the party made a beautiful armor breastplate for the expedition leader, trimmed with the gold and turquoise." This was probably the hundredth time he had told the story to someone, and he had no trouble reciting it.

"Soon after, one of the men and the breastplate disappeared. They think maybe the Indians killed the man and took the breastplate. After they returned to Mexico, Jessie's descendants told the story over and over until it became family history," continued Bannister.

Carhartt listened intently; he always loved a good treasure tale. "How much truth do you think there is in the story?"

"From what we found in our research, we know there was such an expedition, and by the time it had returned to Mexico they had lost several men. We also think they were right here in this area based on the entries and drawings in the logbook of the general in charge. Beyond that, we haven't found another reference to the armor." After ordering another drink, Bannister continued. "They mentioned picking up samples of green stones that could have been turquoise—we also think it's possible that they could be some of the local amazonite stone."

"An interesting story for sure, Jack. Even if it's not real, it is fun to think about."

"Like I said before, it keeps Jessie happy, and if she's happy, then I'm happy," said Bannister with a grin.

After a little more small talk, Jessie came over and grabbed Bannister by the hand. "Come on, old man, I have someone I'd like you to meet; he has a lot of money and I need some of it—so be charming." Jessie winked at Carhartt and put on her prettiest work face and led Jack into the fray. Before the evening was over, she had smiled and flirted her way to thousands of dollars in donations for the museum. Just another day at the office for her.

* * *

Jack, Rocky, and Turner sat around the big kitchen table in the cabin. Stacks of maps of from the mining claims in the district sat in boxes and piles, nearly covering the table. Turner's notes were neatly spread out for inspection, all of them written with a fine purple Sharpie, one of his many eccentricities.

Jack studied the notes closely for a minute. "What stands out to you about the traffic in and out of the mine?"

"Clearly a covert operation," said Turner, trying to add a bit of drama. "Trucks come in the evening, back into the portal, spend about an hour or so, and then leave. A lot of them are riding higher when they leave."

"What else?" asked Bannister, listening intently.

"The same four guys are always there; they come out a couple of hours later and leave. They also work inside during the day, but no delivery trucks come then. When they come out from a day shift they're all dirty and dusty."

Rocky took the notes and copied the license plate numbers to his book. "I'll start running these numbers tomorrow and see if there is any common connection."

Bannister handed him a note with the numbers from Carhartt's chopper. "See what you can find out about this too. Is it leased or purchased—anything you can get."

Suddenly Maggie came out of the bedroom on a dead run, stopping in front of the back door with her tail wagging furiously. The door opened and Jessie came in with her briefcase and a box of museum work.

Looking at the three men at the table, she laughed out loud. "What's going on? It looks like you're plotting against someone and you just got caught . . ."

Jessie went into the bedroom and Maggie followed intently. In a minute she came back in her sweatpants and T-shirt, grabbed a beer from the refrigerator, and sat down at the table. "Well, what have you masterminds been finding out about the old mine operation?"

"We're trying to find out more about your friend Jamie—how he makes his money, and just what the hell is going on in his mine," said Bannister.

"Can't you get a legal warrant to go in and take a look?" asked Jessie. "Wouldn't that be the easy way?"

Jack shook his head no. "We could probably get a warrant to enter, but the DA says it needs to state exactly what we're looking for. We don't really know exactly what we're looking for. If we put down trichloroethylene as our search object, what do we do with the other things we find that aren't called out on the warrant? I'd rather wait a little longer; I intend to find out everything I can about this operation and what we might find down there before we go in."

"Did you meet Jamie's wife, Clarice, at the event?" asked Jessie. "From a woman's point of view you might start looking at her for the money trail. She had at least a hundred thousand dollars worth of jewelry on. She's clearly had a face lift and boob job—a bad boob job at that."

Rocky Batton couldn't help himself, he had to ask. "What exactly is a bad boob job? They're not big enough—or what?"

Everyone at the table was laughing by now, even Jessie. "No, you big dummy, they're noticeably uneven, and one is a little smaller. Between the jewelry, the face lift, and the boobs, she's obviously a high-maintenance woman; I'll bet she has some money of her own."

Bannister turned and looked at Rocky Batton. "I know," said Batton. "Look into her family and her finances, I got it."

Chapter 17

Jessie and Jack sat on the couch nursing the last of their coffee. Maggie was in her normal spot with her head on Jessie's lap, sound asleep. As Jack looked over the notes from Turner, Jessie finally broke the silence. "How are the Russian translations coming along? I was hoping maybe we might have something we could add to the exhibit at the museum."

Bannister shrugged his shoulders. "They're coming along okay, I guess; I can finally read the old script pretty well. The problem is, with the old paper, faded ink, and occasional misspelling, I have to put my own interpretation down. All of my words may not be a perfect translation. And Serinov takes a couple of years to get to Colorado. So far, there's one letter every month or two, and each letter takes about four or five hours to translate."

Jessie listened intently. "Where is he right now? If we can we skip ahead to when he gets here, we can fill the rest in later."

Bannister pulled out the next letter from its neatly tied packet. It was dated April 17, 1894, and posted in Colorado Springs. "Looks like you're in luck; he just arrived in Colorado."

The Drift

After his regular greeting, the Russian miner began to talk of his excitement at finally reaching Colorado, and Bannister settled in to hear the story. "I am now in a place called Colorado City, and it is a great confusion of horses, wagons, and people, most of whom seem to be going to the great Cripple Creek gold camp," wrote Vitor. "I hope to be there soon. The talk here is always about gold, and it's much different from the coal patches where everyone suffered so much. Colorado has bright warm sun and striking blue skies every day, and winter appears to have disappeared already."

The one thing that Vitor liked most was to be able to see clearly the mountain called Pikes Peak every day. It looked almost close enough to touch. He overheard talk from the miners about Zebulon Pike; the man who discovered the peak also thought there was gold there. Maybe he would find Mr. Pike's gold, and maybe someday he would stand on top of the mountain himself.

Vitor found work quickly in one of the dozens of beer halls lining the main street. It was a fairly new, two-story wood-frame building. It was long and narrow as well as dark and very dirty. It looked like most of the other buildings on the block. In return for cleaning, stocking, and general maintenance, he received a sleeping pallet—made of a pile of feed sacks in a corner of the back room—two meals and two mugs of beer a day from the bar, and five silver dollars a week. It was good enough for now, he thought, as he would soon find his way to the goldfields.

Colorado City was built along a small creek and was mostly a collection of clapboard saloons, mining supply stores, and hotels, as well as a few liveries and feed operations. Vitor thought that it was mostly a rough bunch of miners, gamblers, drunks, and those looking to make some quick money. Many of them carried pistols pushed down into their waistbands, and gunshots were common. He wanted out of this town soon; nothing was to be gained by staying.

After several weeks working in the saloon, he decided he would leave in a few more days. He had enough money to take the main railroad to Pueblo and then to Florence. Everyone advised him that this would be a good way to go. From Florence, a new railroad would take him to the Cripple Creek goldfields. He liked this plan; he could ride all the way to Cripple Creek. Just a few more days, he thought, and then he would go.

That night, as he stretched out on the pallet, thinking about his future in the gold business, the window above his head exploded in a shower of glass. Before he could collect his thoughts, a second bullet splintered the front wall and blew out another pane. Rolling onto the floor he crawled toward the back door as fast as his fear would let him. Still on the floor, he kicked open the door and lurched into the alley.

As he explained to Kapeka, "To get killed in a saloon by a drunken man with a gun when I am so close to our future home would be unthinkable—I am leaving for Cripple Creek today." Walking into the Colorado Springs terminal, he dropped his letter into the postal slot and stepped out onto the platform to wait for the train to take him to his new home.

* * *

Bannister laid the letter face down on the pile and picked up the next one dated June 14, 1894. It was posted in Victor, Colorado, Cripple Creek's neighbor on the other side of Battle Mountain. As he started to read, he could sense that this letter had a different feel to it, a greater sense of excitement, but he could also feel a little fear come through in Vitor's words.

The train ride down the Front Range from Colorado Springs to Pueblo was uneventful, the day clear and cool. The most interesting thing was several large groups of wild antelope that often ran alongside the train. "They appeared to be having fun and all the riders enjoyed their company," wrote Vitor. In Pueblo, he took another train to Florence, a small town along the Arkansas River.

On the ride along the river to Florence, he could see the dramatic foothills of the Rocky Mountains grow larger than life in front of his eyes. As the hills turned into mountains, Vitor pulled on his coat and tightened the grip on his bag. He was nearly overcome with excitement for what was around every bend. After two years on the road, he was just a few miles from his and Kapeka's and their new baby's home.

The stop at Florence was short, and Vitor was grateful for that. The town was the center for many gold smelters and a gray-brown cloud hung over it. The acrid smell from the smelters couldn't be escaped. It was not the place for a family, thought Vitor. As he boarded the Florence and Cripple Creek train, he didn't look back at the town. After a few miles the flat, grassy bottoms began to give way to very narrow, steep canyons with many sharp drop-offs and thick brush in the bottom. They were following a small stream called Eight Mile, already beginning to swell with the spring melt, through a place called Phantom Canyon, a fitting name for such a rugged looking place, he thought.

The sides of the canyons were sparsely covered with a few piñon and juniper trees mixed in with giant fractured boulders and rimrock, crumbling into the bottom. The engine pulled steadily up the narrow track, making bends so tight to the cliff that he could reach out and touch the rock. At the same time, he could look out the other side and see straight down for a hundred feet. He heard another passenger say there were 40 miles and 4,000 feet to go; the 4,000 feet was for the elevation gain. The engine strained hard, and great clouds of smoke poured out of it, showering the train with a dark cloud of ash.

Soon they slowed and finally lurched to a stop at a small station for water and wood. Vitor wrote in some detail about this spectacular canyon. "Scattered along the forty-mile trip were a dozen stops like this one called Wilbur. Names like The Trestle, The Narrows, Phantom Point, and Rocky Point may give you some thoughts as to what the scenery is like. Trestles across deep gorges give way to tunnels through solid rock, and bright blue skies would often turn instantly into dark shadows as the train swerved a mean path above the creek."

As the train clattered through the broken canyon, Vitor took it all in. It was the last few miles of his journey and he wanted to be able to remember every detail of it. When he came back down, it would be to meet his wife and daughter; he wanted to share this ride with them.

As they got closer, the sky was still clear blue but the temperature was dropping rapidly. He pulled out his heavy coat from his bag and buttoned it up to his chin. What were once small melting drifts of snow on the dark sides of the canyon now turned into a knee-deep ground cover, and as the canyon widened, he began to see his first sign of people in the district. Piles of rock surrounding faded gray clapboard shacks littered every hill. Smoke swirled from hundreds of dirty black chimneys, and the scene was unlike any that he had seen before.

Passing through the lower hills of the district, Serinov could see the great Battle Mountain gold claims with their giant headframes piercing the sky, and finally, the town of Victor. The train rolled to a stop at the new station, and he pulled on an oversized knit cap that Kapeka had given him just before he left. It felt good against the surprisingly bitter mountain air.

Chapter 18

Darla's diner was empty, the breakfast crowd had left and it would be another half hour before the first of the lunch crowd showed up. Jack and Rocky sat down at the small corner table and waited for Darla to come up front.

"What do you two want—trouble?" said a small feminine voice from the back. "I can give it to you—you know I'm between meals and you're gonna have to wait a while for the lunch menu."

"Now Dar, don't give us such a hard time, we're your best customers," hollered Rocky. "A cup of coffee will hold us until lunch."

"So get it yourself—you know where it's at."

Bannister chuckled at this exchange. He wondered if they would ever take their friendship any further, or—maybe they had and he just didn't know it. Anything is possible, he guessed.

The two men sat quietly for a moment, sipping their coffee and sifting through their notes. Rocky finally broke the silence. "What's Turner up to? Is he still on the job?"

"Yeah, he's still playing mountain man up above the mine," said Bannister. He comes down every couple days to drop off his notes and get some fresh supplies. Jessie feeds him and stocks him up, and then he's off for a few more days."

Rocky shook his head and took another sip of coffee. "He's one tough old bird, I gotta give him that. I'd get mighty tired of sleeping on the ground all those days."

"Well, he sleeps and reads during the day. Whenever there's any activity, he's glued to his spotting scope, taking notes. In case anyone did find him up there, he's on national forest land, and he has an elk license for the next season—he can tell them he's just doing some scouting."

"So has he come up with anything particularly incriminating?" asked Rocky.

"Well, they average about three trucks a week. The trucks all come and go in the dark. The four guys work four or five days a week during the day. They go in clean and come out dirty every day. It looks like routine mining work in the day; at night they come back long enough to unload the trucks. No smoking gun though."

Rocky listened carefully to Bannister, making a few notes. Bannister noticed him staring at Darla, their eyes connecting for a moment. "Rock—hello, you still with me?" said Bannister, poking him in the arm at the same time.

Rocky looked sheepishly at Jack. "Yeah, boss, I'm paying attention."

Bannister had to fight down the urge to laugh out loud. "I can see that you're paying attention to something, all right. Now, about the job at hand, can you get with your new miner friend, Dave, and buy him a beer or two?"

"I'm sure I can catch up with him, something specific you want me to find out?" asked Rocky, as he poured another cup of coffee.

"Yeah, see if he'll give up any info on his boss, the big obnoxious one—or even his coworkers would be good. I'd like to find out what I can about all four of them."

"Got it. I suspect that a few beers will loosen up his tongue a bit," said Rocky, making several notes in his book. "By the way, I found out that the trucks I tracked down were rentals, all from different parts of the Northeast, and all from different rental dealers. So far the IDs of the drivers appear to be unknown, probably fake, and the rentals were paid for in cash and returned clean and full of gas."

Lost in thought for a minute, Bannister watched the traffic move by the small diner for a moment. "Rocky, it looks like we have a real sharp businessman running this deal. The trucks come back with no reason to question anything, or any way to track the renter. Keep looking into that end of things. These guys are real smart, but so are we. With that many drivers, they may slip up somewhere along the line and we'll be ready." Bannister closed his file and stood up. "Bye, Dar, I'll leave you and Rocky alone now, I've got work to attend to."

"Bannister, you're a pain in my ass, just go—and don't call me Dar!"

* * *

A.J. Rogers pulled out a large map and unrolled it on Bannister's kitchen table. "Basically, Jack, the gold bearing area is a large volcanic caldera. It's roughly round in shape and the Black Mule operation is on the very northeastern edge of that zone. Most of the drifts in that mine would probably run more or less in a southwest direction."

Staring at the map, Bannister took in all the information A.J. was giving him. "So you don't think they went back northeast toward Pikes Peak at all?"

"I would suspect that they tried all directions early on," said A.J.

"But their geologist would have stopped them when he didn't find anything promising. And of course, they would have been stopped by the boundaries of the original claim."

"You told me before that most of these claims are interconnected. Do you think that might be the case here?"

A.J. nodded his head. "I'd almost bet on it. But nobody really knows the shape of those old operations. Over the years there have been a couple of earthquakes, and a hell of a lot of indiscriminate blasting down there."

"But you do think there is a chance that it could be connected by a passable drift to another mine?"

"It's possible," said A.J. "But at what level or which drift? There are some old operations that installed heavy iron doors to stop the high graders; you could run into one of those. Jack, you aren't thinking about trying to get into it from another mine, are you?"

"No, not now," said Bannister, recalling his last trip through the drifts of the Black Mule operation. "But I'd like to know what options might be available, just in case. When we were looking down into the open-pit operation, you pointed out the drifts that had been exposed along the sides of it. Do you think a person could make his way from one of those to the Black Mule?"

"Again, I guess it could be possible—but I think it's pretty unlikely after all these years."

"A.J., would it be a lot of work to completely close off a drift with one blast?"

"Not at all," he said, rolling up the map. "A good powderman would just drill the appropriate holes and pack them right. One big bang and the drift will be nearly impossible to open again."

"Nearly impossible, but not impossible?" said Bannister.

"Well, you could always go in with a team and start digging, but it would depend on how much of the tunnel was brought down. As to how long it would take? Days at a minimum."

Bannister digested the information for a moment and finally spoke.

"A.J., if I get access into the Black Mule operation, can I hire you as a consultant, so I know what I'm looking at when I get down there?"

A.J. nodded. "Sure, I'm always up for a little adventure. Are you thinking of trying to find a back entrance to the mine?"

"No, it looks like it will have to be through the front door; when I'm just about ready I'll give you a call."

"You got it," said A.J., thrusting out his hand toward Bannister.

"Thanks, A.J. I appreciate all your help." Bannister shook his hand firmly, thinking what a fortunate turn of events it was to have met him.

* * *

Rocky Batton sat in the end booth, with his laptop plugged in and a file folder open in front of him. It was his third trip to Driller's Casino in the last week, and he had yet to see his new friend, Dave. The waitress and the bartender remembered him from the baseball bat incident and took good care of him while he worked. Shortly after he got his food, the young miner came in. When he spied Rocky, he headed for the booth with his hand stuck out.

"Rocky, my bodyguard—how's it going? Still trying to save the minnows?"

"Still at it, Dave. How's work down in the hole?"

"Still dark and dusty, not much ever changes down there." Rocky waved him over to the booth and motioned to the waitress. "Can you get my friend, Dave, whatever he wants and another draft for me please?"

Dave emptied his beer in an instant and ordered another one. "It takes a couple of beers to make me feel human again." In five minutes' time, the young miner was on his third beer and starting to get talkative, just the way Rocky wanted him.

"You want some food to go with the beer, Dave?"

"Well, maybe a few fries might be good." Rocky ordered the fries and another beer for his new friend.

After two more beers, the miner relaxed a little and began to pick at his french fries, now buried in a giant pool of catsup. Rocky closed his laptop and pushed it aside. "Tell me a little about what it's really like down there in the dark. How long does it take to drill the right amount of holes and pack them with the dynamite?"

"We can usually drill them and pack them in a day or two; it's not really that difficult."

"It must be a bit scary constantly handling all that dynamite. It's pretty dangerous stuff, isn't it?"

"I don't handle the explosives, other than hauling the boxes down—the boss does that."

"So the boss sets the charges after you drill the holes? Are you guys down there when he sets it off?"

"No," said Dave, cleaning up the last of his fries. "He has it on a timer that can be set off from up in the portal, or pretty much anywhere for that matter. We leave before the blast. That way, it will be relatively clear the next day, and the headaches aren't nearly so bad."

"Sounds like a tough way to make a living to me. So are you finding some gold down there?" Rocky realized that his question must sound a bit nosy to a miner and tried to smooth it over. "I'm sorry, that didn't sound right, I'm not really trying to see how much gold you're getting, I'm just fascinated by the business I guess. Although—I really don't want to work down there."

"That's okay, I don't think there is much gold down there anyway. They say we're just exploring for signs of good ore; we just do what the boss says."

The miner started another round and Rocky thought it might be a good time to press him for a little more information. "What kind of guy is the boss, is he good to work for?"

"Just another boss I guess, mostly an arrogant asshole—if they still allowed whips and shackles, he'd be using them."

Rocky leaned over the table, nearly nose to nose with his tablemate. "What's this jerk's name? I'd like to know in case I ever run into him in a dark bar somewhere—you know what I mean?"

"Asshole, his name is asshole, or Max Atkinson if you prefer, but we just call him asshole—but not to his face or there wouldn't be any job now would there?" Dave said, beginning to slur his words badly.

Rocky had a few more questions but would have to act quickly, before his charge was too far gone. "Dave, do you know who Max reports to?"

"Some rich guy with a helicopter is all I know—he's probably an asshole too, if you know what I mean."

"Dave, old pal, I think it's time to go. Tell me where you live and I'll take you there, you can't drive like this. By the way, what's your last name?"

"DeAngelo, Dave DeAngelo, originally from Rochelle, Illinois—dead flat cornfield country."

Rocky threw Dave DeAngelo over his shoulder like a duffel bag and walked out into the night, now bitter cold and heading into a long winter.

Chapter 19

Bannister hung up the phone and opened his notebook.

"Was that Rocky?" asked Jessie without looking up from her book.

"Yeah, he dug up a little more information about your friend Jamie and his wife."

Closing her book, she turned toward Bannister. "Do tell, what's up with those two—anything interesting?"

"Well, Rock says that Carhartt's financials are extremely complicated, and he had to get a little help from our forensic auditor to find out what's going on. After following a long, convoluted trail, it appears that basically, they're bringing almost no income into the company at all. We already knew that PMV, Inc., the mining division, wasn't making any money."

"How can that be?" asked Jessie. "They live a pretty large lifestyle for poor people."

"It looks like your thoughts on his wife may be the answer to that question. Clarice Carhartt, formerly Clarice Marie Whitford, of the

Boston Whitfords, is the only child of a wealthy, well-known family that started out in the late eighteenth century in shipping, mining, and timber. Today, Whitford, Inc. has one of the largest real estate holdings in the Northeast."

"Did Rocky give you any idea how these two love birds met?"

"Well, from what he's found out so far, and what he's gathered from the two family histories and legends, it looks like the families are old friends—very old friends. Clarice Whitford's grandfather and Jamison's grandfather knew each other."

"Wow, that's really interesting—imagine two families that go back that far."

"Not only that," continued Bannister, "the story is that Grandfather Whitford may have loaned Grandfather Carhartt some money to search for gold in Colorado. Jamison senior was the miner in the family; he worked Cripple Creek for a long time with decent success. Then, after the big bust, Carhartt the second took up the aviation business and let all but a few of his claims go. The Black Mule operation is one of only three they still have left."

"So you think the money to keep them afloat may be coming from the Whitford family?" asked Jessie.

"Kind of indirectly, I guess. The rumor has it that there was a trust fund for Clarice worth about ten million dollars or so, and it was taken away from her, but so far we haven't been able to come up with any information to confirm that. It does look like she is completely out of the picture as far as the family and their business goes," said Bannister looking through his notes. "As far as Carhartt Aviation goes, it appears the helicopter is leased and there are infusions of cash about three or four times a year. My guess is she funds him so she can live her life as one of the social gadflies of Colorado Springs. Mrs. Jamison Carhartt the third—wife of an old-money mining and aviation guru. It may be a little unconventional, even phony, but it's not illegal. It does make me wonder even more what exactly is going on in that mine."

Jess turned back to her book and Maggie adjusted herself accordingly on her lap. "Keep at it Bannister, you'll find a crack in that outfit somewhere, it's just a matter of time."

* * *

The days were getting shorter and colder, but Colorado's brilliant blue skies and lack of wind made for a good day to fly. Bannister slung his camera pack over one shoulder, pulled his stocking cap down over his ears, and headed for the helicopter.

The rotors hummed steadily and blew up a cloud of fine grit from the pavement. He pulled himself into the seat and swung the door closed behind him. Carhartt was already behind the controls. "Hi Jack, good to see you again. You ready to do this?"

"I think so, or I should say Jessie seems to think so."

"Do you do a lot of photography with your job, or is it just a hobby?"

"A little of both actually. I've been interested in taking pictures since I was a kid, plus I have to take a lot of photos for the records of the projects we do."

The pavement fell away rapidly and he pointed the chopper toward the mountains, just south of Pikes Peak. "So what exactly is our mission today? Pictures of Cripple Creek and Victor?"

"We definitely need those, but she'd really like shots that show the whole district, something they can stitch together for a large overall view for the new display at the museum. I have a couple of old vintage maps to help me out. I'd like to shoot all the different roads and railroads in and out of the district, the streams leaving the area, and the mining areas and the open-pit operation too."

"How about Gold Camp Road first? We'll be flying over it anyway, and it was the original bed of the Colorado Springs and Cripple Creek Railway."

Bannister unzipped his camera bag and pulled out his camera, already equipped with a wide-angle lens. Opening the window, he made a couple of adjustments and began to shoot the old road as it wound through the bare granite slopes and steep canyon walls. As they got higher, the trees got thicker and they glided over beaver ponds, small reservoirs, and remnants of early homesteads and cabins. The chopper held slow and steady while Bannister recorded everything they saw.

When the district came into view, they headed for the highest point, hovering above the town site of Altman, on the slopes of Bull Hill. "This is still one of the greatest views in the Rockies—at least in my opinion. If you want, I'll turn us around slowly and you can take it all in with your camera."

"You're right about that, it is spectacular," said Bannister while shooting frame after frame. "I've been to Cripple Creek and Victor a thousand times, but I never really saw it like this, until you took me up. I hope I can do it justice with my rather marginal camera skills. How long do you have today, Mr. Carhartt?"

"I planned for a couple of hours; I just couldn't say no to Jessie, even if I wanted to."

Bannister grinned and nodded his head. "Tell me about it. Some days I think I'm being held captive by a beautiful, benevolent dictator, just do what she says and everything will be fine—cross her though . . ."

"I understand the dictator part for sure," he said, turning the chopper slowly in a clockwise direction. "But just one thing, Jack, you have to call me Jamie, remember? That's what everyone has called me since childhood—Mr. Carhartt was my father and my grandfather, not me."

"You got it—it's Jamie from now on."

The chopper started to follow the roads around the gold bearing area, above towns like Victor, a beautiful old period town with a few hundred permanent residents and a few hundred more workers from the Phoenix Drilling operation. The town had a wonderful, colorful history, every bit as interesting as Cripple Creek's. They followed the blacktop road around the hills, and over to Cripple Creek. Jamie hovered well above the town and allowed Jack to get the pictures he needed.

"Twenty years ago, Cripple Creek was a sleepy little town, with a modest tourist trade, a good museum, and a couple of bars. Any mining business was incidental and most residents were happy living in this high, isolated little community making some money where they could," he said, staring out toward the Sangre de Cristo Mountains to the south. "Then, gambling fever took over the state, the politicians got involved, and Cripple Creek became the only gambling town in central Colorado. When gold went sky high the open-pit operation took over all of the mining. I really miss the old Cripple Creek—but each to his own I guess."

The two men followed high above Shelf Road, one of the earliest stage roads in the district, and Phantom Canyon Road, the site of the former Florence and Cripple Creek Railroad, the first rails into the district and one of the most famous and scenic roads in the state. Talking about history, and flying, was a pleasant way to spend a few hours, but Bannister knew there was a connection between Carhartt and the Black Mule mine, and he wasn't about to let it go.

The last creek they followed was Beaver Creek. Its headwaters started at a small lake near Victor, and eventually emptied into the Arkansas River near Florence. They followed the small creek from the dam as it wound through tight, heavily treed canyons and large broken faces of rimrock. Carhartt pointed out the remains of large old wooden pipes that used to carry water downstream to a now-abandoned electric power plant. "That brick building down in the bottom used to make electricity for Victor."

Jack nodded and stared at the structure alongside the creek. "It sure took some work to get all the bricks and equipment down a canyon that deep and that steep, not to mention the electrical equipment and supplies."

"Not only were those old timers tough, but they liked their comforts too. They hauled down a full-sized, heavy slate pool table and plenty of other creature comforts. The slate pieces are still down there."

Bannister enjoyed the history tour and shot more than a thousand photographs throughout the day. As they headed back toward the district, he went over all that he had seen.

"Jamie, do you really think there's much gold left here?"

"I do, but even at today's high prices it's really expensive to get to it. That's why Phoenix is doing it as an open-pit operation: the larger deposits seem to be deeper and this way they don't miss anything. Not as many hazards as the underground and no bad air problems."

"Did your great-grandfather hit it big when he started out up here?"

"After the first few years he had gathered up about a dozen or so claims. He worked three or four at the same time, until, when he was just about ready to throw in the towel, one of them scored pretty big. It was called Carhartt Number Two. After five or six years it started to die out and he sold it. It's gone now, eaten up by Phoenix. He never gave up looking for another strike, though by the late forties it was pretty much all over for Carhartt gold mining."

Bannister took a break from shooting long enough to take a sip of water and change memory cards in his camera. "You said once before that you still like to do a little looking—have you had much luck yet?"

"No, not really, I have a couple of old claims that I hung on to, just for old time's sake. I like to keep a couple, just to hold on to the romantic idea of finding a big strike, I guess."

"Yeah, that would be exciting; I think that's why Jessie loves the idea of the family treasure story so much. So you eventually went into the aviation business?"

"My father came back from World War II as a pilot; he flew dive bombers in the Pacific and was hooked on flying. When he came back he talked his dad into flying and finally into the small plane and aircraft parts business. After my first time in an airplane, I was also hooked; I've loved everything about it since then."

They had been up nearly three hours, and Carhartt asked if there was anything else he would like to see. "How about flying back toward Pikes Peak so I can shoot back at the district one more time, and you mentioned the last time we were up here about a rock formation called the crack or something like that? I'd like to shoot that too."

"You mean the Crease—no problem; we can catch it on the way home."

Chapter 20

Jack sat at the computer screen going through the photos from the helicopter trip. He called Jessie over to take a look.

"Jack, these are great, they'll make a wonderful display for the exhibit. Copy them to a CD and I'll have one of the volunteers put together a montage we can run in the slide show."

The day was bitterly cold and snow had been falling for several hours. In the last thirty minutes, the wind had picked up and the snow was starting to drift deeply around the cabin. The first big storm of the season was moving in fast.

"What about Turner, you think he's okay?"

"I'm sure he's doing fine, he knows when to come in out of the cold," said Bannister with a chuckle.

As if cued by some unseen movie director, the door slammed open and in walked Turner, with his gray beard, welder's cap, and everything else packed with snow. Right behind him was Rocky Batton. "It's too crappy to go all the way back to town tonight," he said, while pulling off his hat and jacket. "So I decided to stay here and wait it out."

"Yeah," chimed in Rocky. "Me too, way too crappy—you got any food?"

Jessie walked into the kitchen and began to pull out some tortillas.

"Brandy for me please," said Rocky, stepping out of his pac boots and parka.

Turner kicked off his boots and walked into the kitchen, grabbing a couple of glasses for the drinks. "Me too—how about you Jess?"

She shook her head no. "Jack and I already have a little something, thanks."

After throwing on a few more sticks of wood, the fire roared to life, warming the cabin and waking up Maggie who had been sleeping in the bedroom. Heading for the living room, she quickly found her regular place on the couch alongside Jessie and was instantly asleep with her head perched on her lap.

After a bite to eat and a little too much to drink, Turner pulled his damp cap down over his eyes and was asleep on the end of the couch in a minute. Jessie and Maggie headed for the bedroom, and Jack and Rocky sat opposite each other in two overstuffed chairs. Between them was a nineteenth-century flat-topped steamer trunk now used as a coffee table. The same trunk also served as a repository for all the notes and maps on the search for the golden armor. Now it was piled high with notes and files and freshly printed photographs from the recent trip over the district.

"Well Rock, how's things with your new miner buddy?" asked Bannister, sorting through his notes.

"Pretty good I guess—he's a cheap drunk, that's for sure. I ended up taking him home last night; he lives in a trashy old Airstream trailer on the edge of Cripple Creek." Rocky set his notebook down on the trunk and flipped through the pages. "The big guy, the one I think you had the run-in with, is Max Atkinson. I ran him through the system and he has a pretty questionable past."

"Keep talking, I like what I'm hearing so far," said Bannister.

"He's got a history of violence and it appears that he likes guns too. He did a year in the state pen for assault and battery. He beat a gas station attendant nearly to death after an argument over money." He flipped to the next page and continued. "He's been in trouble for illegal gun possession and sales and is a two-time offender in Massachusetts."

Bannister shook his head and took a sip of his drink. "He'll be a tough one to get to, what about the others?"

"My new buddy, Dave DeAngelo, is originally from the cornfields of Illinois—back in your old country—and moved out here in search of work in the gold mines. Thought he might get rich, I guess. After scraping along for a few years this is just about the only job that he could find. He's really not a bad guy; I suspect he's just doing what's necessary to get by."

"What about the other two guys, anything on them?"

"I was able to get the names Tom and Ryan from him, but no last names, before he passed out. I also found out that all three hate Max, the big guy. I think Dave may be our way in. I don't think he'll like the idea of spending a few years in prison for this."

"Bannister paused a moment to gather in all this new info. "So, we have Dave DeAngelo, Tom, and Ryan doing most of the grunt work and Max Atkinson giving orders."

"Max is also the powderman; he wires things up and sets the timers. By the way, Dave did tell me that he thinks Max answers to some rich guy in a helicopter."

"No real surprise there, Rock. I think it might be time to sit Mr. DeAngelo down and tell him what he has to look forward to if he doesn't help us."

Rocky leaned back in his chair and nodded in agreement. "When do you want to grab him?"

Bannister got up and pulled back the curtain from the front window and stared out into the swirling white mess outside the cabin. "No time soon, I guess, I think we'll be here for a day or two by the looks of it." Turning back to Rocky it was obvious the day was over for him; he was already sound asleep and starting to snore.

* * *

The next morning Jack woke up to a cold cabin. Jessie and Maggie had all the covers and the fire was nothing more than a few embers. He had forgotten to turn on the central heat yesterday when the fire was hot, and no one had woken up yet to feed the fire. After switching on the heat, he made coffee and looked out the front window. The snow was drifted halfway up the glass and the truck was nowhere to be seen.

"It's about time you made coffee," said Turner, peering out from under his cap. "I've been waiting forever."

Watching Turner pull himself up and make his way to the kitchen, Bannister filled a large mug and set it on the counter for him.

"I dreamed I was still in my tent, buried under a ton of snow," said Turner. "And I was freezing cold and the coyotes were eating me."

"Turner, I wouldn't worry too much about something eating you. As loud as you were snoring last night, nothing would have come anywhere near you."

Turner grinned and took a big swig from his mug. "I'll have you know that it took me years to develop that skill—as you can see, ain't nothing got me yet."

Rocky was now awake and standing behind Turner. "Hell, Old Timer, if you don't change those socks pretty soon, nothing will ever get near you—in fact, I may just throw you out in a snowbank myself."

"You ain't nearly big enough to get that job done," said Turner, looking up at Rocky with a huge grin on his face.

For the next two days the snow kept falling and the wind never let up. The 100-year-old cabin had seen it all many times before, and would likely see it a few more times to come. One of the worst storms in recorded history had reminded them of the reality of living in Colorado's high country. After two days the snow stopped falling, the wind quit blowing, and the sun came out. It was still impossible to open the door of the cabin. Jack and Rocky climbed out a side window and pushed their way to the woodpile. After an hour of digging, they had a path from the woodpile to the door.

Opening the door for the first time in two days, Jessie hollered out to Jack, "Watch out for Maggie, here she comes!" Maggie shot past them on a dead run and came to a crashing halt against the woodpile.

"At least," said Rocky, "she's a girl that has her priorities right." The bird dog had only been out twice since the storm had started. She ran around sniffing through the snow for a while, took care of business, then reversed herself and ran back through the open door, jumping up on the couch and flopping down in her usual place.

Turner had claimed the kitchen while they were all snowbound, and had been cooking up a storm. Breakfast was his specialty, and his homemade baking-powder biscuits and sausage gravy was his star attraction. Topping it off with bacon, a couple of eggs, toast, and some of Jessie's family's homemade chokecherry jam had the crew lined up with plates in hand. The self-appointed chef shook his spatula at Rocky. "End of the line, fat boy—otherwise there won't be anything left for the others. And, you're doing the dishes—if you want to eat later."

Two days of his kitchen banter was wearing a little thin, but nobody wanted to risk having to do their own cooking, so they just put up with the cranky old man and ate their breakfast quietly. Even Maggie had to stand in line when he was cooking.

* * *

Turner pulled open the front blinds showing a broad panorama of snowdrifts and ponderosa pines with their limbs bent down heavily with snow. "Did you ever notice them goofy damn rabbits after a snowstorm . . ? As soon as it's over and the skies are clear again, they come out and run around in circles like some crazy character from *Alice in Wonderland*—did you ever wonder what's up with them?"

"Can't say that I have, but that is one profound observation to be sure." Rocky's comment didn't faze him at all; he was well known for his unique take on things and didn't really care what others thought. He was generally smarter than most people about the outdoors, and usually right in his observations.

After more than two days together in the cabin, the business of the mystery mine had been hashed out and covered from every direction and angle possible. They had also covered several other ongoing cases that Jack had on his desk. The Headwaters cleanup problem near Leadville and the tailings removal near Bonanza were taking a lot of his time lately. Some new issues with the uranium mines in western Colorado had recently come up, and it was hard to put enough time in on the Cripple Creek problem. He was thankful for this team of rather unlikely looking investigators; without them he'd never get anywhere.

Chapter 21

The town of Victor, Colorado, was larger than Serinov had expected, with several large, solid buildings under construction and clapboard and log buildings as well as canvas tents lining the streets. The train station was new, and many people crowded around the train waiting for someone or getting ready to board themselves. He would later write to Kapeka that his first impression of the great goldfield was—mud. Every street was a maze of twisting, ankle-deep ruts full of thick, sticky mud. They would freeze at night, and by midmorning they were mud again.

His second impression of Victor was of great piles of freight stacked and stored alongside every building and on every wagon. Crates, wooden barrels, and bundles of all sizes were constantly being loaded and unloaded from wagons, and every empty lot was piled full of all types of mysterious-looking pieces of machinery. The town was a nonstop whirl of activity and Vitor knew he wanted to be part of this excitement—he also knew that soon he would be looking for his own gold, and his family could come to join him.

The Drift

Walking alongside the muddy tracks, he found himself in front of a small storefront; the sign identified it as a barbershop. By the time he had reached Colorado, his English was good enough to carry on most conversations without a problem; however, reading the printed word was still a mystery to him. In the window was a copy of a current Cripple Creek newspaper, called the *Cripple Creek Crusher*. The date was April 21, 1894. That and a picture of a mine headframe with two men standing outside the entrance was all he could make out.

As he continued to walk along the crude sidewalks, he saw a large poster with the letters "WFM—Join Today!" Within a few moments a skinny, pock-faced, rough-looking man with a wild shock of curly red hair was leading him inside and telling him of the benefits of membership in the WFM, or the Western Federation of Miners. When Vitor explained that he was new here today and didn't know anything about the district, the man sat him down, handed him a cup of black coffee, and began to fill him in on the details.

The stranger introduced himself as Tommy Flynn, a miner and member of the WFM. Flynn laid out a brief history of the district and explained why a new union had been recently formed. Back in February, the owners of the larger mines, J.J. Hagerman, Irving Howbert, and D.H. Moffett, as well as several others, arbitrarily decided to change the eight-hour workday to a ten-hour workday without increasing the three-dollar-per-day wage. "These wealthy and powerful men have taken advantage of the hard rock miner long enough," explained Flynn.

Flynn's voice began to rise and he became visibly agitated at the thought of a cut in pay. "Those rich sons o' bitches don't care how many people they hurt, they're out for themselves and don't give a big rat's ass about anything but money in their pockets."

The more agitated he became, the more difficult it was for Vitor to understand his thick Irish accent. He was surprised at the passion displayed by this perfect stranger, but had experienced more than his share of bad treatment and greedy mine owners. After a few minutes, he told the miner that he might be interested, but needed a job and a place to stay first, so he would be able to pay his dues. Flynn stuck out his hand and Vitor responded with a solid handshake. There was something he liked about this stranger, so he decided then and there to see what the WFM could do for him.

Flynn closed and locked the front door to the tiny storefront and pointed to a loaded freight wagon pulled by a pair of mules. "Your timing was lucky," said the little Irishman as they pulled themselves up to the seat. "I was just taking this feed up to Altman and stopped here to get some paperwork. Now I got a new miner and a new friend."

"Where's Altman, Mr. Flynn? Will there be somewhere for me to find a job and a place to stay?"

"Call me Tommy, everyone else does—what's your name?"

"I am Vitor Serinov, I am from Russia, and can you please tell me about Altman?"

"Well, my new friend Vitor, Altman is pretty much the center of the universe around here right now—at least if you're a miner." He snapped the reins and shouted at the mules and they started to roll slowly through the streets of Victor. "Like I said, you got here right in the middle of some ugly business between the owners and the miners. Altman is where most of the union miners are living and where all our business is done. Trust me, friend, we will take care of you until this is over and you can get on your feet."

Vitor wondered if this man was for real, but since he had no other prospects he decided to follow along—at least for now. "Tommy, will we be going through Cripple Creek on the way to Altman?"

"No, no need to go there today, but you can see it clearly from Altman—in fact; you can just about see the whole world from up there."

He was disappointed not to be going directly to the town he had heard so much about, but he knew he would see it soon enough. "Are there many mines at Altman, Tommy?"

"There are mines everywhere, Vitor," said Tommy. "At least a hundred and fifty or more, I heard. Some of the best are right near Altman. I heard there are nearly fifty thousand people in the district now. When the strike is settled, they will need every miner they can find—that's why the union wants all the men they can get and be ready to go back to work."

"Are all the mines on strike right now?" asked Vitor.

"No, some are working and some are closed until we settle, it depends on the owner."

Serinov was confused, but decided to wait and see what he found in Altman. It had been a long journey and right now he could use some food and sleep. He would continue his adventure tomorrow.

The mules strained against the harness, and the wagon lurched from side to side, wheels grabbing whichever set of ruts came next. It was a strange world they were riding through. The district was devoid of trees as far as he could see, and the wagon road wound around the flanks of one hill and up the next. The landscape was covered with pile after pile of yellow and brown rock, the tailings of hundreds of mine workings. Run-down shacks mixed in with the gleaming new headframes, sending cables into the depths of the shaft.

As they neared the town of Altman, the views were beginning to become more and more spectacular; Tommy noticed Vitor taking it all in. "One other thing, Vitor—Altman is the highest town in all of America, maybe even the whole world!"

As ugly as the district was, Vitor had to admit the view was definitely spectacular. Snowcapped mountains in every direction, including the famous Pikes Peak, stood out like great, white, shimmering ghosts.

As the wagon pulled into the town, Vitor surveyed the surrounding area and quickly realized why the striking miners liked this spot. It looked like the perfect setting for a natural fort. In a slight saddle between the two highest points in the district, it commanded the high ground for several miles in every direction. Pulling the mules to a stop in front of a small stable, Tommy was greeted loudly by two young men who immediately started unloading the feed sacks.

"Grab your bag and come with me, there's someone you need to meet," said Flynn, walking quickly down the street.

Stopping in front of a white painted door, Vitor asked him what the sign said. "It says, 'Free Coinage Union #19—Western Federation of Miners.' This is the union hall for the district miners. Anyone here?" called out Tommy loudly.

"Just me, no need to make so much noise, Tommy, you're louder than the dynamite." A stout, middle-aged man with sandy-colored hair emerged from the back room carrying a bucket of coal. Dropping it down beside the stove, he stuck out his hand toward Vitor. Looking him hard in the eye he introduced himself. "Hello, I'm John Calderwood; I'm the organizer for the Western Federation of Miners. What's your name?"

Vitor was momentarily speechless, surprised at such a direct demeanor. "I'm Vitor Serinov, I'm from Russia and I'm a miner."

Tommy chuckled at this confrontation. Calderwood was a straight-shooting, look-you-in-the-eye guy, and that made him very good at his job. "John, we met in town. He just got in and needs a place to stay and a way to make a few dollars. Anything we can do for him?"

Dropping a few lumps of coal in the fire, Calderwood motioned for the men to have a seat. "Vitor, as Tommy probably told you, we are in the middle of a strike with the owners of some of the mines. We aren't sure when everything will be settled, but through donations, dues, and various means, we are able to keep most of our men fed and sheltered while this is going on. The majority of our men do anything and everything possible to make some money; it could be shoveling snow, repairing roofs, or hauling wood. Are you up for that?"

"Yes sir, I can handle that," said Vitor.

"Great. We want to keep our workforce intact so we can return to mining as soon as possible. What kind of mining have you done since you came to the United States?"

"Mostly coal, in Pennsylvania and Illinois," said Vitor.

"When I came over from Scotland I worked in the Pennsylvania coal patches too. I think that's the path a lot of us took before we ended up here. Did you like the coal mines?"

"No, sir, they were too dirty and too dangerous, and paid too little."

"That's true enough," said Calderwood. "Tell me, did you ever see the Black Maria?"

This was the first time Vitor had thought of the death wagon since he left Illinois; he was surprised to hear Calderwood mention it. "Yes, sir, I did. More times than I care to remember . . ."

"I got hauled out in it once, but fortunately it wasn't all that bad—as you can see, I'm still here."

"You're a fortunate man, Mr. Calderwood. I never knew anyone that rode out in it alive."

"Safety is one of the reasons I got into the union and became an organizer—that and fair pay and treatment for the men. I think we'll get along well. I think we can help each other and the union. We'll take care of you until you get work."

"Thank you for the opportunity, Mr. Calderwood, I will show you plenty of hard work."

"Glad to have you, Vitor. Tommy, find him a spot in number thirty-one or thirty-two, I think one of them has room."

"You got it." Tommy and Vitor headed out the door and took the short walk to the work camp. Row upon row of unpainted barracks lined the street and men were coming and going in a steady stream. They walked into the barracks building marked thirty-two and found an empty bed near the end of the first row. New electric lights flickered throughout the room.

"The plumbing is in the building out back. They've got good water and showers—and if you get there at the right time you might get hot water. The chow hall is at the far end," said Tommy. "Again—getting there early would be good advice."

Vitor Serinov looked over his first home in the Cripple Creek District. *This will do nicely for now*, he thought. *Very soon I will have enough money to get my own place—very soon.*

Chapter 22

Two days after Colorado's worst blizzard in fifty years, the county was finally beginning to get the main highways plowed between the town's of Divide and Cripple Creek. It would be another day or more before the plows got close to Bannister's cabin. The four captives kept themselves busy trying to stay out of each other's way the best they could. Jessie and Maggie worked on the treasure story, Turner claimed the kitchen as his own, and Rocky and Jack alternated between feeding the fire, going through the photographs, and telling fishing stories.

Bannister printed several photos taken from the last chopper ride. Above the fireplace, he tacked up an enlargement of a tall, strange rock formation. Rocky stared at the photo for a moment. "What's up with the rock-pile picture, something to do with the bad guys?"

"I'm not sure, it's probably nothing, but it's close to the mine operation. I just have a feeling it will figure in—but I'm not sure how. The locals call it the Crease."

The picture showed an unusual vertical formation about 200 feet tall with a definite wide fold or crease in the middle. It resembled a shelf full of books, with the tallest ones in the center and the smaller ones on the ends. On the right side of the Crease, the rock was the common pink stone known as Pikes Peak granite. On the left side it was nearly black, with different, lighter colors mixed in. The ground in front was a flat, barren, semicircle, covered with loose rock for a hundred yards out.

"Right near these rocks is where I had the run-in with big Max and his boys," said Bannister. "It's about a quarter mile from the Black Mule operation, and backs up against the ridge on the east side of their boundary, then drops down a couple of hundred feet."

Bannister's phone interrupted them and he shuffled through the papers until he found it. "Yeah, we're fine, we've got plenty of everything, thanks," said Bannister, listening intently. "We have the driveway shoveled enough to get out after the main road is open." He listened for several minutes before he spoke again. "Where did you find it?" Thanking the caller, he closed up the phone with a snap.

"Who's that, the sheriff?" asked Rocky.

"Yeah, he's checking on some of the residents they haven't heard from, to see if anyone needs help until the plows get to them."

"What else Jack? I heard you mention a truck . . .?"

"It seems like another one of our rental trucks may have gotten snowbound, and by the time the county found it, the driver was gone. The truck was just pulled off the side of the road, half buried in snow." Bannister took a few swallows of coffee and continued. "He's tracking down the rental agency now, and will move it to a secure place. I told him a while back that we were working on a case involving the old mine site and rental trucks, and if anything about them came to his attention, to give me a call. I also asked him not to open it until we got there; he said he'd call when it was in a safe place."

Rocky made a few notes and sat back in the overstuffed chair. "Sounds like old Mother Nature may have given us a little break. I'm dying to know what was in that truck, and really wondering what became of the driver. He'd have been a lot safer staying with the truck, unless he knew he would be questioned by the cops and had something to hide."

Bannister agreed with his assessment of the situation. "If he got out of the truck during the storm, he might not be found until the spring thaw. The sheriff said they would probably have the road opened by late tonight or early tomorrow and we can get a look at it then."

Rocky pulled out his cell phone and picked a name from the list. Darla Rios answered on the first ring. Walking outside, he leaned against the woodpile and visited with her for fifteen minutes before returning to his seat by the fire.

"So how's Dar?"

"She's fine; I just wanted to see how things were down in town."

"And—how are things down in town?"

"Only about a foot of snow. She's keeping the diner closed until next week, it's still cold and things are a mess around the city."

"That's good to hear; too bad she doesn't have someone to keep her warm. Oh—wait, maybe someone is keeping her warm and you just don't know about it . . ?"

"I wouldn't know anything about that, it's not my business," said Rocky, his face beginning to get red.

About ten thirty the next morning the county plow and snow blower finally roared down the road, releasing the prisoners from the confines of the cabin. Jessie decided to stay home one more day and Turner blasted off toward his home in Black Forest. After taking a short call from the sheriff, Jack and Rocky headed for Cripple Creek.

* * *

The Drift

The truck had been towed to a county maintenance shed at the edge of Cripple Creek. The sheriff had tracked down the rental company and they said to do whatever was right and let them know when they could reclaim it. It was just another average-looking truck, now covered with muddy, dripping ice, and snow. Both front doors were locked, and the rear door was secured with a heavy-duty padlock.

The local locksmith opened the front driver's door, and one of the county workers provided a pair of bolt cutters for the padlock on the rear. Rolling up the back door exposed twelve fifty-gallon drums. They had all been cleaned of any identifying marks or labels. Each individual drum was secured with a locking ring and a padlock, and strapped to a wooden pallet. The men stared inside for a minute, and finally Jack reached up and pulled the door down. "I think maybe we should call the HazMat guys before we look at what's inside of them. Rocky, you want to give them a call?"

Although Rocky really wanted to open them, he knew this was the right call, it was always safety first. When he finished locking the back door, they checked out the truck's cab. It was empty except for a small scrap of paper in the ashtray. On it was the words "Black Mule mine-Max." Rocky handed it to Jack; the rest of the truck was empty.

After a couple of hours, the Colorado Springs HazMat team arrived at the shed. After introductions and explanations, the team got to work setting up a secure area to offload the drums. Borrowing the county forklift, they removed each drum and built a plastic shack over them.

Dave Sandvik, captain of the team, pulled on his white exposure suit, and waited for the other three members of the team to gown up. "This may take awhile. Please don't enter the tent unless we tell you it's okay." As soon as all four men were dressed, they picked up a toolbox and walked inside.

Rocky, Jack, and Martin Jewell, the newly elected Teller County sheriff, walked into the small office and sat down. "Well, Sheriff, it looks like you're really getting your baptism under fire these last few days. Still want the job?" asked Rocky, only half jokingly.

"Under fire is right," replied Jewell. "Two weeks on the job and a major blizzard, and this mystery here. I'll keep the job but I'll definitely need a vacation when all this is over."

After nearly an hour, Sandvik tapped on the office window and motioned for them to come out. Bannister waited for them to get out of their suits before he spoke. "What do you think, Captain? What's hidden in our mystery barrels?"

"I'm not sure about all of them; a couple have trichloroethylene. A few others have chemicals I haven't been able to confirm yet. I have my suspicions, but I need to get an expert in the field—and the FBI."

Jack wasn't surprised about the trichloroethylene, it was a common cleaning agent left over from the early days of the electronics' manufacturing boom—the same as they found at the site of the earlier rental truck crash, and the same as had been detected in the Arkansas River. "You can't give me some idea what was inside the others?"

Sandvik shook his head no. "Sorry, I have to follow protocol. The FBI will have to take it from here. I've already called them and they're on their way."

Bannister shook hands with Sandvik and thanked him. "Did they say how long it would take to get here?"

"A two-man team will be here by chopper from Denver soon, and they'll take it over. Meanwhile, I have to oversee and secure the site and wait for the agents to tell us what the next step is." Trying not to let his frustration show, Jack walked back into the office with Rocky and the sheriff right behind him. "I guess all we can do now is wait."

Chapter 23

Two days after he arrived in Altman, Vitor found work as a laborer helping a carpenter recently hired to build several new barracks buildings for the miners. Rows of faded, white-canvas tents were slowly being replaced with new, wood-frame buildings. His job was hauling wood and digging foundation holes for each new building. He was more than happy for the chance to work outside. The air was cold and crisp, but much better than what he had experienced in the coal mines. The view still amazed him every day, and he began to look forward to the news chores that kept him outside.

The job came on a recommendation from the union hall. They wanted all the qualified miners they could get for when the strike was finally settled. They also needed the men because there was safety in numbers, and things had deteriorated badly between the owners and the union. Vitor wrote to Kapeka that there were "guns starting to be seen all about the town, and hearing gunshots was now a common thing."

The labor talks had failed to produce an agreement, and since

The Drift

February, smelters and other related businesses were running only part-time or closed altogether. A few mines like the Granite and the famous Gold King finally gave in and returned to the eight-hour, three-dollar-a-day wage, but the bulk of the big producers had bowed their neck and said no to the old wage.

The situation in the district was getting tense, and Vitor told Kapeka he was getting concerned for the safety of the miners. "After only two weeks in the town of Altman, I now see that most men carry one or more guns with them, and talk loudly about what they will do to the mine owners if they ever catch them. There had been some violence before I arrived, but it is sure to get worse very soon."

Vitor's prediction came true much sooner than he thought it would. On May 24, as he was standing on the roof of one of the new barracks buildings, a tremendous explosion rocked the building, almost knocking him to the ground. The sky to the south was filled with a large cloud of dust and smoke. Almost before he could comprehend what had just happened, a second explosion filled the sky with chunks of iron, wood, rock, and lengths of steel cable, all raining down on the mines at the edge of town.

In his next letter, he explained to Kapeka that "I was lucky that day. I was not close enough to be hurt by the explosion. Some miners, frustrated by the strike, set dynamite bombs in a mine called the Strong Mine and blew it up. The town of Altman has taken on the appearance of an armed fortress. The men are an imposing group, ready to do whatever is needed to get their way, and hundreds of men hired by the owners patrol the district, equally ready to do what they have to for their bosses."

In an almost unbelievable turn of events, the governor of Colorado, a large, controversial, white-bearded man by the name of Davis H. Waite, stepped in and declared an end to the violence. He forced the owners to disband their group of illegal deputies and broke up the fortress at

Altman. On June 4, the owners and the union reached an agreement on the contract. The owners resumed the eight-hour three-dollar-per-day wage. Also, there was a negotiated, no-retaliation clause for both sides, but it took several more weeks for things to resume to normal. It was a victory for the miners and the union, and a solid blow to the owners.

After nearly six months, the arbitrary decision of the owners to try to get more work from the miners for no more money had succeeded in gaining nothing but violence, lost wages, and bad blood between the groups.

"I would not have imagined the workers doing such a thing in Russia," wrote Vitor. "I think I will like this place, I will start working as a real miner very soon."

A few weeks after the settlement, Vitor and Tommy were sent to Cripple Creek for building supplies. After looking down on the town for the last several weeks, this was his first trip into the city. As the empty wagon rattled into town, he was surprised at the size and quality of the buildings along Bennett Avenue. Several large brick buildings stood among dozens more of unpainted wood construction. Hotels, saloons, and stores of all kinds had large windows displaying everything a person could ever want in a high, cold place like Cripple Creek.

Vitor was amazed at all the new poles carrying a maze of electric wires into every building. The streets were so crowded with freight wagons, horses, and mules that it was nearly impossible to get through. They stopped on the west end of Bennett Avenue to buy a load of fresh-cut lumber. Flynn expertly backed the wagon up to the dock, tied up his reins, and jumped down. The manager came out and greeted him with a slap on the back and a big bear hug. "Ye beat them sons o' bitches good, Tommy," said the man, referring to the end of the strike against the owners. "Now we can get along with the business of making a livin' again."

Tommy nodded at the man in agreement. "You surely got that right!" The men loaded the wagon with the lumber and two kegs of nails, the manager making notes on his pad what they took. After a few more purchases, they pulled back into the street. After a block or so, Tommy found some room for the wagon and stopped the team abruptly in front of a beer hall. "Come on, my Russian friend, we got time for one quick nip before we head back."

"But I don't have any money, Tommy; I'll just wait out here."

Tommy just shook his head. "Whatever you want to do. I won't be but a minute."

While he waited for his new friend to return, Vitor began to take in the layout of the town. He located an assay office and the patent office on the far end of town. It looked like there were at least two beer halls, a café, and a hotel on each side of every block. People came in and out of every door on Bennett Avenue in a steady stream, and the wagons and carriages threw up a constant spray of mud that coated everything and everyone nearby. Cripple Creek was a busy place, particularly since the strike had been settled, and it was getting busier every day.

After a few minutes Flynn returned, jumping up on the wagon and grabbing the reins in one hand. In the other hand he had a small bottle of whisky. Offering it to Vitor, he called to the mules and started to pull out. "Have a nip on me, it'll be a cold ride home and this'll warm your blood a little."

Vitor looked at the bottle for a moment and finally accepted his offer. "It will be a cold ride home, I guess a drop or two couldn't hurt—thank you."

The two men finished the bottle before they finished the trip back to Altman, and by the time they pulled into town it was dark. Grabbing a few lumps of coal, they walked into the barracks and filled up the stove.

For the next two hours they sat and talked about where they had come from and what plans they had.

"I just want to make enough money to return to Ireland and get me a plump little red-headed bride and settle down and have me a bunch of kiddies," said Flynn, feeling the warmth of the hot fire wash over him. "What about you?"

Vitor had known exactly what he wanted ever since he left Russia. "I want to have my own gold mine, and my own house in Cripple Creek. Then I will bring my beautiful wife and daughter here to live with me."

"You don't ever want to go back to Russia?"

He shook his head no. "Russia is not a good place to live; the czars have made it unbearable for the working people. This strike that was just settled here could never have happened back home. The rulers would just have come in and taken everyone away, and you would never have seen them again."

"That sounds like a terrible place to live, all right. Ireland is not perfect, but it is beautiful and it is home to me and I miss it. I wish you well, my Russian friend, and I hope you get your gold mine."

"I will Tommy; I know for sure I will."

Chapter 24

For two hours, Jack, Rocky, and the sheriff watched as the HazMat team worked to seal up the tent and put in fans with special attachments to filter the air coming in and out of the enclosure. They also set up another tent for a shower and dressing room for the workers. When the FBI chopper finally arrived, there were two agents and two other men with them.

After brief introductions, the team got right to work. The lead agent, Robert Dunn, gave the other three men instructions to gown up and go inside with the HazMat team to open the barrels. One of the men picked up an aluminum case, and the three of them disappeared behind the plastic. Dunn motioned to Jack for them to come into the small office with him. He sat down at the lunch table, set his cell phone down in front of him, and opened up a laptop computer. Next to the computer he had a small two-way radio.

"Give me just a minute here and I'll fill you in as much as I can," he said, making a few notes in his pad and turning on the computer. "Like

I said, my name is Robert Dunn; I'm the lead agent on this investigation. My partner, Tom Monahan, is a field agent specializing in environmental crimes. The other two men are from Homeland Security—one works in terrorism investigation and the other is a nuclear expert."

"Nuclear? You mean like a nuclear bomb?" asked Rocky, suddenly paying much more attention.

Dunn shook his head. "From what the HazMat team has described, we don't think it's a bomb, but we should definitely know soon."

"Do you think there's an element of terrorism here?" asked Bannister.

"Not really, but that's why I brought an expert—I want to rule that out as soon as I can."

After forty five-minutes, a voice came over the radio and said the men were on their way out. The three men cleaned up in the makeshift locker room and walked into the office. "What have you got for us Tom?" asked Dunn, opening his notebook.

"Well, there're two pieces of good news: one—there is no bomb, and two—there is no evidence that this has anything to do with any domestic or foreign terrorists. What you have here are six drums of chemical waste, which the HazMat guys had already determined. After our forensic team gets through, these will be taken care of by the local team. However, the other ones are a problem."

Sheriff Jewell shifted uncomfortably in his chair and finally asked nervously, "Please don't keep us in suspense any longer, do I have to evacuate the city?"

"There are five barrels that contain what appears to be some kind of nuclear waste."

The room was silent for a moment while everyone digested this newest piece of information. Dunn made another note in his book and then looked at his partner. "Tom, are they safe as they sit there now?"

"They're safe for now," said Monahan. "The materials are very small pieces, in sealed glass vials. The vials are enclosed in heavy glass tubes about two inches in diameter and six inches long. The tubes are capped with lead seals and stainless steel caps and clamps. It's a pretty standard method of handling this kind of waste. The tubes are in fitted-Styrofoam packing and closed up in fiberglass cases, two per barrel. Whoever packed these knew what they were doing. Someone just needed to get rid of their waste without going through proper channels. It's safe for now, there's no sign of leakage, and the NRC guys will handle that part of cleanup."

"Isn't there one more barrel, Tom?" asked Dunn.

"Yeah, the last barrel has a dead guy in it," said Monahan bluntly. "He looks to be white and maybe middle-aged, that's about all I could tell for sure. The guys sealed it back up and are setting it aside for the local coroner."

The table was quiet after this last revelation. Finally Bannister broke the silence. "Will the FBI handle all of the forensic work on this, Robert?"

"We will, but it will take a couple of days to get the necessary team together and get it done. Sheriff Jewell, can I get a couple of local officers to help watch over this place until they get here?"

"No problem, we'll keep it covered twenty-four seven until you tell us otherwise." With that, the sheriff got up and walked out to his patrol car.

"Earlier," said Dunn, "you gave me a little about an investigation you guys were working; you think these trucks have something to do with it?"

"Maybe. All of these mines in the district are drained by tunnels dug under them years ago. They eventually drain into the Arkansas River about fifty miles from here. Traces of toxic chemicals not typically used in the mining industry have been turning up in the samples lately. Last spring there was a rental truck, similar to this one, that wrecked on one of the gravel roads not far from here. By the time we got there, the driver was dead."

Dunn made note after note and continued to question Jack about his investigation. "Did you find anything of value in that truck?"

"Just a couple of empty barrels with a trace of trych in them and the dead driver. We've also been investigating a hundred-year-old mining operation called the Black Mule mine on the northeast edge of the gold-bearing district. It had recently been refurbished, and a lot of these rental type–trucks had been coming and going during the night for a long time."

Dunn listened intently to Bannister's information. "You don't think they were hauling anything out of there, do you?"

"No, we've been watching the mine and logging all the traffic and people that have come and gone for several months now. They go in full, and come out empty; that much we're sure of."

"So tell me exactly what you believe is going on in that old mine right now, Jack-how does this truck connect to all this?"

Bannister hated to get the FBI involved any more than necessary, but with Rocky as his only paid investigator, he knew it would be good to at least try to keep the agency waiting in the wings if he needed them. "I believe they're running some kind of a trash-collection business for things that no one can get rid of any other way. I think they haul in the stuff, packed in sealed, fifty-gallon drums, to the ends of the old drifts, and blow them up to make everything disappear."

"Do you have any hard evidence that they actually took illegal material down? Or any evidence that they're actually covering it up by blasting?" Asked Dunn.

Although Bannister knew for sure about the blasting, he also knew he couldn't tell Dunn exactly why. As for what was in the drums, what he saw today was more than enough to remove any doubts as to what was going on. "We're still putting all that together, Robert, but as soon as we can get enough evidence for a warrant, we'll be scouring every inch of the mine to see what's down there."

"Right now, the agency can't do much for you as far as what may be happening in the mine, because there's no solid connection between the truck and the mine. But, we'll handle this mess here and keep you in the loop as far as the forensic work goes," said Dunn. "Also, if there is anything our lab or our research guys can do, just let me know."

Just like that, the truck was someone else's mess, and, just as quickly, the FBI had washed their hands of the mine problem. Bannister thought it was just as well. This new information, plus what they had already gathered, might be enough to move a judge to action. If not, they were about to have what Turner liked to call a Come to Jesus Meeting with Rocky's new miner pal, Dave. He knew it was just a matter of a short while before they got into the mine.

Jack and Rocky walked back to the Blazer and climbed in. After starting the engine, Rocky turned the defroster on full blast. When things began to warm up, he turned to Jack. "Agent Dunn said they couldn't help on the mine problem because there wasn't a link between the truck and the mine—right?"

"That's right—so?"

"We have the piece of paper, remember? The one with the name of the mine on it—from the ashtray? That's a connection . . ."

"Oh yeah—this piece of paper?" Bannister pulled it from his shirt pocket and held it up. "I guess I forgot all about this little piece of paper. I suppose it could be a connection—couldn't it?"

Rocky had never doubted his boss's methods before, even though they sometimes seemed a little far out at times, but this was a little different; he was holding out on the FBI. That was a little extreme, even for Jack.

The Drift

He decided not to press it any further.

Jack could see this was making his old friend uncomfortable and he tried to smooth things out a little. "Rock, this is personal. We're going to get the son of a bitch that's doing this, and I don't need the FBI in the way right now. You sure you're okay with this?"

"You know you don't have to ask, boss—let's go get these bastards . . ."

Chapter 25

It was Vitor's first trip down a Cripple Creek gold mine, and he was both nervous and excited standing in the first line of the morning. He had all new gear provided by the union, which he would have to pay for after his first few weeks. Before he entered the shaft house, he was also given a small, rectangle, brass tag with the number "409" and "V. Serinov" stamped on it. He had to carry it with him at all times down in the mine. If it wasn't hanging on his hook after the end of his shift, they would know that he hadn't come up.

As he stepped into the packed elevator cage, the operator pulled a cord several times, ringing a loud bell. As the cage started to drop, Vitor felt a strange feeling in the pit of his stomach, different from anything he remembered in the coal mines.

All the coal mines he had worked in before were entered through a main tunnel, with tracks going down to the work area. In Cripple Creek, every mine was entered by going straight down hundreds of feet, and in some cases a thousand feet or more. At the start of every shift, miners waited in the shaft house until the elevator brought up the previous crew. When the cage emptied, it returned below with the fresh crew. The routine never varied. *Three eight-hour shifts were really the best way to run the mine*, thought Vitor.

The main shaft was one straight drop with horizontal drifts at different levels. By skillful use of the bell system, the operator dropped the cage down until he reached the level he wanted. Vitor's cage had stopped smoothly, and he stepped out into the gloomy chamber marked "L400." As his eyes began to adjust to the darkened scene, another miner tugged on his sleeve and pointed down the drift.

After a five-minute walk down the long drift, he noticed something else that was very different from the coal mines: the air was much fresher, and a slight, cool breeze seemed to move through the drift. Later he would find out that most of the mines were connected and the air generally moved freely between the different claims. He would also find out that on certain days, in the right weather conditions, it could reverse itself and the air would go bad. Although he really didn't understand how they could tell, he knew the miners watched it closely and wouldn't enter if things weren't right.

Vitor fell into the routine quickly and wrote to Kapeka: "I am now working steadily at gold mining and making three dollars per day. After I pay for my bed and necessities, I still have money for our future. I have started an account at the district bank; it will be for our life in Cripple Creek."

As he grew comfortable in the job of a full-time miner, he began to take advantage of the beautiful summer days to learn all he could about the district. When he wasn't listening to all the miners talk about the gold in the area, he would walk the district every spare day, mile after mile, until he knew it as well as his own home. Everyone in the district knew him, often referring to him as the Wandering Russian. He took in every detail of the geography in the area: who owned which claim, and if they were making a profit. He always kept a notebook in his pocket, marking down new observations every day. Very little about the district escaped his eye. By the end of summer, he had his future narrowed down to three small claims that he found were not well attended to by the current owners.

By the end of September, the mountains were at their prettiest. The beautiful yellow and gold colors of the aspen trees, called quakies by the locals, surrounded the district, and an early, light snowfall concealed the real Cripple Creek Mining District. The reality was a landscape that looked like it had been through a terrible war, with barren hills and piles of mine tailings as far as the eye could see. There were more than 150 mines compressed into a few square miles. Aside from the gold, there was nothing pretty about the Cripple Creek Mining District.

If the district was busy before, since the end of the strike Cripple Creek had become a frenzied rush of humanity, descended upon by tens of thousands of people of all kinds. Every person that had something to sell or a new scam to try out landed in Cripple Creek. Everyone looking for a handout or a job in town crowded Bennett Avenue, clogging the streets and sidewalks to the point of hurting some of the retail businesses.

Meyers Avenue, the next street south, was rapidly becoming as busy as Bennett, but for a different reason. Dozens of parlor houses, mostly wood-frame buildings thrown up quickly, lined the narrow street. Each had their own group of girls, saloons, and casinos, and the citizens of the district took full advantage of the competition between them.

Real-estate sales were booming, and in some places, like the town of Victor, even city lots were being marketed and sold as potential gold mines. Mining claims in the district became chips in a high-stakes gambling game. The claims were being bought, sold, and traded like horses. Many shrewd investors had never set foot in a mine before, but understood how to market what they had, and how to horse-trade these claims to make big profits. It was just another type of gambling to them.

Vitor Serinov, twenty-seven years old on his last birthday, decided this was how he would get his own claim. He wrote to Kapeka about this new plan: "I have found three claims that I believe have the possibility of good gold. When I get enough money in our bank account, I will find who the best claim belongs to, and try to purchase it." He continued to lay out his plan, devised from his knowledge of the area and his own calculations. "Of the three claims, one has a beautiful rock formation that could be a perfect place for our home; it also has a commanding view of Mr. Pike's famous peak."

Vitor was still living in the work camp at Altman, and after checking things out thoroughly, he could find nothing cheaper and decided to stay where he was. Once a week, he went into Cripple Creek to deposit his money in the newest bank in town. It was three floors high and built of sturdy red brick, brought in all the way from Denver. The inside looked like a safe and secure place for his money, with a giant black vault door and marble on the walls and countertops. There were bars on the windows and between the customers and the tellers. Vitor felt very good about coming here.

In Altman, he built a box out of scrap lumber from the last building he worked on and put a lock on it. He built it to fit under his bed. He kept his work gear, extra clothes, and necessities locked up when he wasn't around, as was the custom of all the men in the barracks. Also, like the rest of the men, he kept any money he had left after his weekly deposit with him at all times.

As winter began to show up in full force, he volunteered for any overtime that he could get. He told Kapeka, "Deep snow and cold weather have made me something of a hermit. I go from the camp to the mine and back again almost every day. Every Saturday, I walk to the Cripple Creek Bank, then to the dry goods store and back to the camp. There is little to do when not working in the mine, so I try and find some extra paying job somewhere to keep busy. This also helps by adding money to our bank account for our future."

As for the work, it was just dirty, backbreaking, hard labor like most mine work. Vitor was a mucker, a man that hauled the rock out after the blast. He shoveled it into small cars that were moved to the cage and brought to the surface. He knew it was the bottom level of the operation, but he was working steady and learning the business while he waited for the chance to buy his own claim.

The next level job would be the driller, the man who operated the air drill that put in the holes for the dynamite crew. They drilled the face full of small, deep holes so the blasters could pack them with dynamite. They also wired the charges and set them off. Each setup moved them about ten feet. After the blast, the muckers cleaned the hole and the drillers set up and did it all over again. As far as Vitor was concerned, this was still cleaner and safer than coal mining and even paid better. One of the most common complaints from the miners was the constant headaches from the blasting, but it was just accepted as part of the job.

The winter of 1894 in the district wasn't much different from those Vitor grew up with as a boy. A lot of snowstorms and below-zero days were common in Russia as well as Colorado. The big difference to Vitor was that here, on the days in between the storms, there were beautiful, warm, sunny days, and the temperature could go from bitter cold to pleasantly warm overnight.

Vitor could remember only long, cold winters and gray skies where he grew up. Even the summers there weren't as warm as some of the winter days here. Here, the men would often sit outside in their shirtsleeves and smoke and tell stories. The barracks buildings had one door and one window in each end. On nice days, the windows were opened and fresh air would blow through the building, carrying most of the odors from the workers, the stale tobacco smoke, and the coal dust around the stove, out the window. He could not remember ever opening a window in wintertime Russia.

At the end of April, he wrote to Kapeka: "It is showing a little more life around the district now. The snow is melting rapidly and the old familiar muddy ruts now consume every road in the district." It had been one year since Vitor arrived and he had been dutifully working and saving every dollar that he could. "We are getting a nice savings for our future; maybe in one more season we will be ready to build a home at our own claim."

As the weather dried up the countryside, Vitor once again went back to his walking, looking for a place he could eventually call his own. The Wandering Russian followed every road and stream in the area. He climbed every peak and continued to fill his book with notes. The more he studied the area, the more he became interested in the flat spot below the strange rock formation.

He told Kapeka of his travels and about his notes and how they all led him to the same place. "I think I have found us the right place to make our fortune and raise our daughter. I hope, by the end of the summer, we will have enough to make the deal."

Throughout the summer, he worked all he could, and walked several times a week to his choice of claims. By the middle of summer, he had been promoted to driller and was gaining more experience that he would use in his own mine. He also began to spend time in the assayer's office and the patent office, learning what he had to do to file a claim if he could not buy one.

His letters to Kapeka had become more and more positive, and finally in July, he wrote, "Perhaps you and our daughter should consider preparing for the trip to Colorado next summer; I believe that we are getting close to being a family again."

Chapter 26

When Bannister and Rocky returned to the cabin, Jessie had just finished unloading groceries and supplies. Bannister gave her a quick hug and hung up his coat. "I can't believe you went out with the roads this bad."

"Someone has to keep this crew in groceries; you ate us out of house and home. Besides, I had a couple of things to check on at the office."

After a couple of hours, Turner drove up in his old green Willys. Walking into the cabin, he pulled off his boots and jacket and entered the living room carrying a large cardboard tube under his arm.

"What you got there, old man, lunch?" asked Rocky, poking a little fun at him.

Turner dropped the tube on the trunk, knocking some of Rocky's notes on the floor. "Don't start in with me fat man, you ain't been whipped yet today, and I'm just the man who can do it."

"Forgive me," said Rocky, forcing down a laugh. "I forgot just who I was talking to here."

Opening the tube, Turner pulled out a large U.S. map. "While you were all cuddling together by the fire singing "*Kumbaya*," I was doing some real work on this problem." He rolled out the map on top of the trunk; it was covered with purple Sharpie marks all ending in Colorado.

"I took all the license numbers from the rental trucks and did a little of my own research. With that, and the information Rocky gave me, I found out something pretty damn interesting—you want to know what it is?"

Bannister knew he had to allow for a little drama when Turner was talking; this time was no different. "Come on, Turner, get on with it—I don't want to wait till the snow melts to find out."

Taking out his Swiss Army pocketknife to use as a pointer, he motioned to where all the purple lines converged in Cripple Creek, Colorado. "Most of the rentals came from the northeast part of the country. The New England states had the most, especially Massachusetts, New York, Maine, New Hampshire, and Connecticut. There are a few from other areas, but most are from a long ways away."

Although Bannister had already decided that the loads were not from around here, the map did confirm it. "That's great, have a cup of coffee and I'll fill everyone in on where we are on the mine deal."

As they all sat down around the trunk, Bannister laid out to everyone what they found in the abandoned truck.

When he was finished, Jessie asked the obvious question on everyone's mind. "What's next? Can you finally go in and get this shut down?"

"I think we may have enough to do it, but Rocky and I are going to confront the miner that's the lowest man on the totem pole, Dave DeAngelo, and explain to him that he has a chance to get right here—if he gives up the others. Add that to what we have, and I doubt there will be a problem. What do you think, Rock?"

"I don't see any problem with him. He's just a go-along kind of guy, and I know the thought of prison will scare him to death."

"Jess, when's the next event at the museum?" asked Bannister.

"Next week we're having a small private deal, mostly for the larger benefactors. It's to thank them and get input on the direction the museum will be going for the next few years."

"Will the Carhartts be there?"

"She usually attends everything; he comes when he can get away I guess."

"How about giving them a little extra attention; I'd like to know more about their history."

"Both of them?"

"While we're looking, we might just as well look at both of them individually, and their history together. Anything you learn could be helpful. Just be subtle, Jess, we don't want them to know what's going on."

"Bannister, you ever known me not to be subtle?"

"You're right. What was I thinking?"

* * *

Jack and Rocky pulled up to the front of the Airstream trailer. It was a model from the sixties, parked in between the trees and surrounded by junk. It was a rental that miners had been using for generations, and it looked like it was on its last legs. The top was covered with a blue plastic tarp and taped to the sides. A woodstove had been added years ago for heat, and one side of the trailer was piled high with firewood.

The pickup truck parked beside the trailer was nearly as old, and just as rough looking. After putting on their badges and guns, they walked up to the door, and stood on either side. Rocky pounded on the door and identified himself. After no response, he repeated the process, much louder this time. Finally, a stocky, scruffy, half-asleep Dave DeAngelo pulled open the door. "Hey, Rocky, what's up?"

Slipping his foot inside the doorframe he looked at DeAngelo. "Dave, I need to come in and talk to you right now."

DeAngelo shrugged his shoulders and ran his fingers through his hair in an attempt to look halfway acceptable. "Sure, Rocky. Who's your friend?"

"This is my boss, Jack Bannister. We have something to talk to you about."

"Come on in and sit down."

The inside of the trailer was cluttered with piles of newspapers and magazines, topped off by stacks of empty beer cans. Dirty clothes were all thrown in one big pile, and the sink had several days' worth of dishes needing to be washed. In the front of the trailer was a nearly new fifty-two-inch flat screen TV and an assortment of DVDs. Squarely in front of the TV was an oversized recliner.

After he put in a couple of sticks of firewood, he sat down at the table with the two men and offered them a beer. Looking at Rocky, DeAngelo suddenly noticed the badge. "Aw, shit, Rocky, you're a cop?"

"Always have been, Dave, I just had no reason to show you until now. Like I said, this is Jack Bannister, he's my boss, and he's also a cop. In a nutshell, everything I told you before about testing the rivers was true. The problem is, I found things in the water that shouldn't be there, and, they're coming from somewhere in the district—that's what we want to talk to you about."

"Rocky, I'm just a miner; I don't know anything about contaminating the river."

"I know that, and I know you work for PMV. I also know your boss is Max Atkinson and that you guys drill out old drifts and prepare them for the blasting." Bannister paused for a moment to let DeAngelo soak up what had been said. "I also know that several nights a week rental trucks from all over come into the shaft house and unload sealed fifty-gallon drums, and you take them down into the mine."

DeAngelo slumped in his chair, staring at Rocky. "I just drill holes for the guy. I don't know what's in the drums."

"You know what else I know, Dave? I know that you take those drums to the area of the drift that's been recently drilled and packed with the charges. Then, you blow up the drift and the barrels are gone and you do it all over again. Anything I missed here, Dave?"

DeAngelo nervously tapped his heel on the floor, his knee bouncing uncontrollably. By now, most of the color had gone from his thin face. "Rocky, I swear to you I never saw the contents of even one of those barrels. That was always the rule set by Max—no unsealed barrels could even come onto the property, nobody knew what was in them. We used to make jokes about it—like maybe Jimmy Hoffa might be in one"

"Well, Dave, what if I told you we have one of the trucks in custody right now. Would you like to know what we found inside?"

"Sure, I guess so—what did you find?"

"We found twelve barrels, Dave. Six of them had poisonous chemicals, like what we're finding in the river—does that bother you?" DeAngelo just nodded his head meekly. "We also found five barrels of radioactive waste material, Dave—does that bother you?" DeAngelo remained quiet while Rocky continued. "And, do want to guess what was in the last one Dave? Well you don't have to guess here, I'll just go ahead and tell you. We found a dead guy. We found a dead guy all cut up and stuffed in one of those barrels—what do you think about all this, Dave?"

DeAngelo couldn't answer; he just looked away and hung his head. Finally, he said quietly, "I didn't know, Rocky, honest. I didn't know what was in the barrels. I just needed a job."

Finally, Bannister bent over very close to the miner and spoke to him directly. "Dave, neither Rocky nor I think that you're a bad guy, but you took cash for doing a job that you knew was something less than legal. You joked about what was in the barrels with the other guys. You helped unload the barrels; you helped take them down to the drifts that you helped prepare. The jury's not going to care just because you say you didn't know what was in them."

DeAngelo looked at the two men sitting across from him. He knew it was over and they weren't leaving the trailer without him. "Okay, I got the picture, what happens now?"

Bannister laid out a pad and paper and told him to start writing everything he knew of the operation, starting with the day he first met up with Max. "Dave, if you cooperate with us in every way, I can guarantee that you will be treated fairly and your help will factor into what the DA does with you."

"What's the worst I could expect if I don't help?"

"Well, I can't know for sure, but I can tell you that the FBI and Homeland Security are involved. If they connect you to the radioactive waste, I doubt if anybody will ever hear from you again."

DeAngelo picked up the pen and began to write. For the next two hours, they talked about everything he knew, and he wrote everything down on the pad. When Bannister was satisfied, DeAngelo signed and dated the letter.

When they were ready to go, DeAngelo looked at the two men and shook his head. "I'm really sorry. Never in a million years would I have thought there could be something that bad in those barrels. I would never want someone to get hurt by this. I was just broke and needed a job bad."

Rocky handed him his coat and told him to put it on, then he snapped on the cuffs. "I believe you, I really do. If you help us clean up this mess, we'll do the best we can do for you; you have my word on that."

"We'll take him to the jail in Colorado Springs instead of here. It might be a little safer. Plus, I haven't been in the office in a few days," said Bannister, "so I need to stop there."

"Good enough, I think I'll drive down myself."

"Hungry for a little diner food are you, Rock?"

Batton refused to rise to the bait. "A little biscuits and gravy couldn't hurt anybody, could it Jack?"

Chapter 27

By the end of the summer of 1895, Vitor Serinov was well known to most of the people in the district. He was a regular at the bank every Saturday, and he was becoming one of the most knowledgeable people in the district on the subject of the different claims: who owned them and exactly where all the boundaries were. He had covered more miles on foot than most locals had done with a horse or wagon.

At the mine, he was known as one of their best workers, always ready to help anyone do whatever job was necessary. When he wasn't working or researching a claim, he and his friend Tommy Flynn would get together for a drink and a little conversation. Near the end of August, they walked down to the town of Gillette, located four miles to the north of Cripple Creek.

The talk around the district was that there was going to be a real Wild West Show in town for three days, and the pair thought they would spend a Saturday watching the excitement. A man named Joe Wolfe and his partner, a seven-foot-tall man named Arizona Charlie Meadows, put together a plan to use the racetrack at Gillette for the show. To make it an even bigger extravaganza, they decided to hold a genuine Mexican bullfight. They imported four matadors from Mexico, and when they couldn't get Mexican fighting bulls into the United States, they bought eight bulls from local ranchers.

It was the first time that Vitor had spent any of his earnings for frivolous entertainment. He wrote to Kapeka, "I saw what is called a wild western show today; there was shooting and tricks on horses and tricks with ropes. It was all very exciting; the man in charge was a giant called Arizona Charlie. He was much taller than anyone my friend Tommy Flynn or I had ever seen, with hair even longer than yours." Serinov left out the part about the bullfight, as he did not think that Kapeka would like to hear of the killing of a bull.

On the way back to their barracks, Vitor took Tommy to the piece of land that he wanted for himself. As they stood looking at the strange rock formation, Tommy finally spoke up. "My wandering Russian friend, do you positively think there may be gold here?"

"I do," said Vitor with confidence. "I have looked nearly everywhere, and I believe this place has been overlooked by all the big-shot experts. I believe that the two different kinds of rock are hiding something very big beneath them. And I have a good place to build my home right here as well," he said, pointing to the fine, pink granite scattered beneath their feet.

"But," interrupted Flynn, "it isn't your claim, Vitor."

"No, but I believe that it will be mine soon, hopefully by spring I think."

"I hope you're right, my friend—maybe I can come to work for you when you get it?"

"I think it would be good to have you, Tommy, when I hire my first worker, it will be you. I will also name my claim—the Crease, because that's what it looks like to me, a very large crease in the rocks. And I will name the house I build—Kapeka's House."

Tommy looked at the rocks and the surrounding gravel, wondering just what Vitor saw in this barren piece of ground. "I hope you are right, Vitor, I hope you find your fortune here."

"When you are finally back in Ireland, with a family of your own, I will send you a photograph of my house and my family. You will see; this is where I will find my gold, and raise my family."

As they stood talking, they suddenly felt a jarring, vibrating sensation in the gravel they were standing on. "Sometimes," said Vitor, "when they are blasting in the next claim to the west, you can feel it here. Last month, I was leaning against the rock and it appeared almost to move slightly when I felt the blast."

"How close is this next claim to this one?" asked Flynn.

"We are neighbors, right next to each other," said Vitor, already referring to the claim as his. "Their claim stops less than one hundred yards to the west of these rocks. I plan to begin my mine by digging right at the base of the Crease. I think that will prove to be a good place to start."

Tommy knew that Vitor was ambitious, and anxious to get his own mine started, but wondered if his Russian friend really knew what he was looking at. "It looks like you could almost crawl down into the crack at the base of the rock right here, or at least with a small amount of digging, Vitor. But I don't see anything but this pink gravel here, no sign of anything of value."

Vitor kicked at the gravel at the base of the rock and looked up at his friend. "Tommy, look at what I have found just lying on the ground." Pulling a small leather pouch from his pocket, he emptied the contents into his hand. There was a broken piece of white quartz crystal with a tiny thread of gold in it and several pieces of what was known locally as Amazon stone, a dull, light-green stone similar to turquoise. "I found these, right where we are standing. The green stone is the same as we find back where I came from in Russia. It can be used for jewelry. I feel that the Crease is hiding something, and I will find out its secret."

As the two men walked back to Altman, they talked about gold mining and their families and what their futures might be like. Vitor had been here about a year and a half and hoped that he would have enough savings by spring to secure his claim. Tommy had been here about a year longer and was having trouble saving much money for his family back in Ireland. He was very undisciplined with his money, and often spent too much in the local beer halls to have anything left to save.

Vitor was aware of his friend's weakness, and finally one day marched him down to the same bank where he saved, and helped him open an account of his own. On the small book the bank provided for his records, he had the teller write "Tommy's Ireland Fund," so it would help him remember to deposit every week. Every Saturday he would take Tommy along with him and make him deposit into the fund whatever he had left from his recent carousing.

As the winter weather caught up to the district, Vitor invested in a new pair of boots and a heavy winter coat. He still wore the cap that Kapeka had made for him; it was the only thing that he had left from home. Folding up the new coat, he placed it inside his storage box and saw the hat lying next to it. It momentarily flooded him with memories of home: Kapeka and their baby—a baby he had not yet seen.

It had been more than three years since he left home, and he was still looking for a place of his own—a place to bring his family that he could be proud of. Sliding slowly down the wall next to his bed, a sudden, heavy sense of sadness overtook him, and it made him feel lonely and small. It was as if for the first time since he left Russia, he realized how far away from home he really was. The thought that he might never see his family again was more painful than he could handle, and he began to cry softly in the darkened corner of barracks.

* * *

The next morning, as Vitor and Tommy walked to the mine for their shift, Tommy ran ahead and stopped at a beer hall he often frequented for his morning shot. While he was inside, a large, open freight wagon pulled by a pair of huge black draft horses, was unloading coal to the stores on the main street. At the sound of random gunfire from behind the nearest saloon, the inside horse reared up on his hind legs and came crashing down on the outside horse causing both horses to bolt. Veering into the center of the street and gaining speed, coal flew wildly from the rear of the wagon, and suddenly the tongue of the wagon snapped.

The remaining piece of tongue still attached to the wagon dropped down and dug deep into the dirt. The wagon flipped over and came down hard on the horses' hindquarters. One of the big blacks went down and the second one crashed onto him. The horses rolled through the street, with the wagon flying through the air, throwing coal in every direction, and disintegrating as it rolled and bounced through the deep ruts.

At the same moment they reached Tommy's favorite saloon, the little Irishman bolted from the front door moving fast to catch up with Vitor. He was instantly caught in the middle of the melee and disappeared into the carnage. One of the giant black horses had an obvious broken leg. As he kicked and flailed wildly, trying to release himself from the harness, he managed to kick and roll over Tommy Flynn again and again.

In less than a minute, the teamster had dispatched the injured horse with a shot to the head and it was over as quickly as it started. The second horse was already dead, with a broken neck, and Tommy Flynn lay dead, pinned under the horses and the remains of the wagon, mangled so badly he could hardly be recognized. Coal, coal dust, and road dirt covered much of the wreck, making the scene almost unrecognizable to anyone who hadn't just witnessed it.

Vitor was stunned at what he just saw happen. His friend of nearly a year was gone in an instant. For the second time in as many days, he sat down and cried. He wrote to Kapeka about how sad he was, and that he could not go much longer without his family with him. "I need to have you and our beautiful daughter with me; it can be very lonely here. I miss Tommy; he was my good friend here in this rough place. I will know soon if I have our mine, and I will dedicate it to him."

Vitor made an extra trip to the bank the next day and told the manager what had happened. He told him he would take care of the undertaker and funeral expenses for his friend, and asked what they would do with Tommy's bank savings. The banker told him that as soon as the county released the account, they could send his money home to his family. Vitor shook hands with the manager. "Tommy was a very good man, sir, thank you for your help."

The manager responded by nodding his head and squeezing his hand again. "You are a very good friend, Vitor, he was lucky to have you."

Chapter 28

Sheriff Jewell readily agreed to transfer the prisoner to the El Paso County Jail in Colorado Springs, as it would be one less headache for him. Bannister was glad to get him away from Cripple Creek. He didn't want to take the chance that someone would try and intimidate him into not talking. He left instructions with the El Paso County Sheriff's Department that the prisoner was to get no visitors except his lawyer. As he was clearly intimidated by Max and company, DeAngelo himself seemed good with this and agreed not to accept any visitors.

Pulling back into the long driveway of the cabin, Jack could see that Rocky and Turner were already there. He had called Sheriff Jewell and A.J. Rogers from the Springs, and they were on their way to the cabin. Walking in, Bannister could smell Jessie's green chile cooking and noticed the pile of fresh tamales on the counter. Within a few minutes, A.J. and the sheriff arrived at the cabin.

After the introductions were made, everyone grabbed some food and found a place close to the fire to settle in. The trunk was piled high with notes and maps and a few photographs. Bannister decided it was time to lay out everything to the group and come up with a plan to get this glorified trash collection scam shut down.

After going through everything they had found out about the mine, the trucks, and what DeAngelo had told them, he asked Sheriff Jewell if he could come up with a cover story as to what happened to the prisoner, and why he wasn't in the Cripple Creek Jail.

"That shouldn't be any problem," said Jewell. "I'll just tell anyone that asks that I arrested him for drunk and disorderly, and he got belligerent with me. We lost our power for a while during that snowstorm, and I decided he would be better off in the Colorado Springs lockup."

Bannister nodded his head in agreement. "Also Martin, if you could make a note of anyone who might be inquiring about him, I would appreciate it."

"You got it. What else can I do?"

"Do you have enough deputies to spare a couple for this job?"

"I can give you two, and myself, if that will do the job."

"That would be great," said Bannister. "I need you to help with the arrest at the shaft house and to secure it when we go down. We don't know how many of these birds might be in the shaft house and how many might be below. One more thing, A.J. is going to go down the mine with me to identify the areas that have been blasted shut; I'd like you to deputize him. I know he can take care of himself, but I'd like him to carry a weapon legally. We don't really know what we could run into down there."

"I'll take care of it," said Jewell.

Bannister looked at A.J. for confirmation. "You good with that?"

"No problem—it wouldn't be the first time I've carried a gun in gold-mining country."

Turner had listened patiently while Bannister laid out the plan, but couldn't hold his tongue any longer. "What about me, what will I be doing?"

Bannister knew he wanted to be involved, and after all he had done already, he deserved to be. "Well, I have a special job for you, if you're interested."

"Shit yes, you know I am. I'll do whatever you want, just lay it out."

"Okay, here's the deal," said Bannister. "After we bust the guys in the shaft house, I want you to work with Sheriff Jewell and his men to document everything you see in the building. You help him record everything in sight. I want all the information on all the vehicles inside the fence, the info from the rental truck, and any firearms they have. Have your camera ready too."

"Sure, Jack, if that's what you need. But can I go underground to see what's been going on down there too?" asked Turner.

"As soon as it's safe, we'll give you a personal, in-depth tour." Jack knew how badly he wanted to be a part of this, but he also didn't want to put him in harm's way. "One more thing, I need you to make a large, clean copy of the map you made, and a copy of all your notes. This is for the FBI; they could use your help."

"A couple more things I want to bring up while we're all here. I talked to the FBI about the radioactive material we found. In North America, it's really difficult to lose track of any spent reactor fuel that comes from power plants or from the military," said Bannister, shuffling through his notes. "But the information I got from the agency says that there are many small organizations all over North America that use the stuff for other purposes, like research and medicine. This small of an amount most likely came from one of them. Also, the DA had no problems with the search warrants. They'll be ready whenever we are."

They had been at it for several hours and they were all getting a little tired. Rocky shifted position in his chair, trying to find a comfortable spot for his large frame. "When do we plan on doing this? With DeAngelo missing, they might get suspicious."

"I want to be ready to do this when we're sure that they have a truck inside. Turner, can I get you to do a spot check every now and then? You can stay here while we're waiting for one to show up. When they do, you call us and we'll move. Although it does look like it may be a couple of days before the roads are clear enough."

"I'll be here when you need me," said Turner, standing up and stretching his legs. "I think I'm gonna head home and get started on that map."

"Sounds good. Oh—and one more thing while you're all here. As I found out a long time ago, these are real bad guys, they carry automatic weapons. I'm sure if they have a chance they will use them. No one goes inside the fence without a protective vest—no one," warned Bannister.

As Turner put on his coat and got ready to leave, he couldn't resist one more dig at Rocky. "Hey, fat man, you better buy two of them vests-it'll take more than one to cover that belly!"

Rocky shot back quickly, "Turner, you worry too much; you can hide in my back pocket if you're scared."

Opening the front door, Turner stopped short, turned, and announced to everyone, "If you all want to get home anytime soon you better get moving. Otherwise it looks like we might all be hunkered down here for a while." Another six inches of snow had fallen since they returned to the cabin, and it was still coming down hard.

* * *

Closing the door, Bannister looked around the cabin; it was the first time it had been this quiet in ages. Before he could get away from the door, Maggie was standing alongside him, wiggling her stubby tail and looking up at him. When he opened the door again, Maggie shot outside and ran around for a few minutes. Jack followed her out and grabbed an armload of firewood, depositing it in the bin next to the fireplace.

When Bannister sat down on the couch next to Jessie, it was more than Maggie could take. She jumped up and forced herself into the narrow space between them. "Well, you and Maggie were pretty quiet this afternoon—is everything okay Jess?"

"Everything is fine; I liked hearing about the mine and what's going to happen," said Jessie. "I almost wish I could be there myself, it sounds real exciting."

"Well, I'm not really hoping for any real excitement, just a smooth, easy arrest." Bannister reached up and started to run his fingers through her hair, trying to release the clip holding it all tight to her head. "Want to mess around a little?"

"Go away—you stink. No way would I mess around with someone that smelled like sweat and wood smoke. You need a shower."

Bannister dropped his head in mock shame. "Okay, I give up, I'm a beaten man, and I admit it. I'm headed for the shower." Walking into the bedroom, he stripped down and walked over to the shower, opening the glass door and turning on the water full blast. Stepping inside, he leaned under the showerhead and let the hot water beat down on him for several minutes.

Finally, he began to lather up, closing his eyes while he did. He never heard the bathroom door open, nor did he hear the shower door open and close. He didn't realize that someone was in the shower with him until he felt her soft hands slide slowly across his chest and realized her lips were caressing his neck.

For a few moments, Bannister tried to ignore her, pretending he didn't notice. The more he ignored her, the more her hands explored him, and the more places her lips found to caress. She playfully nipped at his ears and lips, and ran her leg up and down the inside of his thigh. Finally, he couldn't take it any longer and turned toward her, pulling her tight against him. Jack looked into her intense, dark eyes for a long moment. "Well hello stranger, fancy meeting you here . . ."

"Oh, so I'm a stranger, am I?" said Jessie. "Well, I guess we'll just have to get to know each other a little better. You certainly wouldn't want to live with a stranger now, would you?" She spun slowly around, facing away from Jack, at the same time pulling his hands up and pressing them against her breasts. She squeezed his hands tightly around them. "These are just for you Jack; you should get to know them—that is, if you really want to get to know me a little better."

Bannister felt the softness of her breasts and slowly traced the outline of her nipples as the warm soapy water followed each swirl and touch. His hands explored every inch of her smooth olive skin. After a few minutes, the water began to cool, but they hardly noticed. Finally, they managed to get out of the shower, and headed for the bedroom, still locked in each other's arms—still covered in warm soapy water.

They were together in an instant, first with Jack on top of her, moving slowly and steadily, not wanting anything to break the moment. Soon Jessie was on top, still together and moving rhythmically but getting faster and faster. Jessie leaned down and kissed him, her perfect breasts lingering for a long moment against his skin. Then she brushed her breasts across his lips and collapsed on his chest shaking softly, kissing him deeply.

The rest of the day went by quickly, with Jessie walking around in nothing but the sheerest black nightgown that Jack had ever seen, one that she had never worn before that day. She was, without a doubt, the most beautiful woman Bannister had ever been with; for that matter, the most beautiful woman he had ever seen.

As Bannister sat on the couch in his shorts, Jessie walked between him and the fireplace. Standing perfectly still, she was silhouetted against the flickering light, and Jack could see every curve and detail of her body. Her long black hair fell seductively over her shoulders, framing the picture perfectly. After a minute, she let the nightgown slip from her shoulders and fall to the floor. "Well stranger, are you ready to get to know me a little better—again?"

Chapter 29

The spring of 1896 was a particularly bad one for the Cripple Creek Mining District. At the end of April, almost every building in Cripple Creek burned to the ground.

"They say a gasoline stove overturned and started a fire," Vitor wrote to Kapeka. "There are now very few buildings of wood left. Downtown, there are still several good, solid, brick buildings standing high above the rubble."

There had been two separate fires just three days apart. The famous gold camp had been devastated, with many killed and several thousand injured and left homeless. In an extraordinary display of compassion, nearly every city and town in the state came to the aid of the residents. Even Colorado Springs, their old adversary, jumped into action. W.S. Stratton, with the help of Spencer Penrose and several other mine owners, formed a team to start gathering supplies and sending them to Cripple Creek. Stratton told the team, "We've got to move and move fast! No time to get money pledges. Charge everything to me. We'll divide the bills afterward."

"Kapeka, it is unbelievable that so many good people came so quickly to help, that within a day or two, everyone had a warm, dry shelter and food to eat. This will be our home for sure," wrote Vitor.

He didn't tell her that he had been concerned that all his money may have been lost in the fire. Vitor still felt somewhat ashamed that he would have had such a thought with all the suffering going on. Like all the other residents in the district, he had worked for days to clear the burned-out rubble and help distribute the steady stream of donations from Colorado Springs. He also set up rows of white canvas tents, and installed small stoves inside of them. Along one side of each would be a pile of coal and whatever scraps of wood that could be recovered from the burned-out buildings.

Just three days after the last fire, Vitor's bank reopened, displaying a very large Open for Business sign in the window. The new brick building still stood tall in the middle of so much ruin—as a testament to proper building procedures. Vitor hurried into the bank and the first person he saw was the manager. "Hello, Vitor, your money's safe," he said, answering his question before Vitor could get the words out. "The fire only damaged a small spot on our roof."

Vitor's relief showed clearly on his face. "Thank you, sir, I hope you and all of your family came through this all right."

"We did, Vitor; we live northwest of town a few miles and were spared by the fire. Thank you for asking."

"Sir, could I talk with you sometime about a business I have in mind?"

The banker, dressed in a dark, three-piece wool suit and easily six inches taller than Serinov, looked so official and intimidating to Vitor. He thrust out his hand and formally introduced himself. "Vitor, I'm John W. Lasser, I would like for you to call me John, if that's okay with you."

Vitor was startled at the giant hand pointing at him, but took it and shook it firmly. "Yes, sir, I would like that, sir." Correcting himself quickly he added, "Thank you, John."

"We can go into my office right now and visit a bit if you would like," said Lasser, motioning him into his oak and glass office.

Together they walked into the large office with high ceilings, dark, wood-paneled walls, and enormous windows facing Bennett Avenue. Lasser walked behind his desk and took his seat. The bank manager still looked a bit intimidating to Vitor, and he had not seen many rooms this beautiful in his whole life. There were two long, leather couches, several matching chairs, and a large table containing a stack of maps of the district.

Behind the manager's head hung a painting of Grover Cleveland, the U.S. president, a stout, mustached man with a bow tie and a stern look on his face. Above it was a new-looking flag. Vitor quickly counted forty-five stars on it.

"That's my new flag, Vitor, it just arrived the day before the first fire, it's the biggest one I could find. Do you like it?"

"Yes, sir—er, Mr. John, I like it very much."

"Have a seat and tell me what you would like to talk to me about."

Vitor sat in the big leather chair closest to the desk, took a breath and started to tell the banker about his home and family, how he traveled here to find gold, and how he planned to move his wife and baby here soon. He explained what had happened since he got to the district and how he had been researching claims and found a piece of ground that he was interested in. He explained that he thought it showed promise and would also be a good homesite for his family.

"One problem," said Vitor. "I don't know if the owner will sell, because I don't know how to locate him or how much money he might want."

Lasser stood up and walked to the table, "Vitor, can you show me on the map where this property is?"

"Yes, I can show you," he said, now leaning over the table next to him. "It's right here, next to the Black Mule claim, right against the east boundary line."

Lasser looked at the spot Vitor was pointing to. "I know some of the owners around there, Vitor. Why don't we take a ride up there tomorrow and take a look at it?"

Vitor was starting to get excited at the prospect of the banker's interest and suddenly blurted out, "How about taking a ride up there today, Mr. John?"

Lasser got a laugh out of this exchange. "Sure, Vitor, why not. Do you have a horse?"

"No sir, just my boots, I'm used to walking, though."

"Well I'm not used to walking, so why don't we take my buggy. It's a nice day for a ride, don't you think?"

"Yes sir, Mr. John, a very nice day for a ride."

The two men left the bank and walked the block to the stable. Lasser spoke to the blacksmith for a moment and walked back to Vitor. "He'll have the rig ready in a few minutes, and we'll be on our way to see this special place of yours."

"I know you will like it, Mr. John, but I am worried about how much money I will need to buy it, and if the owner can be found."

"Let's look at the spot first, and we can talk about that part later."

It was Vitor's first ride in a fine buggy like this, and the banker was very good at making the young bay horse respond to the reins. They headed east down Bennett and turned north at the end of the town. The horse pulled easily up the hill and headed out of town. Moving past the Molly Kathleen operation, he headed toward the property Vitor had pointed out on the map.

"Mr. John, how much does a buggy like this and a good horse cost?"

"Well, they're not cheap, that's for certain. The buggy was a gift from my wife, and the horse is one I raised from a colt. The horse might be worth twenty-five dollars, but the buggy would cost at least two hundred."

"I guess I will still be walking when I get the mine," said Vitor, knowing he couldn't afford such a high price.

Lasser told him how nice the buggy was, but he also offered some advice. "You don't want anything like this for mining, Vitor, this is just for pleasure. You will want a good mule or two mules if you can afford it when you start out, and a decent small freight wagon to haul your supplies."

Looking up at Lasser, Serinov grinned. "Or—a large wagon to haul out all of my gold!"

"You never know, Vitor—you just never know."

As they rounded the last corner, Vitor pointed out the rock formation to Lasser. "There, Mr. John, right there at the base of the rocks!"

Lasser pulled the buggy up to the rocks and wrapped the reins around the branch of a small aspen tree. The banker put his foot on the step and swung his large frame down to the ground. "So this is it, these strange rocks and this gravel pad is where your fortune is hiding?"

"Yes, Mr. John, this is it. These rocks are hiding something wonderful, and I plan on finding out what it is."

They walked the property and Vitor pointed out the boundaries, explaining how close it was to the Black Mule operation and that sometimes he could actually feel the blasting from their work.

Lasser pulled himself back into the buggy and motioned Vitor to get in. "Okay Vitor, I always make it a point to be dead honest with people in these kinds of deals, it's the best way of doing business. I have to admit I don't see much future in this spot; it looks mostly like granite to me. It's a very marginal piece of land . . . I doubt if it was really missed by all the geologists, and it just doesn't look like it would produce anything. Tell me again what makes you feel so good about this place."

Vitor could tell that his claim might be slipping away and knew he needed to do something else to try and convince Lasser. Pulling out his leather pouch, he dropped something in the banker's hand. "Mr. John, this is what I found when I scratched around at the base of the rocks the first day I came here."

Lasser picked up the white quartz crystal and held it up to the light. It was about an inch long and three quarters of an inch wide, with a typical point on one end. Running along one side was a fine wire of pure gold. The banker stared at it for a minute and handed it back to him. "Come to the office at nine tomorrow morning. Bring your crystal and we'll talk about this. Will you do that, Vitor?"

"Yes, Mr. John, I will be there waiting for you, I promise."

After a long, sleepless night, Vitor finally got up long before the sun and went down to Cripple Creek and took up a spot next to the front door of the bank, just below the Open for Business sign, and waited. Just before nine, Vitor saw the manager walking toward him along Bennett Avenue, stopping to visit and shake hands with a few people along the way. At precisely 8:55, he stepped up to the front door of the bank and put his key in the lock.

Vitor stood up and waited for him to open the door before he spoke. "Good morning, Mr. John, I am here like you asked."

"Good morning, Vitor, have you been here very long?"

"For only a couple of hours. I couldn't sleep well, so I just came down."

"Well, come on in and have a seat, let me stoke the stoves and we'll talk."

Lasser opened the blinds and put the coal in the stoves and stepped into his office. Hanging up his coat and hat and leaning his cane in the corner, he settled into his chair and looked at the young miner across from him. "Vitor, I have done a little checking around about your special piece of ground, and learned who owns it. I also learned he will sell it for the right price."

"That's good—right Mr. John?"

Lasser drummed his fingers on his desk quietly, momentarily lost in thought. "Well, yes, Vitor, it's good we know who owns it and how much they want for it, but I don't think you will be able to buy It yourself."

Vitor's shoulders sagged, and he slumped down in the chair, unable to keep his face from showing his disappointment. "Mr. John, how much longer do you think I will have to work before I can afford to buy it?"

"The owner wants six-hundred dollars for it. After all the time you've been saving, you have about two hundred and forty dollars right now."

"Mr. John, can I make a loan with you for the money? I am a hard worker, I will always pay you."

"Vitor, I have been watching you for a long time now, and you are very hard working, very smart, and very honest, and I'm not the only one that has noted that. Everyone in Cripple Creek and Altman has noticed it also. So, I would like to offer you a deal, a partnership between you and me to buy and develop your mine. Do you think that might sound acceptable?"

Vitor was surprised and a little unsure of what the deal might be like, but he trusted the banker and wanted to hear what he had to say. "Please, Mr. John, tell me how this partnership thing works."

"I think the best way might be for me to buy the claim for six hundred dollars, and I will lease it back to you. We will agree on a way of paying off the mine either by regular payments or a percentage of your profits. I will also grubstake you for four hundred dollars more out of my own pocket to get set up. This part you only have to pay back if you make a profit."

Vitor's head was spinning and his face felt flush; he had never heard of this kind of deal. Although he wanted the mine to be his alone, he understood he needed more money than he could make in the mines to do it. "Mr. John, I have to be able to mine it in any way I want. And I have to be able to name it, and I have to be able to build my home there, before I can say yes to a partnership."

"Okay Vitor, I will draw up the papers with the terms and we will finish it up next week. There is something else; I will expect you to keep adding to your savings account on a regular basis. I don't care how much, as long as you keep it active. You will always need to have a little something put aside for a rainy day."

This time Vitor thrust his hand out to Lasser, shaking slightly with the excitement of the moment. "Mr. John, just one other thing—can we draw up our partnership today?"

"No, not today, this will take a little time—so it will be next week."

"What day next week, Mr. John?"

"Wednesday, Vitor, Wednesday at ten o'clock."

"How about nine o'clock Mr. John, I can be here at nine o'clock..."

"Okay Vitor, you win, nine o'clock it is."

Chapter 30

Bannister woke up early the next morning with Jessie buried under the covers and Maggie jumping on the bed, reminding them that she needed some time outside. He walked into the kitchen and swung open the door, and Maggie bounded out with her usual enthusiasm into the fresh snow. Making a pot of coffee, he grabbed an orange and began to peel it while he waited for the dog. After a few minutes, she came back in, covered in snow, with a small piece of firewood in her mouth. She was ready to play if she could get someone's attention.

Tossing the stick out the door, their game continued for a few more minutes. She was finally starting to wind down and Bannister closed the door. Using an old bath towel, he wiped her down and they headed into the living room. Grabbing the map that Turner had made, he put his feet up on the chest, and Maggie found the warmest spot next to him she could and burrowed in.

After a few minutes, Jessie came out, poured a cup of coffee, and sat down next to them. Her hair was pulled back in a ponytail, and she had on a baggy sweatshirt and an old pair of flannel pajama bottoms.

Bannister looked at her outfit and just shook his head. "Well, damn, I was hoping for that sexy black nightgown this morning."

"Not a chance," said Jessie. "You were just lucky yesterday; I was experiencing a weak moment, combined with a little too much red wine. I doubt it will happen again."

"Well, then, how about a little red wine with breakfast?"

"Get over yourself, old man; it'll take a lot more than that to get me back into that nightgown."

"What exactly would it take?"

"I'll make you a deal—you find the golden armor, and you can ravish me any way you'd like."

"Really? Any way I want?"

"I'm yours—any way you want me."

"Consider it found, my lady, and you will be my prize!"

After all these years together, he still loved Jessie's playful nature and strong will. This kind of teasing was one of the things he loved the most about their relationship. He knew she could make anyone do anything she wanted, and watching her work that charm on others was one of his secret pleasures. He also noticed that she had already worked it on Maggie, who was now curled up tightly in her lap.

Jessie held out her coffee cup, batting her large, dark eyes, and looked at Bannister.

"Another cup of coffee, and put a shot of foo-foo in it, please." Foo-foo is what Bannister called the sweet, flavored cream she liked so much.

"Foo-foo coffee coming up my lady—one shot or two?"

"One and a half shots and a piece of dark toast with Chokecherry jam, and don't put too much jam on it. You always put too much jam on the toast—you don't want me to outgrow that nightgown, do you?"

"No way, I will work hard to see that you fit that nightgown perfectly,

I don't want it so tight that I can't get it off easily."

"Just stop talking, old man, and get me my coffee and toast."

* * *

As they finished breakfast and relaxed in front of the fire, Jessie worked on some notes for the upcoming expansion of the Cripple Creek Mining District exhibit. "Jack, are you about through with the Russian letters? I'd like to get the last of them put in our database."

"I'm about to do the last one. Maybe we'll get a clue as to what happened to Vitor; It's dated August 8, 1896, and was posted in Cripple Creek."

"You know, it's kind of sad about him, don't you think?"

"How do you mean?"

"Well, he's spent years traveling the world, looking for a new life for his wife, and his baby that he's never seen. He sounds like a good man, but he's still got a regular miner's job, and not much more. I think what's really sad is that we haven't found a single reference to whether his wife got any of the letters or ever wrote back if she did. He still doesn't seem to know his baby's name—or even if there really is a baby."

Bannister nodded his head in agreement. "You're right; his life was pretty tough, like all immigrants of the time—or even now for that matter. In his last letter, it sounded like he was finally about to get a piece of ground of his own. It also sounded like he was getting ready to try and bring his family out."

"Still—it's a pretty sad story, but I'm glad we got the donation of the letters. It really makes the story of the district come alive for the time he's there. I think we'll get another exhibit later about the immigrant experience from them too."

"I'll probably get to the last one today or tomorrow, and then I'll make you a disc with the whole story. Do I get anything extra if I finish it up today?"

"Just go to work. Maggie and I are going to take a little nap—and no, you cannot join us."

* * *

After supper, Bannister asked Jessie how her conversation went with the Carhartts at the recent sponsor dinner. "Jamie was there for about an hour, Clarice was the first one there and the last one to leave, pretty typical."

"Did you find out anything interesting about them?"

"Well, I didn't uncover any big secret, if that's what you mean."

Bannister settled into the couch and opened his notebook. "Jess, tell me everything you know about Jamison and Clarice. Rocky gave me what he found out; maybe we can add a few more pieces to this puzzle."

Jessie warmed her hands on the hot coffee mug and leaned back. "I met Jamie almost immediately after I took the job at the museum. He was a patron then—and still is for that matter. I met Clarice within a few weeks at a party set up to introduce me to the board and the patrons."

"What was your first impression? Did you like them?"

"I liked Jamie right away. Clarice, on the other hand, has been hard to get to know very well. Jamie comes across as up-front and honest in his love of history and the mining district. In my personal opinion, though, he may be a bit weak, as far as Clarice goes. I've seen her order him around pretty roughly a few times."

"Any other observations about him you think might be important?"

"There is one thing that I thought was kind of funny, or at least a little odd. He doesn't like it down in the mines; he says he's claustrophobic. I asked him if he has any mine work going on right now."

"And what did he say?"

"He told me he's had a small crew working his remaining claims for him for a couple of years now, but that he hasn't really found anything to brag about."

Bannister listened intently, making a few notes in his book. "Apparently, since he doesn't go down in the mines, he trusts his small crew, or at least his foreman, to tell him what's going on."

Jessie nodded her head. "The truth is, I think he just loves history and flying—he can talk about them all day. I think keeping the old claims is just a way for him to feel close to his own history."

"So, let's talk about Clarice for a minute. Rocky says she's part of a very early, old-money family from Boston. Did she ever talk much about her history to you?"

Jessie chuckled at this. "The only time I get much of that kind of information is after the third glass of wine. Do you know the old saying, with wine there is truth? Well, it seems to be true in her case. Since I knew you were interested, I had her stick around after the dinner and we polished off the better part of two bottles of wine. After that, she got pretty gabby."

"Jess, you're a woman after my own heart and one damn good investigator. So what did our little rich girl have to say?"

"After she got started, I could barely get a word in edgewise. She is the only child of the family and something of an outcast, I guess. She says her father wanted a boy to take over the family business. When she was growing up, he decided she would never be smart enough or tough enough to run it herself. After that, she was basically shunned—that's her word, not mine—by her father and kept away from the business."

"The Whitfords sound like a really sweet bunch, I can just about imagine what the rest of them are like," said Bannister. "What else do you know about her history?"

"She's not dumb at all. In fact, she got a full ride scholarship to Yale for business, and graduated fourth in her class. After she got out, the family still didn't recognize her potential, so she says that caused her to run away from them and into the drug business for a while."

"Wow, that fragile little blonde woman, a drug dealer? You never really know, do you?"

"You're right about that, it surprised me too. She said she sowed her wild oats for a couple of years, but she paid the price. After getting busted for possession and intent to deal, she served six months in jail. It was really small-time stuff, but when she got out, her family had locked up most of her ten-million-dollar trust fund, which she was supposed to get when she was twenty-five. She only got fifty thousand dollars a year."

"So what's happened between then and now, besides marrying Jamison?"

"By the time we hit the end of the second bottle we were both feeling the effects of the wine and she was slurring her words pretty good."

Bannister chuckled at the thought of the two women, sitting alone in that big empty museum, and getting high on red wine. "What's this? My top investigator getting a little too deep undercover to do her job?"

"I was fine, just a little buzz is all, not enough to cloud my memory. She said she used her first fifty thousand to start a small business.

"Really? Did she say exactly what it was?"

"No, not specifically, but after her last glass, she said it was doing well. She also said that she had built it up from nothing, and she was proud of that, because her father and uncles had just inherited all their money; they never really worked for it."

"Jess, you might have stumbled onto something interesting here."

"Bannister, I did not *stumble* onto anything. It was my highly tuned investigative skills that dug up the information!"

"Really?" asked Bannister. "How about we break out a fresh bottle of red wine?"

"Just shut up, old man."

Chapter 31

Bannister experienced a slight twinge of sadness when he opened up the last of Vitor Serinov's letters; he really did hate to see the story end. It was dated August 8, 1896, and had been posted in Cripple Creek.

It started like all his letters had for the last four years. "My wife Kapeka and our beautiful baby daughter, I have very wonderful news. I have purchased a mine and a place for our new home. I have already started work on the mine and will soon build a place to live."

Vitor went on to say that the banker had explained how he might get the claim he wanted right now, and that just working as a miner, he would never be able to save enough money to purchase it. "Mr. Lasser, the manager of our bank savings, has offered to help us get our home and claim started. He owns the claim and the property that we are going to live on. I believe he is a very good and honest man, and I agree that I will never be able to save enough money just working as a miner."

He explained how he signed a paper that says the banker will own the claim for ten years. The claim cost the bank $600, and Vitor would have to pay back ten-percent of the principal and two-percent interest every year, or, ten-percent of the profits of his mine each year, whichever was greater. After ten years, the claim would belong to Vitor free and clear; if he was unable to pay, the bank would keep it. Although this kind of transaction was foreign to Vitor, others told him that he was getting a good deal from the bank, and that Mr. Lasser could be trusted.

"Kapeka, I feel a kind of freedom that I have never felt before. No czars telling me what I can and can't do, just the possibility of a wonderful and free life on our own property. As it is getting late in the season, I would like to see you and our daughter come to Cripple Creek in the month of May, next year. By then I would have a place built for us."

Vitor had talked with his boss and explained to him that he wouldn't be able to work any more overtime, or do any other extra jobs they may have, as he had been doing for them since he started. He began working just the first shift, eight hours a day, and spent every waking moment laying out his dream at what he now called Tommy's Crease.

As Cripple Creek started to rebuild from the fire; the population of Cripple Creek had begun to find more permanent places to live. The temporary tents and small stoves were now available everywhere. Vitor bought two of each for four dollars to put on his claim, and a fellow miner with a mule and wagon hauled them and a few other supplies to the site. Within a few days, he had a tent for sleeping and living, and another one for supplies. He had decided to stay a little longer in the barracks in Altman because the camp was less than a mile from the mine he worked in, and he knew he would miss the showers if he left. He had grown accustomed to a shower every day; where he came from that was a real luxury.

He set his tents up extra solid, and laid in all the coal and scrap wood he could find. Every free minute was spent at the claim. In a few weeks, he had nearly everything he needed to start his mining, except the explosives. Vitor had walked the claim so many times he knew every square inch and exactly where every boundary line and corner was.

He knew right where he wanted to start digging. Every day he studied the rocks in front of him. In his own methodical and precise way, he would measure them, climb on them, and even put his hands on them, as though the rock would tell him exactly where to find the gold.

After two weeks on the claim, he was certain that his first intuition was right. Every time the mine next to him blasted another set, he could feel faint vibrations in the rock. With one hand on the pink granite face and the other one on the rough black face, when a blast was set off at the Black Mule mine, the granite sometimes appeared to give off a fine pink dust that would coat his hand and sleeve. He realized that all the dust and fine gravel in front of the Crease must have come from thousands of years of the ground moving and other things, like earthquakes.

Vitor went into the supply tent and came out with a piece of coal the size of a small book. He walked over to the rock and stared at it one more time. Then he took the piece of coal and began to draw an outline on the rock. Starting about six feet high, he drew a line from left to right, ten feet long. At the ends of the horizontal mark, he drew vertical lines down to the ground. Then, he dragged a stick across the gravel, scratching out a mark about ten feet square. Standing back, he looked at the first work on his new claim. "This is it," he said out loud. "This where I start, this is where I will find my gold."

For the next few weeks, Vitor kept busy accumulating tools and supplies and making his camp comfortable. He had started to dig at the base of the rock, but the loose granite was deep, and it was hard to keep out of the hole. Finally, he found some old timbers from a bridge that had been replaced after the fire. Again, he depended on his friends and fellow miners to help him get the wood to the site. He knew it was just about time to get his own mule and wagon, but he was hoping to hold off until next spring, so he didn't have to care for it through the worst of winter.

Mr. Lasser's $400 grubstake money was going quickly and he needed a saw big enough to cut the large timbers he would need in the shaft. A friend gave him an old freight wagon with bad wheels and hauled it to the claim. Vitor removed the wheels and turned it into a small shed, a place where he could lock up his most valuable tools.

His days were starting to fall into a steady routine, eight hours in the mine, then walk to his claim, work until dark, and walk back to Altman. By the time he got back to the barracks and showered, it was already ice cold. For the next month, he dug his shaft in the loose granite, shoring up the sides with the timbers to keep the gravel from sliding in. The rock face continued straight down, and the fine gravel kept sliding in, nearly as fast as he could shore it up.

After several weeks of work, he had the first ten feet of his shaft dug and shored up. Standing in the bottom, he put his hands on either side of the Crease, like he had done many times before. After a minute, he felt the familiar vibration of the blasting from the neighboring mine. Suddenly, he realized that the gravel had started to slide back into the shaft, through the cracks in the timbers, just covering the toes of his boots.

Climbing out, he grabbed a long, pointed steel bar and a shovel, and threw them into the shaft. Climbing back down, he realized he would probably have a constant problem with this fine pink rock, and would need to work harder to keep it out. Back in the bottom, he dug for the next two hours, clearing away the newly deposited gravel and a few more inches of fresh ground.

Clearing away the rock face, he noticed that the granite was beginning to look rougher, even shattered into large chunks, and starting to pull away from the black rock next to it. Vitor felt this was a good omen. If he could remove the shattered chunks of granite and keep the fine gravel away, he believed that his fortune might be very close at hand.

Using his bar, he chipped away at the broken rock, driving the tip into the cracks repeatedly, until large pieces popped off. With a large sledgehammer, he broke the big rocks into smaller pieces and tossed them out of the shaft. After a long day, Vitor was tired, but excited. Locking up his tools, he made the long walk back to Altman and to the shower.

After his next shift, he hurried quickly back to the mine, ready to see what the Crease would bring him today. When he looked into the shaft, he was shocked to see more gravel in the bottom—nearly a foot more than when he left it yesterday. Throwing his bar and shovel back into the hole, he climbed back down and started shoveling. When he got it cleared, he realized that the gravel came in from under the bottom timber and through the cracks in between the timbers. The ground was just unstable, and every time there was a blast, it made it worse.

He knew he had to find more timbers when he got out of here, but for now, he continued to chip away at the granite. Breaking off one last piece, he pulled it back and saw what looked like a small void in the rock. It was too small for his hand, so he used the bar to chip away at the opening. It was getting dark, and Vitor couldn't see into the hole, but he put his hand into the opening nearly up to his elbow. He ran his fingers along the sides, but couldn't feel any bottom. He knew it was too late to do any more today, but tomorrow was Saturday, and after he went to the bank, he would have all day to explore this new development.

At 9:00 A.M. sharp, Vitor was already at the front door of the bank when John Lasser stepped up and pulled out his keys. "Good morning, Vitor, how's the claim coming along?"

"Very well, Mr. John. I think that I will be able to show you some gold very soon," said Vitor, setting his weekly deposit on the counter.

After the transaction, Vitor pulled out the letter to Kapeka that he had begun a few weeks ago. He wanted to finish it and get it posted today; he also wanted to tell her how excited he was. As he wrote in his familiar, flowing Russian script, he explained how far he had gone with the mine and how he missed them both. "Soon, we will be together, our little family under one roof, just like it should be." He didn't mention the loose gravel that was causing him concern, or just how difficult life in the district could be. He didn't want to worry her any more than he needed to.

Vitor waved to Lasser as he went out the door. "Good-bye, Mr. John, I'm off to mail a letter to Kapeka—and to find my gold."

Lasser looked up from his desk and waved back. "Good-bye, Vitor, see you next week."

Chapter 32

Bannister walked out of the El Paso County sheriff's office and drove over to the diner, pulling in next to Rocky's Blazer. He could see Rocky through the window, and Darla leaning against the counter talking to him. After a minute, she spotted him and backed away from the counter, grabbing the coffee pot and filling Rocky's cup. Then she motioned with the pot for Jack to come inside and join them.

Bannister walked through the door and sat two stools away from Rocky. "I don't want to interrupt you two lovebirds, so carry on with whatever you were talking about—just pretend I'm not here."

"Jack, I always pretend you're not here," said Darla. "In fact I'm pretending we're not even talking right now."

Rocky listened to their friendly banter for a minute and finally spoke up. "Okay already, don't make me come over there and break you two up, or I'm gonna get real mad."

"Big deal, you think we're scared of you?" said Darla, playfully turning the tables on him. "Just drink your coffee and shut up, or you're the one who's going to get hurt here."

The diner was empty except for the three friends, and after several cups of coffee and a little more joking, they finally got around to business. "Rock, we're going to take down the mine operation in the next couple of days, depending on the weather, and if a truck is inside the shaft house with a load that night."

"You don't think we could just pick those guys up outside the mine, do you?" asked Rocky.

"No, the DA said that if we don't catch them in the act, it will be hard to prove who did what inside the mine. Catching them in the act will put them away for good."

"Do you have all the necessary paperwork ready to go?"

"Yeah, I just had a meeting with the district attorney," said Bannister, "El Paso County, Teller County, and the state police are all on board. We have warrants that are good for all the principals, their property, the mine, and Carhartt Aviation—all good for fifteen days from today. I'd like to have you and Turner meet me at the cabin tomorrow morning about ten. I'll have the rest of the team there as well. By the way, Rock, not that I think there's going to be a problem, but you and I are sworn federal officers, and there shouldn't be any issues over who's in charge here. Sheriff Jewell not only agreed to that, but was relieved to have us do it."

"I'll be there, boss. Any chance Jessie will be cooking breakfast for us?"

"Would it matter? You'll probably have had at least one breakfast here before you even get up the mountain."

"Well, one extra breakfast couldn't hurt anything."

"Good-bye kids, feel free to pick up where you left off . . ." said Bannister, stepping out the door.

Leaving the diner, he drove the few blocks to his office. After an hour or so, he finished up the last of his paperwork and listened to his messages. Unlocking the bottom, right drawer, he pulled out a box of .357 Magnum shells and a small-frame revolver in an ankle holster. Walking to the door, he looked back at the mess in the office. "Next week," he said out loud with a laugh. "I'm going to clean this place—next week for sure."

* * *

The next morning, Bannister sat at the kitchen table with a large map of the district laid out in front of him. Around the table, Rocky, Turner, Sheriff Jewell, and A.J. Rogers listened intently while Jack brought them up to speed on the operation. "I've filled in the FBI on what's going on, and although they aren't participating in the bust, they've made their resources available to us for whatever we need. They're also working hard on tracing the trucking end of things. Turner, they said the map you made and the information you recorded really helped."

His face lit up like a schoolboy's at Christmas. "Always glad to help those federal boys out, they usually can't find their ass without a map."

Bannister decided to address the Teller County sheriff's part first. "Martin, what I think might work best is, after we confirm that there is a truck inside the shaft house, and the overhead door is down, we cut the lock on the gate and go in. If we're quiet about it, I think we can slip in and reach the building undetected; there's only one man-sized door on the south side and the overhead door in the front, and it doesn't have any windows. There's really nowhere else for them to go, other than down the shaft."

Jewell listened intently and made a few notes in his book. "With DeAngelo in the can, do you think they may have recruited another guy to replace him?"

"I haven't seen any evidence of it, but I think we should plan on the chance of more than the three bad guys and the driver—you never know. I want to go in fast, and go in loud. I want to startle them and disorient them as much as I can. If the side door is locked, Rocky will use a sledgehammer to bust it open. I'll throw in a flashbang grenade and go in. You and your two deputies will be the next in, Rocky will follow us. Martin, you said your guys are up for this, you still good with that?"

"No problem, both of them have SWAT team experience. Bill was on the Denver team for two years before he moved up here, and Rick has all the necessary training. You might want to let Bill make the first entry, he's done it before."

Bannister thought about this for a moment. "That's good to hear. How about if Bill follows me and Rick comes in next, then, once we clear the doorway, you and Rocky come in?"

"That sounds good. They both have their own gear and have been filled in on what's going to happen. They're ready for this."

"That's great. Rocky, I want you in last because I don't want you off balance after swinging the hammer, and I want the biggest guy in the doorway last, in case someone gets close enough to the door to try and escape."

Rocky knew that his boss wasn't giving him a hard time about his size; it was just practical thinking on his part. "Got it, boss," he said quietly.

"A.J., I'd like you to be outside the shaft house, find a safe spot, and watch the corner where you can clearly see any activity at either door. If anybody comes out except one of us—use your own judgment."

A.J. nodded his head. He really liked Bannister, and was impressed with the way he took charge and did business.

"Turner, I want you outside the fence in a safe place. When things settle down inside, we'll let you know, then you and A.J. come on inside."

"I'll be there—I'll be ready."

"You're going to be the key to this thing. We have to be ready to go on an instant's notice. I need you checking the shaft house while you're concealed somewhere above that's safe. We're going to do this on your signal. When you see a truck go in, and the door come down, you call and we'll be there in less than fifteen minutes, ready to go. You can handle that alright?"

"Shit, Jack, you know damn well I can do it."

"Okay then, there're couple ways that I see the entry going down. One, all the bad guys are in the shaft house and unarmed and no shots are needed to make the arrests—but somehow I doubt that will be the case. Two, some or all of them could be in there, and there's a lot of shooting, but we still confine it all to the shaft house," said Bannister. "The third scenario could be the worst. If one or more of the bad guys are in the mine and we have to hunt them down in that endless maze of drifts, it could get really ugly."

"If someone's down there, we'll most likely know what level they're at by where the cage stopped," added A.J. "We can bring the cage up from here, but it's getting out of the cage down there, into the unknown, that'll be pretty spooky."

"No doubt about that, A.J., I think you and I have to talk about that problem separately, after we get the rest of this ironed out."

A.J. nodded and continued to listen intently. Bannister laid out the rest of the details of his plan. "Once A.J. and I figure out how to get us out of the cage without getting shot, he and I and Rocky will go down with Martin's two guys. Rocky and I will team up with one of them. A.J., I want you to hold the fort near the cage and be the communication guy with topside. Even though they have nowhere to go, they will undoubtedly be well armed. I don't think they'll give up easily—particularly Max, the big guy."

"What about me, Jack, what do you want me to do?" asked Turner.

"I want you to assist Martin with anything and everything he needs in the shaft house. Martin, I'd like you to be command central, communicating with A.J. at the bottom, and calling for any other help or supplies we might need."

"You got it. I already have the safety gear at the office," added Jewell. "You guys come by in the morning and familiarize yourself with everything. If you've never used night vision equipment before, you need to try it first."

"Night vision equipment?" asked Rocky. "You thinking of going after them in the dark?"

"I really hope not, but we'd be better off having it with us." It had been a long day, with Bannister going over and over the details, trying to find any cracks in his plan. "There are just a few more things I want to run by everyone. Between what we've dug up and what the FBI has found, most of these trucks have originated in and around the New England area, most within five-hundred miles or so of Boston. With the heavy population up there, there are thousands of small to medium companies that use all kinds of exotic chemicals, gases, liquids, and poisons. The FBI thinks this is a freelance criminal enterprise that will dispose of nearly anything for a price."

"The bottom line is, we don't know what we might find down there after we secure the area. A.J. will be along to identify any potential hazards in the mine itself. He'll also be looking for booby traps and explosives, and to try and identify areas that have been blasted closed. After things are secured, and A.J. looks everything over, the HazMat boys will go down. From then on it's in their ballpark. Does anyone feel like we've missed anything?"

Rocky spoke up. "I think it would be good to have an EMT team on standby."

"Good thought, Rock. Martin, can you arrange that? By the way, the state patrol will set up a roadblock out of sight of the mine. They will also be available for any assistance we might need. Turner, you're the man right now. You need to start watching right after sundown for the next few nights. Based on what we know from your notes, probably until about midnight or so. You'll have a cell phone and a radio with you. As soon as you verify that a truck is in the shaft house, we'll be there."

Bannister knew that Turner wouldn't have any problem; this was just his kind of thing. He had spent a lot of time camping outdoors in the winter, and this would keep him out of harm's way. He also knew that A.J. could take care of himself in any kind of situation, and was the right person to have down in the mine. "If we're all good with this, we should probably get a little sleep," said Bannister, standing up and stretching his legs. "The next couple of days could get a little stressful. Hey, Rock, it would be good if you and Turner plan on coming up and staying here tomorrow, until this is over. A.J., hang in here for a few minutes, will you?"

"Sure, no problem."

Bannister sat down on the couch next to Rogers and handed him a cold beer. They had become good friends in the last couple of months, sharing a few war stories and talking a lot about their love of western history. Bannister had filled him in on Jessie's family treasure stories and the letters from the Russian miner. A.J. read every one as soon as they were translated; he had become an official member of the golden armor treasure-hunting team.

"A.J., you know this is our job, to find these guys and secure this mine, but you don't have an iron in this fire. I'm grateful for all of your help, but you really don't have do this. There's a good chance things could be dangerous down there."

"Don't worry about it, Jack—I've spent most of my life in those kind of places. Things have been a little boring lately anyway."

"Well," said Bannister, "I don't think this will be boring. It might be more like what the tunnel rats did in Nam."

"Guess where I got my love for the underground? Hell, I still have my 1911 Colt that I used back then—still works great too."

Chapter 33

Turner sat with his back against a rock, well concealed behind a pile of brush. Covered with a wool blanket, the cell phone and radio lay next to him. On his other side was a thermos full of strong, black Lapsang-Souchong tea, something he had learned to love while working on the Alaska pipeline job in the seventies. With his spotting scope on a tripod between his knees, he was comfortable and ready for the night.

He had a good view of the entrance to the shaft house and another hundred yards of road leading into it. The black Jeep and a pickup truck were inside the fence, but there was no sign of a rental truck yet. It had been snowing lightly for about an hour, and no fresh tracks were anywhere to be seen. About 11:00 P.M., three men walked out of the side door, and one of them went to the gate and unlocked it, swinging it wide open. After the pickup headed out, the Jeep pulled through. The man on foot closed the gate and climbed into the passenger side, and the pair headed down the mountain.

Turner waited for a few minutes to be sure they didn't come back, and called Bannister to fill him in. Then he packed up his gear and headed back to his own Jeep, making his way back to the cabin. He repeated the same routine the next day— also a bust. On the third night, about 8:00 P.M., a yellow rental truck pulled up to the gate and waited. The big guy they called Max came out and opened the gate and spoke to the driver for a minute. After the driver pulled in and turned around, Max locked the gate behind him and walked back inside. The overhead door started to roll up and the truck backed in. Picking up the cell phone, Turner dialed Bannister while the door was closing.

Within minutes, the team was near the site, stopping just short of being able to see the shaft house. The Colorado State Patrol immediately set up a two-car roadblock just behind them, providing four officers for the job. The five men pulled on their vests and helmets, checking their primary weapons and their backup pieces. In one hand, Rocky carried a shortened Model 12 Winchester pump shotgun loaded with buckshot; in the other, a sledgehammer. After talking with Turner on the radio, Bannister decided to give it another ten minutes, then if it was still clear, they would go.

The five men walked silently in single file along the edge of the trees, their breath freezing in the air as they went. When they got to the gate, they waited another minute or two, then cut the lock and removed the chain. Opening it slightly, they entered the compound and made their way to the shaft house and around the corner to the small door.

As the men lined up on either side of the door, Bannister used hand signals to place them where he wanted them. The window had been painted over since the last time he was here, and he couldn't see anything inside. Gently turning the handle, he found It was locked. Stepping back, he checked the team to see if they were ready; they all gave the thumbs up and nodded their head yes.

Rocky leaned the shotgun against the building and grabbed the sledge with both hands. Bannister pulled the pin on the flashbang grenade and nodded his head. With one powerful blow on the handle, the door swung open violently and slammed against the wall, the window glass shattering in the frame. Rocky tossed the hammer away and Jack threw in the grenade as far as he could. Within two seconds it was chaos, the men inside screaming at each other and looking for some kind of cover. Bannister entered while the smoke was still clearing, the team following him in perfect step. With his Browning in one hand and a small flashlight in the other he moved forward, making room for the others. In the haze, he saw a figure diving into the cab of the truck. In an instant, the man was hanging onto the open door, firing a pistol wildly at the intruders.

Bannister and one of the SWAT members each fired three times, and the figure dropped his gun on the concrete and fell in a pile alongside the truck. For a second, it was quiet, and then suddenly gunfire erupted again, bullets piercing the tin building and the truck. The mirror and windshield exploded, sending a shower of glass in the air, and a bullet penetrated the overhead door. Another bullet glanced off the concrete floor and hit the doorjamb next to Rocky just as he touched off the Winchester. Bannister felt the muzzle blast behind him, and the buckshot hit its mark low in the front of the shooter, piling him up in a bloody heap on a coil of steel cable in the corner.

Rocky jacked another round into the Winchester and the room went silent.

Bannister called out to the team, "Everyone sound off—is anyone hurt?"

Everyone answered with a loud okay here! The driver was dead, hit by five slugs. The miner, the one named Ryan Allworth, was lying in a pile, with his hands clenching his belly, trying to stop the blood flow. Rocky was standing over him with the muzzle of the 12-gauge tight against his forehead. "Who's in charge of this operation—talk now you asshole, or your brains are gonna end up on the floor."

"Don't do it, Rocky," yelled Bannister over the confusion, "we need to talk to him." Jack put one hand on his shoulder and one on the barrel of the shotgun. "Take it easy, it's all over."

Rocky Batton was running on autopilot, his training, combined with past experiences, had kicked in. He finally relaxed enough for Jack to take over.

Bannister bent down alongside the wounded man. "Tell me who's down below, and I'll get you to the hospital."

The miner turned slightly with blood running from his nose and mouth, "Just Max and Tom, but they'll never give up . . ." After a long, hacking gasp for air, he exhaled slowly, blowing a fine blood spray on Bannister's sleeve as he died. After clearing the rest of the shaft house, Bannister called to A.J.: "Come on in—can you shut down the cage and tell us what level it's stopped at?"

"Sure, looks like you guys did good here; everyone all right?"

Bannister nodded his head yes. "Everyone but these two bad guys, they're kind of hurting right now."

"Only two?"

"Yeah, it looks like we're going to have to go below and dig out the others."

The names had been given up by Dave DeAngelo, the man they already had in custody. He had made a deal the first day in jail. They knew that Allworth had a long criminal record, and had a felony warrant still outstanding in Massachusetts. Tom Belt, who also had a long record, and the big guy, Max Atkinson, were next.

"Rocky, call Turner and tell him to come on down and bring his camera. Martin, let the state patrol know they can pull the roadblock and come on inside the fence and set up here. They can provide some security for the place, and help out with the scene."

Walking the whole shaft house, it was clear that they were in the middle of taking a load down when the flashbang went off. There were four more drums left in the truck, and two sitting in front of the entrance to the cage, waiting to go down.

Calling the team together, he noticed that Rocky had a small trickle of blood running down the side of his shoe. Rolling up his pant leg, Rocky found a three-inch long splinter of wood from the doorjamb embedded in his right ankle. Pulling out the splinter, he let out a small sigh of relief. "Shit Bannister, I think I'm going to get me some of that workers comp money for this."

"If you're lucky, there might be a Band-aid in the truck; if not, you'll just have to cowboy up, big guy, there's no comp money in your future." Everyone had a good laugh at this exchange, breaking the tension of the moment.

Bannister motioned Rocky to go outside and they leaned against the building, taking in the cold night air. After a few minutes, Jack finally spoke. "Some of the old demons still hanging around Rock?"

Batton nodded his head. "Jack, do you remember the last time we made an entry like that?"

"Yeah, I remember it all too well," said Bannister, unconsciously running his finger along the scar on his chin, "but I don't dream about it as much as I used to."

Rocky ran his fingers through his hair, and paused to catch his breath. "Sometimes I don't think of it for a couple of months at a time, then it just comes roaring back with a vengeance. I'm sorry, Jack, I didn't mean to freeze up like that at the end."

"Don't worry about it, Rock, everything went fine. We all have a few things in our past that come back to haunt us at the worst possible time. Besides, old friend, you saved my ass back there."

Rocky looked at Jack for a moment, "Well, I'm glad it all worked out, but we're still not quite even on that count."

When Turner arrived, Bannister started him photographing the scene just as it was before anything got moved. He was a good photographer, and with his new digital outfit he was able to take several hundred photos from every possible angle. When he finished, Sheriff Jewell and his men bagged up the bodies and moved them outside in the cold night air.

"What else can I do, Jack?" asked Turner, closing up his camera bag.

"Just work with Martin on whatever he needs. When we go below, we'll be communicating with him and he'll run the show up here. For now, you can put on some gloves and help him gather up all the loose evidence material in the truck and in the building. By the way, everything went perfect, you did a great job."

He just nodded and smiled. "Thanks, I'm just glad it went down safely and no one got hurt."

Bannister and Rocky walked over to the entrance of the cage. A.J. had secured the cage and figured out the system quickly. "It's pretty straightforward," said A.J., pointing to the electrical panel. "Right now, the cage is at level two-twenty, meaning it's not all that deep as far as these mines go. I have it set on hand operation, so I can override any local controls in the cage and do with it whatever we want."

Bannister thought about this for a minute. "Well, unfortunately, I think we all know what has to come next: we have to go down and dig out these bottom feeders. I don't see much chance of them giving up voluntarily. I'm sure they figured out that something bad happened up here and that's why they didn't try to come up."

Bannister gathered up the team and explained that they were going to bring up the cage, and they didn't know if anyone would be inside it when they did. Turner stepped outside and the team spread out in a small semicircle outside the cage door with their weapons in hand. "Okay A.J., turn it on and bring it up so we can see just what we got."

As the cage came to a stop in the shaft house, the door remained closed. The top part of the door was made of a heavy steel screen, and Bannister looked inside with his Browning pointed in front of him. "All clear—A.J. shut it down again and let's talk about our next move."

Everyone agreed that going down was more than just a little dangerous, but that they really didn't have much choice. Finally, Bannister laid out his plan. "A.J., is the power for the cage on a separate circuit from the lighting in each level?"

Walking over to the breaker panel, A.J. looked down the list of circuits noted on the door. "It looks like we can shut them down separately. There's a light inside the cage too, but we can kill it easy enough."

"Okay, shut down everything but the lights in this building for now."

A.J. reached up and threw all the breakers except the one for the shaft house. "Well, that ought to make them a little nervous."

"Let's give them another hour, so they can get even more nervous down there in the dark. Everyone relax awhile and have something to eat or drink. We're going down in the dark; it's our best chance of seeing them before they see us."

Chapter 34

After an hour or two, the team was rested, and ready for the next part of the job. Finally, Bannister told them to gear up and get ready for the trip below. In addition to the regular equipment, they each carried the latest and greatest technology provided by the FBI just for this job. They were also outfitted with a helmet that contained the cutting edge of night vision technology, combined with a new infrared illumination system, a high intensity light and a built-in communication system.

"Everyone put on the helmets and get used to the controls. Even with this technology, there won't be enough light to make it look like daylight down there," said Bannister, putting on his helmet. "Also, the internal radio is pretty much a line-of-sight system. If it's too dark to see clearly, I have these small light sticks we can use. Everyone put a couple in your pocket. When you use one, throw it as far down the drift as you can. And remember, if you can see them without the night vision, they can see you too."

Next he handed each man a small foil packet. "This is Atropine, like the drops your eye doctor gives to you before a checkup. The military gives it out to their teams that have to work in extreme darkness. The more light we get into our eyes the better. Any questions?"

"Guys," said Bannister, "anyone who doesn't want to go down there, feel free to stay up top, no one will think less of you for it. Going down in the dark, with the night vision goggles is the only way that we can get the advantage. If we go down with our regular lights turned on, we'll be sitting ducks. Both these guys are convicted felons, with long criminal histories and gun violence in their past. I also know for a fact that they have at least one MAC-10 machine gun."

"When you step out at level two twenty, it runs straight for about a hundred yards," added A.J. "Then it stops and goes ninety degrees to the left where it runs about a hundred and fifty yards before it turns again. Also, at the end of that first tunnel, it turns right for a short ways, then left again. These old maps are pretty accurate for the start of the mine, but after that, it's anyone's guess just what it might look like."

"Anything else we might look for, A.J.?" asked Bannister.

"A couple of things: watch for abandoned stopes shooting off the sides of the drifts. These could easily conceal one or more men that could ambush us."

"What exactly is a stope?" asked Sheriff Jewell.

"It's a smaller excavation that takes off from the side, usually following a vein. They are much smaller, and generally angle upward," said A.J. "Also, a big concern here is explosives. We know they're routinely drilling out areas that they prepare for blasting, to cover their next load." He let this sink in for a minute and then continued. "These could be detonated from just about anywhere, depending on what they're using and where they are. They could easily be used as a booby trap. Look for wires; look at the top and sides of the drift for charges and wires hanging down.

Avoid anything that looks like dynamite boxes or electronics."

As they all walked toward the cage, Bannister asked one more time if anyone wanted to stay on top. No one spoke; they all just stepped into the cage and waited for him. After a few more instructions to Martin, he handed him a walkie-talkie and told him he would put the other one in the cage at the bottom. With that, he joined the others. A.J. closed the door and they began the slow ride down into the darkness.

As the cage went down, the men did their best to adjust to the eerie, grayish-green world they saw through their goggles. Running the cage with the controls in manual, A.J. began to go slower and slower, stopping just a few yards short of the level 220 opening.

Momentarily switching off his goggles, Bannister tried to make out anything in front of him. The darkness was like some all-consuming nightmare, kind of what he remembered from his last trip down this hole. It was as though he was in a heavy damp cloud, and he felt his old fear of the underground beginning to engulf him. He quickly switched his goggles back on and decided he preferred the strange-looking landscape in front of him.

When the cage rolled slowly down to a stop at the landing, everyone stood dead still, staring down the long drift. It was difficult to be sure, but with a little light coming down from the top of the shaft, they could see nearly all the way to the end. After a few long minutes, they opened the door and stepped out.

Slowly and silently they began the walk to the end of the drift. So far, all they saw were a few empty pallets and a four-wheel cart; there was no sign of the bad guys. When they came to the end of the first drift, Bannister called a halt. He motioned for Rocky and his partner to take the drift on the right and go to the end where he could see around the corner and wait. Bannister and his partner went down the drift to the left and told A.J. to wait there until he reached the end. When Rocky was in place, Bannister asked him what he saw.

"Not much," Rocky whispered quietly into his helmet mike. "It only runs another twenty or thirty yards and then kind of peters out into what I think might be one of those stopes A.J. talked about."

"A.J., check it out and see what you think. If you can't see back in there, it might be a good spot to toss in one of those light sticks. We might lose contact when you go around the corner, so I'll wait for the all clear before I go in any farther."

"Got it, I'll let you know what I find." With that, the three men walked to the end of the drift where it pinched down into a narrow tunnel not high enough to stand in. Looking inside, there was hardly enough light to see three feet.

"It probably goes quite a ways back, Rocky, I'll need to go in to be sure it's clear," said A.J. flatly. Removing his vest and helmet, he stepped into the opening with his Colt in one hand and a flashlight in the other. "It's way too tight with all that gear on, you can hold down the fort while I'm gone."

Rocky stared at the skinny little miner in disbelief. "You're outta your fuckin' mind, A.J., you can't go in there in the dark!"

"Don't worry so much, I've got my trusty flashlight, and my forty-five. I'll be back in a bit."

Rocky watched as he started crawling into the stope, small flashlight beam moving slowly, piercing the blackness, and finally disappearing out of sight. About ten minutes later, a sliver of light appeared in the back of the stope. A.J. had opened one of the light sticks and pushed it into a crack in the rock to make the return a little easier. In a minute, he was back in the drift putting his gear back on. "Nothing up there but rock and a few old timbers." Rogers clicked off his flashlight and turned on his night vision. "This area is clear. Let's go find some bad guys, Rocky."

"A.J., for such a little guy, I gotta say, you got a real set of stones on you. I'm surprised that you could get them into such a tight place."

He chuckled at Rocky's comment. "It wasn't really all that tight. I've been in lots of tighter places than that." "You talking metaphorically or literally A.J.?"

"Both, Rocky—many times."

The men returned to the main drift and filled in Bannister on what they had found. He had them move up to his position on the opposite side of the drift. "We're going to move slowly. You guys stay on the left side in single file, and we'll do the same over here. Look for any movement, or any indication of a light source, no matter how small. It will be our guys."

They moved along painfully slowly, seeing nothing for the first hundred yards. When they came to another turn, they repeated the procedure until, after a few yards, they found another stope heading up into the darkness. A.J. walked up to it and looked inside. It was much like the last one, but angling up at a forty-five degree angle. A.J. stripped off his safety vest, just like the first time. "I'll try it with the night vision for a ways; I'll only use a light if I absolutely have to."

Bannister said nothing, and Rocky realized this must have been in the plan all along. As A.J. started his climb up the stope, the men waited silently with their backs against the wall. After fifteen minutes, not a sound had been heard from the entrance to the stope. Then a loud pop and the sound of crashing rocks came from the stope, echoing through blackness.

The rest of the team tensed up, prepared for any possibility, but Bannister told everyone to remain still and give him a few more minutes. Five minutes later, A.J. emerged from the opening. "I'm sorry guys, I brushed against an old timber and a rock sitting on top of it fell off and dropped about five feet. It knocked a few others loose when it rolled down." He picked up his vest and put it on while he was talking. "It's all clear, no sign of anyone in there in decades, but I don't think we have much chance at surprise now."

The team started to advance down the drift again, staring hard through the goggles, their senses even more strained than before. Within a few more steps, another opening appeared on the right, and the team fanned out on either side waiting for their instructions. Bannister and A.J. communicated with a mix of hand signals and whispers. "I think there's someone in this one," said A.J. "I can smell something that seems a little out of place, I think someone took a piss in here, and maybe was smoking."

Looking in the opening, Bannister pointed at two butts lying on the ground a few feet inside the opening.

"What do you think? You want me to go in?" whispered A.J.

"Not yet, A.J.—maybe he's scared enough to give up if we make ourselves known." Bannister had Rocky and the two SWAT guys watching down the drift to cover their back. Then he and A.J. stood along the sides of the opening. Picking up a baseball-sized chunk of rock, he nodded at A.J. and threw it as far as he could into the stope.

The reaction was instantaneous. The drift lit up with orange and red fire, and slugs began tearing off chunks of rock and ricocheting in every direction. The smell of gunpowder filled the cavity and shards of hot lead and small pieces of rock screamed in every possible direction, small fragments hitting nearly everyone in the team. The noise was terrifyingly loud, and the helmets with their radio systems seemed to amplify everything by a hundred times. It stopped almost as soon as it started.

"Probably a thirty-round mag, I wonder if he has any more . . ." Before Bannister could finish, another round of chaos began, with fire, lead, and rock flying everywhere. Then it went quiet again. Finally, Bannister spoke loudly to the man in the hole. "Listen, we don't want to kill anyone, you can come out now and be in a warm comfortable cell in thirty minutes. Besides, I'm betting that you don't have another clip for that MAC-10."

"Maybe," hollered back the stranger. "Maybe not. Why don't you come on in and find out for yourself, asshole. You scared?"

After a few minutes, Bannister threw in another rock. Within a few seconds a single shot popped against the opposite wall.

"That sounded more like a thirty-eight. My guess is that he has a revolver with five more rounds left," said A.J.

"Let's hope you're guessing right—you sure you want to do this?"

A.J. nodded his head and removed his vest again. "Never really sure, Jack, but we'll find out in a few minutes. Besides, I got this magic helmet on, how can I go wrong?" With that, Rogers pulled out his Colt, cocked the hammer, and stepped calmly into the cavity.

For five minutes, everything was quiet. Then several shots, obviously from two different guns, erupted, followed moments later by a single shot, then silence again. In a few minutes, they could see A.J. picking his way down to the opening. "All clear, one bad guy down and one to go." Dropping a .38 revolver and a MAC-10 in the dirt, he suited up again and put in a fresh clip in his Colt. There were three more clips on his belt and a smaller pistol strapped to his boot for backup. "I'm ready to go if you guys are."

Rocky shook his head as he took it all in. Like he thought before, one big set of stones.

As they continued down, Bannister caught a tiny movement and a faint sliver of light about fifty yards away. Moving straight for him was a large bulky figure, advancing as fast as possible considering the conditions. It was the missing man named Max, and he hadn't spotted the team yet. He was pointing a miniature flashlight, the type you might have on a keychain, at the ground in front of him.

Bannister yelled for him to stop and drop his gun. The startled man froze for a second then turned and disappeared back down the drift. Advancing forward as quickly as possible, he saw the man turn right and disappear. Following him as fast as he could in the murky light of his goggles, he saw a row of barrels lined up along the wall. As he moved past the barrels, he noticed a car battery and a wooden box on top of one of them, with wires disappearing into the darkness.

The team was about fifty feet behind Bannister when he went around the corner. Ten seconds later the world exploded. Rocks, dust, and rushing air blew out of the drift and covered everyone. Choking and scrambling, the team couldn't have outrun it even if they could see. Despite having night vision, it was twenty minutes before they could see anything.

When it finally cleared up enough to investigate, the four team members walked to the end and surveyed the damage. The drift had been completely sealed; rocks of all sizes tightly filled every inch of space. Both Bannister and Max were gone, and they had no way of knowing how far back the explosion went, or if there was anywhere to hide on the other side.

Chapter 35

When the dust had cleared enough to see what had happened, A.J. jumped into action, instantly issuing orders to the team. "Everyone shut off the night vision and turn on your regular lights. Rocky, head back to the cage and go up and get the rest of the group. Have the sheriff call in my guys and bring down everyone that can lift a rock. Have him turn on the lights down here and bring down whatever other lighting he can get his hands on. Tell him to get some picks and shovels and bring some bottled water while you're at it."

Rocky was already halfway down the drift by the time A.J. had finished talking. Leaning his shotgun against the wall, he stepped into the cage, closed the door and started up. When he opened the door at the top, he didn't wait for questions; he just started giving his own orders. "Sheriff, A.J. says to call in the guys that work for him, you know who they are?"

"I do, I'll call them right now."

"Turner," continued Rocky, "we need a lot of bottled water, and something for the guys to eat—can you take care of that for me?"

"I'm on my way, Rock—is Jack okay?"

"We really don't know right now, but someone set off a blast. Jack and one of the bad guys are missing and we have to dig out the drift before we can go any farther."

"I'll be back as fast as that Jeep will carry me." With that, he disappeared out the door.

Rocky opened the electrical panel and turned on all the breakers. Next he asked Sheriff Jewell if he could call in any miners he might know to help.

"Already on it, what else can I do?"

"Talk to the troopers and see if one of them can cover security up here and if any of them would volunteer to work down below. I'd like you to coordinate things back and forth between the crew down there and the people up here."

"You got it." The sheriff talked with the four troopers; two of them agreed to help on top, and the other two said they had never been in a mine but were willing to give it a try.

Within an hour, they had extra lights and tools, and the men were already moving rock. Turner had returned with his Jeep sagging to the springs with cases of water and food for the team. After unloading the supplies, he walked over to Rocky. "Rocky, can I go below and see what it's like down there?"

He could see the concern in the old man's eyes. Although he didn't want him to get hurt, he deserved to see what was going on. "Sure, I'm headed back down right now, come on with me."

In a minute, Turner, Sheriff Jewell, and Rocky and A.J. stepped out into level 220. The two troopers followed them down next. Lit up, the drift looked larger and much cleaner than it did with the goggles on.

He stopped when they got alongside the stope where all the bullets had started flying and explained what happened, including A.J. pursuing the bad guy in the dark.

One of the troopers asked if he got the guy when he went in.

"Sure did," said Rocky, "I'm still amazed at what had happened. The crazy bastard crawled up there with nothing but a forty-five in his hand. He came back with the guy's guns—the bad guy is still up there somewhere, but I don't think he'll be coming back down on his own."

They continued to the site of the blast where A.J. and the crew were removing the rubble, one rock at a time. The place was full of men, covered in dust and sweating heavily, with long gritty streaks running down their faces.

After filling in the men about what happened, Rocky pulled Turner aside. "It looks like they need some water already. How about bringing the food and water down right away, and keep them well stocked. And see what you can do about some dust masks for everyone."

He nodded his head and took off for the cage.

Rocky touched A.J. on the sleeve to get his attention. "Tell Sheriff Jewell, or me, what you might need as this goes on. Turner is bringing water and food down now, and he's looking for dust masks. Anything else you need right away?"

"Not right now," said A.J. "We'll do this in two-hour shifts, four guys moving the rock out of the blast site and four moving it down the drift to get it out of our way."

Rocky finally asked the question no one else really wanted to. "Any thoughts on how long it might take to get through to the other side?"

"No way to know. I can't tell how much of the drift was blasted, so I couldn't say for sure. From past experience, I know that in a worst-case scenario, a stretch a hundred yards long could take as much as a couple of days."

The Drift

* * *

Not for one second did Bannister think he would ever find himself in this position again. Sprawled facedown in the dirt, in total blackness, his head was pounding and crashing uncontrollably. His thoughts were being drowned out by the overpowering scream in his ears, and he was covered with several inches of dust and small rocks. He lay still for a long time, trying to take stock of his situation. His helmet was still on, but the night vision goggles were missing. The helmet may have saved his life but he was still not sure if everything else still worked.

Moving each arm and then each leg, it looked as though most of his body functioned properly. Trying to roll over, a quick, violent pain shot through his side from his lower back, and he gasped audibly, falling back on his face. He recognized the pain from past experience—probably from broken ribs pushing up inside.

After a few more minutes, he remembered his small emergency flashlight and the extra light sticks he was carrying. Gritting his teeth for the pain that was about to hit him, he rolled himself over out of the dirt and onto his back. When he finally caught his breath, he started to dig around in his pockets for the lights. Just as his fingers wrapped around a light stick, he heard a long, low growl of a sound coming out of the blackness.

Releasing his grip on the light sticks, he lay still and strained to hear any more sounds. After a few minutes he heard the sound of a small rock hitting the wall close to him. Out of the darkness a rough voice called out, "Hey buddy, you alive out there? I know you were hot on my ass when the charges went off."

Bannister could hardly believe what he was hearing. The same guy that caused him trouble that day on the road, the same guy he'd been staking out for months was lying a hundred feet away in a pitch-black hole talking to him—it was a surreal situation that even Hollywood couldn't come up with. He felt for his back-up revolver. Finding it still in place, he decided to see what this guy had to say. "You're Max—right?"

"You got it. How about your name? I mean as long as we're both prisoners together down here, I think I should know your name."

"Bannister—my name's Jack Bannister. You hurt, Max?"

"Yeah, kinda busted up, I think it's my back, I don't seem to be able to feel my feet."

"You in charge of this trash collection business, Max?"

"Nope, just second in command. If I was the boss, someone else would be here right now and I would be safe and warm sitting in front of a fire somewhere drinking a cold beer."

The voice coming from the darkness was course and raspy, creating a weirdly unnerving sound that Bannister strained hard to hear clearly. "So who is your boss, Max, anybody I might know?

"Hell, Jack, if I told you that, what would I have left to bargain with? We both know the DA is already arresting everyone they can find that's connected with this thing, but he needs someone to point to the head guy."

"Well, shit, I thought you might help out your old buddy, you know—make my life a little easier."

"I don't think a few minutes together in a black hole qualifies us to call each other buddies."

"You don't remember our last meeting, Max?"

"If we'd ever met before, I think I would remember it."

"You're getting old, Max; it was on the road right above us. I had just climbed up a hill and was bleeding—I asked you for help. Do you recall how you helped me that day? Don't remember, Max? 'Cause I have trouble forgetting it."

Finally the voice from the dark spoke up. "Is that what this is about? You getting roughed up a little?"

"That's what put you on my radar screen. I'm a federal officer, and it didn't take very long to realize you were just another dirtbag working some kind of scam."

"Fuck you, Jack; I'd shoot your ass right now—that is if I could see you!"

The outrageous humor of the situation caused both of them to burst out in uncontrollable laughter. Two enemies, a hundred feet apart, unable to see each other, at least one of them not even able to walk. "You're a real funny guy, Max; you even got a gun?"

"That's for me to know and you to find out. You ready to find out?"

"Well, the way I see it, this will end one of two ways. One, by the time the rescue team gets here, we'll both know who you're working for and we'll both get out of here alive. Or two, when the rescue team gets here, I won't know who you're working for, but I'll get out of here alive and you'll get out of here dead. It's all up to you, but I guarantee, that's the way it will go down."

"Well, Jack, my old friend, I ain't got shit to say to you, but I think you're right about one thing: one of us ain't gettin' outta here alive."

Chapter 36

The action in the mine shaft had been going nonstop for several hours, and daylight was just starting to show. After coordinating the excavation all night, the team was working well together and A.J. finally took his two longtime miners up top for a break. The three men rested for a while, had something to eat, and then stepped outside for a little fresh air.

The shaft house had become a little Grand Central Station, with supplies stacked everywhere and men waiting to take their turn moving rock. Jessie had arrived several hours ago and was assisting Turner with the food and drinks, and anything else she could do. The work kept both their minds off of the problem below and was probably the best thing for them right now. Dozens of people from the district had showed up offering their assistance. Many offered food and drinks and others brought cots and bedding. One local mining outfit brought hand tools, electric jackhammers, and four men to help move rock.

A.J. called his two guys over to the corner of the building, sat down on one of the cots, and spread out an old mining district map on his lap. After marking a spot with a red pencil, he handed the rolled-up paperwork to his men and they left the building. A.J. fell back on the cot and was asleep instantly, feet still dangling over the edge. Jessie walked over and lifted his legs onto the cot and threw a blanket over him. In seconds he was snoring loudly.

The workers brought down the electric hammers and several hundred feet of cords. A local electrician rigged up a temporary outlet panel with a dozen outlets and some new lights. For now, everything was going smoothly, and the supplies were coming steadily. At the end of a two-hour shift, the next group of men were already standing by, waiting to go. The one thing that everyone knew and nobody talked about was how much rock was left, and how long would it take to get through. Although many of the men in this group had been through this kind of thing before, and knew that the odds were probably against finding someone alive, that didn't stop them from putting their backs into every rock they moved.

By midmorning, A.J. was back in the hole, supervising and hauling rock. The waste rock was being piled up against the walls of the main drift, leaving just enough room for the small carts to get through. Rocky began redirecting them to the short drift that they had checked out on their first trip in the dark. They could pile the rock wherever they wanted in that end and not have to worry about running out of space.

Although a lot of material had been moved, the task they faced seemed nearly impossible. A seven-foot wall of rock was always in front of them. They had to watch for unexploded charges, blasting caps, and tangles of blasting wire. A.J. watched every piece that was moved, looking for anything dangerous. He also knew that there could be some barrels buried under all this rock, and had to be ready to bring down the HazMat team as soon as he spotted one. The team settled into a routine;

it was going to be a long, grueling job.

* * *

Bannister still lay on his back, engulfed by the total blackness, wondering exactly what his next move would be. Although he had no doubt that there were people on the other side working to get through, he had yet to hear them. He was also concerned that the rest of the team may have been hurt in the blast. His hearing was starting to improve, and he could hear his adversary back in the tunnel breathing. He was also badly in need of water. He hadn't been able to clear all the dust from his mouth, and he knew he would be here awhile and had to keep himself from dehydrating.

Finally, he decided to try and sit up. He planted his right hand in the dirt, mustered up all the strength he had left, and pushed. Letting out a muffled scream, he found himself lying flat on his back, with his left arm pinned under him. Jerking it out from under him, he settled back into the dirt and took a deep breath. The pain from his ribs softened a little in this position, and his breathing became easier.

Everything else appeared to be working all right, so he used his legs to push himself an inch or two at a time toward the side of the drift. As he scraped along in the dirt, he stretched his arm in front of him searching for the wall. After a few minutes, he made contact and slowly began to pull himself up into a sitting position. Sitting upright caused the pain in his ribs to return with a vengeance, and he soon found himself lying back down for relief.

The last time he had broken ribs, the doctors wrapped him up tight with a girdle-like brace and sent him home telling him to take some aspirin and relax a few days. Finally, he grabbed at the straps on the side of his bulletproof vest and pulled them as tight as he could; the pain nearly causing him to pass out. He remembered something his old friend and rodeo mentor told him years ago when he was learning to ride bulls and bucking horses: you have no choice but to set the fear and the pain aside and do the job at hand, or you will never succeed. Then he grabbed the straps again, gave one more hard pull, and sat upright with his back against the wall.

The deep raspy voice called out in the darkness. "You all right over there? Sounds like you're dying on me. You're not dying are you, Jack?"

"No such luck, Max, I'm just sitting here drinking champagne and eating caviar. You ready to tell me what I want to know? Or do I have to come over there and beat it out of you?"

"Come on over, I definitely have a little something for you, my friend."

"I'll bet you do, Max. Why don't you just tell me about your boss? You know who I mean—the guy in the helicopter that's running all this," said Bannister, fishing for whatever information he could get.

"Well, Jack, if you got it all figured out already, what the fuck do you need me for?"

"I just need you to fill in a few small blank spots; I hate to have a puzzle with missing pieces."

Bannister's breathing had returned to normal and he seemed to have a grip on the pain. If he didn't breathe too deeply, he could keep it in check. After a few minutes against the wall he realized that his right hand felt wet. Moving his hand around in the dirt, he noticed that it had turned to mud and the wall was damp. Reaching his arm out as far as he could down the wall, he felt more water and it was icy cold. Pulling himself along on his butt, he followed the water along the wall for a few feet, finally coming to a deep fracture in the rock. He could stick his hand in the crack about a foot or so and the water was trickling slowly from the opening.

Holding his hand in the crack for a minute, he let the cold water wash off his fingers. Cupping his hand and catching what he could, he raised it up and splashed it on his face. It was just about the best thing he'd ever felt in his life. As cold as it was, he realized it must be snowmelt: he knew they couldn't be too far below the surface, or the water would never have reached this spot. He also realized that the fracture might have appeared with the recent blast, because it looked as though the water had just started to collect.

Bannister spent twenty minutes alternately drinking and washing out his eyes and throat. It was amazing what a little cool water could do for a man. Removing his helmet, he tore out the padding and turned it upside down, jamming it against the rock. In a few minutes he had an inch or two of water collected. He took a swallow and rinsed out his mouth the best he could, then he drank what remained. Pushing the helmet against the rock again, he drank all he could and repeated the exercise several times, until he began to feel a little more alert.

"Hey, Max," he hollered, with his newfound strength. "You still with me?"

"Yeah, Jack. I'm still hanging in—were you hoping I was dead by now?"

"Hell no, you can't die before you tell me what I want to know. By the way," added Bannister, "what the hell were you thinking when you set off that blast?"

"I set the timer for a couple of minutes and planned on hiding in one of the stopes," said Max, his voice obviously getting weaker. It was now taking him a minute to gain his breath between sentences. "I figured if the blast didn't get you, it would be enough of a diversion that I could get better hidden. That is, until I realized you were standing in front of me—were you wearing night vision or something?"

"You got it, the latest and greatest thing going today," said Bannister. "When I realized you were there, I had nowhere to go but back in the drift that was wired. I hadn't counted on you being back here with me; I thought you'd be buried."

"Max, here's the deal. I think maybe you're dying, and maybe I'm dying as well, but I've got a little water here. I'll bring some over if you don't try and shoot me."

"Dying huh? You sure know how to cheer a fellow up in his hour of need. But the water does sound good. What the hell, I can't get to my gun; it might be underneath me somewhere. All I can move is my head and my right arm, nothing else seems to work. I won't be shooting at you—you got my word."

Bannister thought about this for a minute and decided to give it a try. Using his legs to assist him, he pushed his way up the wall and stood up for the first time since the blast. He called out to tell Max that he was going to break a light stick and throw it his way.

"You got light too? Damn, you seem to have all the luxuries, don't you?"

"I also got a .357 in my hand Max, so let's keep this friendly—okay?"

Bannister fished out a light stick, broke it, and pitched it toward the voice. "You see that, Max?"

"I do, for a while I didn't think I was ever going to see anything again. Looks kind of comforting actually, or hell, maybe it's the light at the end of the tunnel?"

"You should have been a comedian; you're pretty good at gallows humor." Bannister flicked on his small flashlight, relieved to find that it still worked. The small beam seemed to evaporate into the blackness, holding him to about ten feet of visibility. Picking up the helmet full of water and holding the pistol and light in the other, he picked his way through the scattered rock and toward the injured man. "Keep talking, Max; it'll help me find you."

"I hear you; you must be out about twenty feet or so. I see your light-after all these hours down here, it looks really bright."

Bannister found him lying flat with several large chunks of rock covering his legs from the knees down. His left arm was bent at a grotesque angle and turned back under his shoulder. As he sat down next to him, his ribs caused him to give out a painful grunt. "Shit, Max, we're quite a pair, between us we couldn't swat a fly if we had to."

"Good to finally meet you, Jack, or meet you again, I guess. If we'd been meeting up top, we'd probably be shooting at each other."

"Probably so," said Bannister, nodding his head and settling in alongside him.

"You said something about some water?"

"Right here—you might want to rinse out your mouth a little first." Bannister lifted his head slightly with one hand and held out the helmet with the other. The injured man pulled it toward his mouth and started to take large swallows of the water as fast as he could until it was gone.

"Okay, Jack, looks like you win, I got nowhere to go. For another drink of water I'll tell you anything you want to know."

Bannister rolled the heavy rocks off of his mangled legs and straightened his broken arm alongside his body. "If I'm hurting you too badly, just say so."

"That's the strange thing, Jack, my head hurts some and I hurt inside a little, but no major pain. I'm pretty sure my back is broken too or I would hurt a lot more. Anyway, ask all the questions you want, and Jack—I got a feeling you better hurry."

The two men talked quietly for the next twenty minutes, covering as many issues as Bannister could think to ask about. Before he could ask his last question, Max's hand reached up and grabbed Bannister's arm. Hanging on to it for a few brief moments, he slumped down quietly and was gone.

Bannister made his way back to the water and shoved the helmet back under the trickle. Lying down and finding the most comfortable position he could, he dropped off into a restless sleep, waking up now and then to find a more comfortable position. After a couple of hours, he woke up again, not because of the pain, but because of an unusual sound. After listening for a while, he realized that there was also a strong vibration in the drift.

Before he could figure out what was happening, about ten feet down the drift a small chunk of rock popped off the ceiling and a long steel drill bit emerged right behind it. As the bit started to back out, he sat back against the wall in amazement. *Damn, I might really get out of this mess after all,* he thought.

Within minutes, a cable camera with a light, like the type used in exploring piping systems, came out, along with a wire taped to it with a microphone on the end. "Hello, is anyone in there—can anybody hear me?"

He recognized A.J.'s voice immediately. Pulling himself up the wall again, he walked over and took the camera and microphone in his hand and screamed at the top of his lungs, "What in holy hell took you so long?" Laughing out loud, he kept peppering the listeners with nonstop chatter and profanity.

Finally, when things calmed down enough for a regular conversation, Bannister told him that he was hurt but would be okay. Then he asked if the rest of the team was alright.

"It was a close call, but everyone's okay," said A.J. "Half the county is down there digging you out."

"Tell the diggers that there are several barrels under all that rock, all of them along the left side as you go in, so be extra careful."

"I will. This is only a four-inch hole, it's the largest bit I could find in a pinch. What can I send down there to make your life more comfortable?"

"Lights, batteries, and water, a lot of water, along with some food. Maybe Jessie can whip up something that will fit down the hole. A couple of blankets would be good if you can fit them in. Send down some strong pain pills, like all those rich celebrities use, and have the doc fix me up with some kind of antibiotic, I've got a lot of cuts and scratches."

"Got it, what else?"

"Just tell everyone I'm okay."

"I will. Hey, I forgot to ask, what happened to the bad guy?"

"He didn't make it."

Chapter 37

A.J. walked into the shaft house and gathered everyone around. "Everyone listen up. We drilled a test hole into the back of the drift that exploded—Jack Bannister is alive . . ." For a moment it was silent, and then the room exploded in a frenzy of cheers, hugs and high fives. Jessie hung on to Rocky, and finally broke down sobbing. She had been holding back until then, determined to keep it together.

A.J. pulled Jessie, Rocky, and Turner aside and filled them in on what he knew. He told them about Jack's condition, and what he needed to stay comfortable for a few days until the diggers broke through. "Oh, yeah, Jessie, he wants to know if you can whip him up some food—he's hungry."

Jessie wiped her tears away, but couldn't wipe the smile off of her face when she heard that. "Of course—he's always hungry! I swear, all I ever do for him is cook and clean. Well, I suppose if I have to, I can make him something."

Darla Rios had arrived at the shaft house a couple of hours after the word got out about the search, two enormous pots of her homemade red chile and a pile of tortillas in hand. "Come on, Jessie, you and I can whip him up something special."

"Remember girls," said A.J., "it has to fit down a four-inch hole. So be thinking of some kind of container to lower down on a string that will hold the food."

"I'll take care of that part," said Turner.

"Good, and grab a couple cases of water and get them down to him as quick as you can. Whatever he needs, you're in charge of getting it to him. Rocky, he wants to talk to you ASAP; he can't even stop working this case long enough to rest."

"Welcome to Jack Bannister's world—if he's on the trail of the bad guys, he's pretty single-minded."

A.J. went below and filled in the team working at the site. After another explosion of cheers, he filled them in on what Jack had said about the barrels on the left side of the drift. "We're going to remove the rock off of the top three or four feet of the collapse; keep away from the barrels as long as we can. I know that will be a much tougher job, but we can't take a chance of exposing a damaged barrel."

A.J. had one member of the HazMat team and an EMT at the site at all times. Everyone worked in two-hour shifts, and since the announcement, the pace had picked up noticeably. When they finally started to remove just the top layer, it proved to be even tougher than they thought. The guys on top moved the rocks to the man behind, and the last guy in line rolled the rocks down to the guys waiting to move them. If a rock was too big, they broke it up with the electric hammer. The first guy in also had to watch the ceiling and clean off any loose rock. It was dirty, dangerous, and physically demanding work, but if anyone was weakening, no one showed it.

Rocky and Turner headed up top with a load of supplies, stopping at the county maintenance building to grab a piece of PVC pipe and a few fittings. When they got to the drill, it was set up close to the rocks everyone called the Crease. After unloading the supplies, Turner cut off two feet of pipe, plugged one end, and drilled a small hole in the side of the other end. Running the end of a piece of quarter-inch nylon cord through the hole, he tied it on. Then he put four bottles of water inside and slid it down the hole. After a few minutes, he had lowered most of the supplies, including the painkillers and antibiotics; it was about forty-five feet to the bottom of the drift.

The drill operator dropped the camera and microphone back into the hole, and for the first time he and Rocky could see a murky picture from the drift displayed on the screen. In a moment, Jack came into view.

"Who's up there sending me all these goodies?"

"It's me and Rocky. What else can I send down?"

Bannister was glad to hear his old friend's voice. "Is Jessie making me something to eat?"

"Yeah, her and Darla are whipping up some goodies for you right now, they should be ready soon."

"That's great. Put Rocky on for a minute, will you."

"Sure. Hey, what happened to the bad guy?"

"He's dead."

"Good, serves his sorry ass right—here's Rocky."

Rocky took the microphone and keyed it to talk. "For someone who professes to hate those nasty black holes, you sure are spending a lot of time down there."

Hearing Rocky give him a hard time cheered Bannister up, even more than seeing the drill bit punch through into the drift. "Well, Rock, someone needs to do your job, you were just too fat and slow to do it yourself."

"Hold on a minute while I piss down this little hole will you?"

"You'd be damn lucky if you could even find that tiny little thing, let alone hit this hole."

After a few more minutes of badgering each other, Bannister got back to the business at hand. "Rock, you got your notepad?"

"Got it right here, boss, fire away."

For the next few minutes, Bannister filled him in on what Max had told him and what he wanted to do next. "Rocky, make all the calls right away and be sure they know we have the necessary warrants in place. And be sure the jail understands clearly that they have to be kept separate and confined alone."

"Will do; see you in a couple of weeks, boss."

"Couple of weeks my ass, now get moving."

Turner took the mike from Rocky and spoke to Jack. "I'll figure out how to get you some blankets, meanwhile, I'm gonna send you something right now."

"Okay, go ahead."

When the PVC pipe slid out of the hole, Bannister grabbed it and turned it upside down. A dozen candy bars and half a roll of toilet paper fell out of the tube followed by a tightly rolled up magazine. Unrolling the magazine, the name *Playboy* jumped out at him. Stuck to the cover was a yellow sticky note and written in purple, it said, "I know how much you like the articles—Turner."

After nearly sixty-hours of confinement, Bannister heard the faint sound of an electric jackhammer pounding against the rock. Getting comfortable on the pallet of wool blankets Turner sent down, he drank the last of a bottle of water at his side and just watched and listened. The pain in his side was nearly as bad as it had been when he tightened the vest up, but the pills had helped enough to make it tolerable.

About an hour after he heard the first sound, he heard a rock roll down his side of the cave in. Soon several more came down, and then he heard a voice: "Can you hear me? It's A.J.—we'll be in there in a few minutes."

Bannister didn't really realize just how tired and weak he was until he tried to stand up. Instead, he settled for sitting against the wall. "I'm here, A.J., take your time, I'm not going anywhere."

Finally the last of the rocks came down and A.J. Rogers climbed out of the hole, pulling a rope with a litter basket tied on behind it. Two EMTs followed him out of the hole. Placing the litter alongside Bannister, the medics checked all his vital signs, and then the three of them put him on the litter and strapped him in securely.

Lifting the litter up to the top of the opening, they pushed him as far in as they could. Someone else tied a rope onto the other end of the basket and began to pull him through. When he finally began the trip up to the surface, the EMT started him on an IV, and gave him a shot of pain medication.

When the cage door opened, another cheer erupted, and everyone crowded around him. Rocky and Turner squeezed in next to him, making room for Jessie and Darla. Jessie kissed him on the cheek, and whispered something in his ear, then kissed him passionately on the lips.

After a few minutes, they wheeled him toward a waiting ambulance where they transferred him to a gurney. The fresh air helped to revive him a little, and he tried to sit up in the ambulance only to find he was strapped down there too. "Let me out of this thing, damn it—I don't need an ambulance ride . . !"

Rocky stepped up into the ambulance and sat down next to Jack. "Lie down and shut up, Bannister, we're going to the hospital in Colorado Springs and get you squared away, and you ain't got nothing to say about

The Drift

it." Then he waved his hand at the driver to get going.

"Rock, the head bad guy is still out there somewhere and we have to get him."

"The warrants have already been served. Everything you needed has been done. Now just lie back and enjoy the ride."

Before long the meds kicked in and Bannister began to relax. "Rock, everyone did a hell of a job on this—you be sure and tell them, okay?"

Batton nodded his head in agreement. "They all know it, and you'll have plenty of time to tell them yourself."

"How about the HazMat guys—are they all dialed in on their part?"

"It's all theirs now; they've locked down the whole compound and are already getting started."

Rocky could see that Bannister was fighting sleep, unable to get the job off his mind.

"Where's A.J., and the rest of them, Rock? I need to talk to A.J."

"You'll see them at the hospital, Jack, now try and get a little sleep."

"Rock, thanks for being there, you know . . ." Just as they hit the city limits of Colorado Springs, Bannister finally gave in and closed his eyes.

Chapter 38

Waking up In the emergency room of the hospital, Bannister found the small space full of people. The ER team had treated all the minor wounds and rewrapped the area of the fractured ribs. After a thorough exam, a large dose of antibiotics, and more pain medication, he was starting to feel a little better. Although he had several cracked ribs, none had penetrated his insides. "More than likely," said the ER doctor, "the vest saved you from a lot worse injury."

Rocky, A.J., Sheriff Jewell, and a couple of people he didn't recognize were also crowded into the room. Jessie, Turner, and Darla watched from outside the door. "Thanks a lot, doctor, I really appreciate everyone's help," said Bannister, pushing the button to raise his head up in the bed. "Can I visit with these guys for a little while now?"

"Well, if you keep the visit short—at the moment, you need rest more than anything else."

"Thanks, I will." Bannister called A.J., Rocky, and the sheriff over. "Martin, I can't thank you enough for your help with all of this, but I think we left you with a pretty big mess to clean up. Are the EPA and HazMat guys getting things organized up there?"

"No problem, there are about forty guys up there exploring the old mine and locating all the problem areas. If it hadn't been for you, in time, this would have become a major disaster area. Teller County is just providing a little security; the federal boys are pretty much taking care of everything," said Jewell.

Bannister stuck out his hand to the sheriff, "Martin, keep me in the loop please?"

"You got it; I'm heading back up the mountain. Thanks again."

"A.J., I don't know what to say. Without your help, this could have ended up pretty ugly for all of us," Bannister stuck his hand out toward A.J.

"Glad I could help." Grasping his hand tightly, A.J. just nodded his head in understanding.

"Rocky," said Bannister, looking at his longtime partner. "You saved my ass when we entered the building, I never saw the guy behind me." Rocky took his hand and squeezed it between his giant paws for a moment. The three men shared a bond formed by their military experience, something they knew would connect them forever.

"Jack, I'm headed back up to our other project up on the Crease. I'll give you a call as soon as I know anything—it shouldn't take more than a day or two." He turned, and headed out the door, stopping a moment to give Jessie a hug before he left.

Rocky had been listening to the conversation. "What's that all about?"

"Mostly just a hunch of mine, we'll know for sure pretty soon. Are the suspects still in the can?"

"For now, they're locked up and lawyered up, but they're screaming bloody murder to anyone that will listen. Jack, this is Robert Barrett,

El Paso County assistant DA, and Leon Terrell, assistant to the federal prosecutor's office."

Jack shook the men's hands and asked them to fill him in. Terrell spoke first. "Jack, what you have uncovered here is one of the most extraordinary cases our office has ever seen. After the FBI started following all the leads you provided on the rental trucks, they began to unravel a complex crime organization that no one had ever heard of before. They're an all-purpose crime organization that deals in everything: importing drugs from the cartels, stealing and selling prescription drugs, smuggling, robbery, and disposing of anything for a price. They also have their own version of the old Murder, Inc. operating in the New England area. We think they're operating out of the Boston area, but we're still not positive who is giving the orders."

Bannister digested all this new information for a minute. "How close have you gotten to finding the top dog?"

"We have an idea, but the group has a simple method of keeping the law away. There is a top dog and he gives the orders to just one lieutenant, then he gives the order to just one of his lieutenants and that guy makes the deal. Then if the law is getting too close, they just take out one of the links in the chain and, I imagine, stuff him in one of the barrels—then there's no one left to positively ID the leader."

"Leon, can we keep our suspects in the can without bail?"

"Not for much longer, Jack. Robert and I have done nearly everything possible within the law to keep them there until we get them arraigned, and that's tomorrow at 2:00 p.m., but we're already being threatened with lawsuits from some pretty high-powered attorneys trying to get them out."

"Jack," said Robert Barrett, speaking for the first time. "I'll be handling this for El Paso and Teller Counties. The only reason they're still our guests is because of the pressure from the multiple police agencies. We need to sit down with the principals and their attorneys and start hashing this out pretty soon, or they'll get released for sure."

"How about you guys give me an hour or so and I'll fill you in with everything I've learned. I'd like to get it all on tape before I forget it, or before I get hit by a beer truck on the way to court."

Barrett looked at his watch. "We'll go get some supper and be back in an hour."

As they walked out the door, Jessie and Turner came in. "Turner, you doing all right?"

"Better than you, by the looks of things."

"I can't thank you enough; we couldn't have done it without your help. And it looks like your notes have provided the FBI with a road map to breaking up a huge crime ring."

Turner smiled, bent down, and gave him an uncharacteristic hug, something Bannister had never seen him do before. "I told you those federal boys couldn't find their ass without a map!" He turned and walked out the door, passing Jessie. "He's all yours—have at him."

Jessie sat down on the bed and stared at Jack for a moment. Suddenly, the tears began to flow and she sobbed uncontrollably. "Damn you, Bannister, we all thought you were gone," she said, laying her head on his shoulder and sobbing softly. "I was scared, Jack, really scared. You know how much I love you?"

"I do, Jess, I love you too—you know that. You were all I thought about when I was lying in the dirt and darkness wondering if I would ever get out of there. You were what kept me alive."

Jessie lay in Jack's arms until the two men in suits returned carrying briefcases and a tape recorder. Jessie kissed him one last time and left him to the lawyers. Pulling up chairs next to the bed, they set up the recorder and pulled out legal pads, and began to take his information down. After two hours, Bannister had told them everything he could remember leading up to the raid and everything that he learned from Max Atkinson and Dave DeAngelo.

"There's no doubt who's running this, but if you want to round up the rest of the operation, you may have to make a deal—but, that's for you guys to decide."

* * *

At 8:00 A.M., Bannister climbed up the steps to the El Paso County courthouse, his ribs reminding him to go slow and breathe easy. He walked through the metal detector and found the ADA's office. After a long conversation with the state and federal prosecutors, they all got up and headed for the holding cells.

Looking through the window of the interview room, Jamison Carhartt III sat with an attorney on either side, and a pile of paperwork in front of him. When the three men walked into the room, he looked up at Jack, obviously shocked to see him here. "Jack, what are you doing here—what do you have to do with all this?"

"Jamie," said Bannister, remembering his desire to be called by that name. "Do you own the Black Mule mine?"

"Yes, I own it, and two other claims in the district, but I told you that before. They say I was involved in some kind of deal to use it to hide nuclear waste? That's a bunch of crap, I never did any such thing."

Bannister looked at him for a moment. He saw the same, pleasant, easygoing guy that he took the chopper rides with. "Jamie, do you know Max Atkinson?"

"Sure, he's my mining foreman. He has a small crew, and they prospect for any gold that might still be there. But Jack, if he's doing something illegal, I sure didn't know it!"

"You're right, Jamie, I know you didn't."

"Then what am I doing here?"

"I didn't know for sure where you fit in until a couple of days ago. The prosecutors are ready to discuss bail, and maybe dropping the charges at the arraignment this afternoon."

"Thanks—I think," he said weakly.

Bannister and the prosecutors walked about fifty feet down the hall, and entered another interview room. Sitting between two-well dressed lawyers was a tall, slim, almost-waifish looking woman, with short, blonde hair and her hands clasped tightly together in front of her.

Jack and the prosecutors sat down across the table from them. "Hello, Clarice, I don't know if you remember me—I'm Jack Bannister, we met once at the museum."

She stared at Bannister for a moment, and her blue eyes suddenly flashed at him. "I remember, so what?"

"I assume by now you know why you're being held?"

"Some phony crap about a nuclear bomb or something? It's all a load of bullshit, and I'm going to sue you and everyone you ever knew into oblivion if you don't let me the fuck out of here."

"I don't see much chance of that, Clarice," said Bannister. "I see you spending the rest of your life in the nastiest women's prison in the country—that is if you aren't executed."

"You haven't got squat on me. You can't connect me to anything. All that mining stuff is just another one of my husband's hobbies—just another toy for him to play with. Those crappy old mines are all he owns. I'm the one that pays for all his other toys, like the fancy helicopter." Her lawyers tried to get her to stop talking, but she wasn't having any of it.

"Clarice, do you know a guy by the name of Max Atkinson?"

"Never heard of him. Next question."

"Well, I'm going to lay out this whole deal for you, let me know if I get anything wrong. You're the black sheep of the Whitford family out of Boston, a smart but troubled kid; a felony bust for dealing earned you six months in jail. When the family revoked your fat trust fund, you went into business yourself, and now you're a big-time crime boss. Am I pretty close, Clarice?"

"Fuck you—you can't connect me to anything."

"Well, it took a little while to do it, but with some help from the man you claim you don't know—Max Atkinson—I got you nailed to the wall."

Clarice Carhartt began to turn red, and her hands started to shake. "That no-good lying son of a bitch is just trying to save himself. It's my word against his, that's all it is."

"He's your lover, Clarice—has been since your drug-bust days. He had some experience with mining, so you got him set up with your husband when you needed a place to bury things, and to be able to see your lover whenever you wanted. Pretty smart thinking. And poor old Jamie didn't suspect a thing. We got a list from Max a mile long of people in your businesses, friends from college days, and just how your organization works. When he gets on the stand and tells his story, and we follow up with a couple dozen of your old friends, it will be all over."

Standing up and glaring at him, Clarice poured out a steady stream of obscenities at Jack and the prosecutors. When her lawyers tried to restrain her, she screamed at them and started to punch and kick them. "You're goddamn right I'm the boss, and that bastard Max will be dead before he ever gets to court…! And you—you asshole, you're a walking dead man. You'll be dead before you ever see a trial . . ."

Bannister sat back in his chair, shocked to see so much hatred come out of one small woman. She was trying to get across the table to

Bannister, and launched a spitting attack at everyone she could reach. Her lawyers finally pinned her down with the help of two deputies, and she was shackled to the table.

Finally, one of her lawyers spoke up. "I think we're ready to talk about a deal; we'll meet with you guys tomorrow." With that, the two deputies returned her to a holding cell and waited for transportation to the jail.

After the wild melee, Robert Barrett was the first one to speak. "I thought Max was killed in the mine?"

"He was," said Bannister. "I just brought him back to life for the day."

Back at the cabin the next morning, the phone rang and Jessie answered it. "Yeah, he's here, A.J., I'll get him."

"Hey, how's it going with our project?"

"I think you were right, Jack, better have everyone get up here around noon or so."

"Thanks A,J., I'll gather them all up and we'll be there."

Chapter 39

Jack and Jessie bounced along the gravel road until they reached the rocks known as the Crease. On one side was a large pile of gravel with a yellow bulldozer parked next to it. A backhoe was parked at the edge of a fresh excavation, with its boom stretched down into the hole and the engine shut off. They were the last of the team to arrive.

Walking to the edge, he looked down into the hole; the machine had cleaned off the surface of the rock down to about fifteen feet and removed all the gravel for ten feet in every direction. The bucket of the backhoe was propped up on a large slab of rock leaning against the bottom of the Crease.

A.J. walked over to Bannister and put his hand on his shoulder. "What do you think, do you really believe something's down there?"

"Did you find anything man-made when you were digging this out?"

"A piece of a broken shovel and the remains of a few old timbers is about it."

"The answer is yes, I believe something is down there, and we're about to find out exactly what it is—let's get digging."

A.J. climbed into the cab of the backhoe and fired up the engine. Raising the boom slightly, he curled the bucket up and wedged its teeth behind the slab leaning against the rock face. Curling the bucket the opposite way, and pressing the boom down, the slab fell forward with a dull thud and a puff of dust. The group all gathered around waiting for the dust to clear.

Where the slab of rock had rested they could see where the line between the pink-colored granite and the rough black rock begin to separate. A.J. hooked the bucket on the back of the slab and pulled it back away from the crack. Then he took several more buckets of gravel out against the rock wall.

Bannister waved his arms. "Hold on, I want to take a closer look. Can we get a ladder and a flashlight down there?"

A.J.'s men dropped a ladder into the hole and handed Jack a flashlight. Climbing down the ladder very slowly, he gritted his teeth in pain with every step. He walked over to the crack, knelt down, and flicked on his light. Although the opening was getting wider, it still wasn't big enough to crawl inside; another bucket or two with the backhoe should open it up plenty wide.

Bannister watched as a small trickle of gravel started to slide into the opening. His flashlight lit up the inside, but not quite enough to see what might be there. He directed A.J. where to put his bucket and watched as he removed several more loads. Then he gave him the sign to shut it down. Bannister hollered up that he needed more light and a shovel, and for everyone to come on down.

Starting up a generator and connecting a pair of strong lights, A.J. passed them down to Jack, then he threw in a couple of shovels and climbed down. The rest of the team had been pretty quiet until now, but

Turner couldn't wait any longer. "Just what the hell do you expect to find in there, gold? Buried treasure?"

"Maybe, maybe not. But I've had a hunch about this place for a long time now and I figured it was time to find out one way or the other." Everyone else was straining to hear Jack's story. "I needed someone that knew all about mining to help me out, so A.J. and I partnered up and bought this old claim—now we're about to find out if we wasted our money."

The rock continued to separate to a point where it was about twenty inches at its widest and about five feet high, flattening out at the bottom. Shoving the light as far into the opening as he could, Jack and A.J. were stunned at what they saw.

"Holy shit, it's a vug! Holy shit—a huge vug . . !" said Rogers loudly, unable to control his excitement.

Bannister was equally as excited as A.J. but couldn't understand what he was trying to tell him. "A vug—what the hell is a vug . . ?"

"It's a natural opening in the volcanic rock. Think of it as a giant form of geode, with rock on the outside and crystals on the inside. The old Cresson mine on the other side of the district found one full of gold and crystals worth millions . . !"

Taking a minute to calm down, they began to look over what they had found. They estimated the cavern was about eighteen feet long and ten feet wide. The depth was hard to determine because it was partially filled with the pink granite gravel that covered the rest of the site. As they scanned the walls, they could see beautiful quartz crystals of all sizes attached to every square inch of the rock walls. The crystals were shot full of strings of gold winding throughout them like some kind of exotic jewelry.

Backing out of the hole, he handed the light to Rocky and let him look into the vug. In turn, everyone got to look inside and spend all the time they wanted sharing in the excitement of the moment. From somewhere, a magnum of champagne and a stack of plastic cups appeared. A.J. popped the cork and let the sudden burst of champagne splash directly onto the rock.

"Bannister raised his cup for a toast. Here's to the greatest bunch of friends and partners a man could ever have!" As it started to get dark, and the celebration mellowed out, A.J. set up a bunch of construction lights around the project. Climbing back into the excavation, Jack decided it was time to crawl inside and have a closer look. Grabbing a pair of lights, he lowered one down into the hole and hung one in the entrance. Forcing himself through the small opening, he picked his way carefully across the crystals, and finally sat himself down on the gravel in the bottom.

For five minutes, he just sat still and stared. The light swirled and reflected off of the crystals. He felt like he was in some kind of incredible jeweled palace. Finally, he turned his attention to the gravel on the floor. Up against the entrance was a mound of it, oddly out of place in the otherwise smooth floor. Bannister took his shovel and started to clear the gravel, and then suddenly thought better of it.

Using his hand to whisk it away, he began to uncover a whitish colored lump. As he brushed harder, he realized he was uncovering a skull. Moving faster now, he could see that it was probably a full skeleton. Traces of cloth remained on the body, and the front panel of a pair of overalls were still stuck to the rib cage.

For a moment he didn't really believe what he was seeing, but he was sure it could be only one person. Calling to A.J. to gather everyone around, he picked his way back through the opening. When everyone was bent over as close to the opening as they could get, wondering what Bannister was up to, a grizzly white skull popped out of the opening right in front of everyone's face, backlit by the construction light. "Ladies and gentlemen—meet Vitor Serinov!"

Bannister's dramatic presentation made a few people jump back, but mostly they all cheered. After more than a hundred years, the case of the missing Russian miner could be officially closed. He had been trapped in the vug—probably right after he discovered it—most likely a result of nearby blasting from the Black Mule mine. The slab had slid down like a giant vault door, and the fine, loose gravel eventually filled in his small excavation.

A.J. took the skull and set it aside, and as everyone crowded around the opening to see what might happen next, he climbed through the opening and sat down next to Jack. Running his hands across the crystal formations over and over, he could barely speak. When he finally regained his composure, he leaned close to Bannister's ear and said in a quiet whisper, "Jack—we're rich! Do you understand that?"

"I understand A.J., trust me I understand."

"No, Jack, I mean really rich—like really, really rich."

Jack Bannister and A.J. Rogers sat in the center of the vug, square in the middle of the most magnificent treasure either one of them could ever imagine, and they suddenly started to holler and scream like a couple of schoolboys. After they calmed down, A.J. climbed out of the vug and helped anyone that wanted to go inside and experience this once-in-a-lifetime find. Everyone took them up on it except Rocky. At 6 foot 6 and nearly 300 pounds, he knew it wasn't going to happen.

"Don't worry, Rock, we'll open the entrance up a little more tomorrow and you can check it out then."

"No problem, it needs to be made big enough for a real man anyway," he laughed.

Bannister called out of the hole for a trowel and a broom, and Turner went back to his Jeep and returned with the tools. Throwing them into the cavity, he asked if there was anything else he could get.

"Get me a blanket, and I'll be out in a few minutes." No one could see exactly what he was doing because he was on his knees with his back to the opening. They could see him sweeping a lot of gravel to the sides. When he got the blanket he carefully wrapped something in it and set it near the opening, and then crawled out. After a long drink of water, he called everyone in close, and with Jessie alongside him, reached in and pulled out something wrapped in a blanket.

Pausing for a moment, to add a little drama to the situation, he turned to Jessie and told her to pull off the blanket. Jessie grabbed the corner of the blanket and pulled. In Jack's hand was a piece of antique armor, a breastplate from some long-forgotten Spanish explorer. It was trimmed with fine gold woven around the edges, and pieces of turquoise and amazonite were mounted throughout the design. In the center was a crest, also made of gold and set with rubies.

With all the necessary fanfare he could muster, he handed it to Jessie.

"Jessie Lopez, I would like to present you with the golden armor you and your family have been searching for, for more than four hundred years!"

Jessie was speechless, and the team crowded around her to see the armor. Bannister, Rocky, and A.J. leaned back against the rock wall and watched as Jessie showed off the armor. Finally Rocky asked the obvious question: "Jack, are you gonna tell me that you knew all along the Russian miner was down there—and the golden armor?"

"I was pretty sure that the Russian was down there somewhere, after reading all of his letters and looking at the aerial pictures. As far as the golden armor goes, after a few years with Jess, she had me pretty well convinced the story was real. Although I thought there could be a slim chance it might be somewhere around the district, I was shocked to see it down there—that was just an extraordinary piece of luck," said Bannister, downing another cup of champagne. "However, I never thought anything about any treasure on a scale like this. I was really just hoping old Vitor had maybe found a decent vein or something."

"Do you think the armor was hidden in there by someone with plans to return and get it?" asked Turner.

"If I had to take a wild guess, I'd say that the local Indians knew about the vug. It may have been an old source of gold for them, because they were known to have gold ornaments. It could be that they killed the Mexican owner and threw him and the armor in the hole to conceal it. I also think there are some more bones down there. I don't want to dig anymore until we get the local authorities out here to deal with them."

"And you're sure that the skull belongs to the missing Russian miner?" asked Rocky.

Bannister reached in his pocket and pulled out a small square brass tag with a hole in one end and the number "348" stamped on it. Below the number and crudely stamped was the word "TFLYNN." "This was in the pocket of his overalls; it's an ID tag used for checking in and out of the mine—It apparently belonged to his friend Tommy Flynn."

Jack turned to A.J. "Realistically, what do you feel this vug may be worth?"

"Hard to say, but in today's market for raw gold, it should be easily worth maybe fifteen or twenty million—maybe more. There's an additional market for the crystal samples with the gold still in it; museums and collectors will probably pay top dollar for good specimens."

"Well, Jack, looks like you will be retiring to a life of white-sand beaches and topless island girls serving you fancy fruit drinks with little colored umbrella's." Rocky said with a chuckle.

"Hell no, Rock, I'd rather stay here with you and freeze my ass off chasing bad guys—besides, you're rich too."

"No, boss, I don't think so, I don't see any large inheritance in my future."

"Well, when A.J. and I made the deal for the claim, we went fifty-fifty on ownership. My fifty percent is owned by me, Jessie, you, and Turner. The others don't know it yet."

For the first time since he'd known him Rocky Batton was totally speechless, and looked close to tears. Bannister poked him in the belly and grinned. "So don't say a thing you big wuss, just shut up and be happy. A.J., what are you going to do with all that money?"

"I'm going to help out the local museums for one thing, then—I'm going to go looking for some more!" With that, they all had a good laugh and finished off the last of the champagne, shaking hands and slapping each other on the back.

Rocky Batton walked over to Bannister and put his long arm around him and gathered him in tight. "I just remembered something, Bannister. I'll take those Bronco season tickets now."

"My Bronco tickets? What the hell you talking about, fat boy?"

"You said if Carhartt was clean, you'd give me the tickets—remember?"

"I just made you a millionaire—and now you want my tickets too?"

"Bannister, money is just money—these are Bronco tickets we're talking about!"

"Forget it, you can have my money, but you ain't getting my tickets."

"We'll see about that, Bannister," said Rocky, squeezing him tightly. "You just wait and see who will be sitting in those seats next fall!"

After he told Jessie and Turner what he had done, A.J. told him to go on home and he would set up security for the night. When Jessie and Jack finally got back to the cabin, Jack set the armor and the tag on the mantle. These would go to the museum tomorrow. They had a little wine, and after revisiting the day's events, Jessie got up and said she was heading to bed.

"Not so fast, lady, you have something to do first."

"What are you talking about? I'm tired, and I'm going to bed."

"You can go in the bedroom, but you have to come back out wearing the long black nightgown, and model it for me right here in front of the fire—remember?"

"Remember what? What the hell are you talking about, old man?"

"You said, and I remember it clearly, if I found the treasure—I could ravish you any way I wanted."

Without speaking a word, she walked into the bedroom and came out wearing the sheer, black nightgown that Jack couldn't stop thinking about. Stepping in front of the fire, she modeled it provocatively for a few minutes. "So you like this, old man?"

"I like it very much, thank you," said Bannister, unable to take his eyes off of her.

"Well, if you liked that—you might like this . . ." She slid the straps off her shoulder and let the gown fall to the floor, showing off her smooth olive skin, soft curves, and gorgeous breasts peeking out between the strands of long black hair.

"I like that a lot," said Bannister.

Jessie stood completely naked in front of Bannister, backlit by the dying embers of the fire.

"So what are you waiting for old man . . ? Ravish away . . ."

∽ *The End* ∽

Acknowledgments

Even after years as a freelance journalist, taking on my first novel proved to be almost more than I bargained for. Like all writers know, it's the people you meet along the way that make the stories and help you in more ways than you could ever imagine.

Even though I am going to try to list them here, in no particular order, I know that I will forget someone and that bothers me a lot. I'm sorry for those of you that I miss, so please call and yell at me so I can get it right in the next printing. My test readers are friends new and old, and family, all from many different walks of life. They all mostly think I'm crazy, but hung in there with me.

So—thanks to all of you . . !

Nancy Entwistle – My wife and partner, who worked so hard for me and for the book. I'm sure she would like to read some of her own books for a change.

Al Sesserego – My motorcycle photography mentor and friend, who taught me about superbikes and umbrella girls. I will try to get at least one bike and a couple of umbrella girls in the next book.

Bob Baker – My friend and mechanic extraordinaire, who can fix anything on wheels and make it go faster. I'll put a couple of car chases and an explosion or two in the next one.

Don Kallaus – My master book designer, friend, and house-flipping pal, who managed to turn a large pile of word files into this very cool book.

Glory Ann Kurtz – My editor and friend, and the one who helped me make sense out of this huge mass of words, bad grammar and even worse punctuation, I don't know how you do it.

John McKenna – Publisher, writer and new friend, for his sage advice, and for taking on a new author in his publishing house—Rhyolite Press.

Nancy Kelleher – My new friend and overwhelmingly enthusiastic reader who gave me such great feedback.

Pat Turner – My friend and gracious lady. Hope you like how R.D. turned out.

Jess Knight – My long time friend, who claims to never read books. I know he has read at least one, because he called me up and yelled at me for killing off a character-go figure.

Teri Lee – Editor and old friend who bought some of my first work and has had faith in me since I first started writing.

Tim O'Byrne – Editor and good friend who has probably had more confidence in me than I have had in myself at times.

Jody Berman – Book editor and new friend who evaluated the manuscript for me and gave me great insight into fiction writing.

Allison Auch – Book editor and new friend who helped me see the (many) errors of my ways.

About the Type

The Drift is set in Adobe Garamond Pro. Garamond is another of the old-style serif typefaces. It was designed in the mid-sixteenth century by Claude Garamond and refined in the early seventeenth century by another French punch-cutter and printer named Jean Jannon. Unique to the Garamond letter forms are the small bowl of the letter a and eye of the letter e; as well as it's sense of fluidity. Garamond is one of the most legible and readable of the serif typefaces . . . and is noted as one of the most eco-friendly fonts for its precise, sparing and efficient use of ink.

Have you seen
our other
Rhyolite Press
Publications . . .

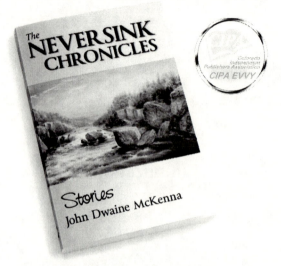

THINK YOUR HOME IS YOUR CASTLE?
... NOT IF THE GOVERNMENT WANTS IT!
READ

THE NEVERSINK CHRONICLES

Seventeen linked stories showing what happens to us, the ordinary folks, when the government takes our property away. It's all about the water . . . our most precious resource and increasingly scarce commodity.

We don't stand a chance . . .

CIPA EVVY Award Winner, 2012
1st prize, Best Fiction

$15 at bookstores everywhere, or direct from the publisher:
www.rhyolitepress.com

ISBN 978-0-9839952-0-3

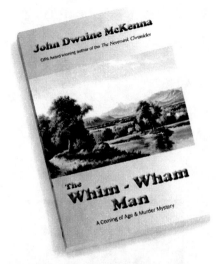

A STORY THAT HAS IT ALL . . .
A CRIME YOU CAN'T FORGIVE
A PLOT YOU COULDN'T IMAGINE
AND A CHARACTER . . .
YOU'LL NEVER FORGET.

THE WHIM - WHAM MAN

The first of a series featuring CSPD Detective Jake McKern, is a coming of age and murder mystery that takes place in 1940 in Husted, Colorado, 12 miles north of Colorado Springs.

It's a helluva yarn!

Don't miss this exciting read!

$15 at bookstores everywhere, or direct from the publisher:
www.rhyolitepress.com
ISBN 978-0-9839952-1-0

Coming in Spring of 2013 . . .

THE COLORADO *Noir* CHRONICLES

"Stories from the other Colorado
Springs . . . the one the tourists aren't
allowed to see . . . where the marginal
ones live and die in
the shadows of affluence."